BLOOD ROGUE

LINDA J. PARISI

CITY OWL
PRESS

BLOOD ROGUE
Blood Rogue, Book 1

CITY OWL PRESS
www.cityowlpress.com

Cover Design by Mibl Art. All stock photos licensed appropriately.

Edited by Tee Tate.

For information on subsidiary rights, please contact the publisher at info@cityowlpress.com.

Print Edition ISBN: 978-1-949090-97-0

Digital Edition ISBN: 978-1-949090-96-3

Printed in the United States of America

Manuscripts are born into the world then they are molded and shaped into final form. BLOOD ROGUE is dedicated to Tee Tate, my awesome editor at City Owl Press, for helping me make my work more than worthy of becoming a book. Thank you from the bottom of my heart.

Chapter One

CHAZ

Every city has a pulse, a vibration, a sound. Take New York City, for instance. The city that never sleeps; it's unstoppable, frenetic, and definitely treble. Then there's the *new* New York. Hoboken, New Jersey, the land of thirty-something's tired of living four to a one-bedroom apartment, the city across the Hudson, anchored in the bedrock of the Palisades. Hoboken pounded out bass, slow, deep, rhythmic, and solid, like the beat of a human heart, the one organ a nine-hundred-year-old vampire would never take for granted.

Charles Tower, Chaz to those who knew him best, stood in *Beans* — his guilty pleasure. He stared at the rows of jars with black beans, brown beans, beige beans, appreciating that in his human life, coffee would have been as foreign to him as a heavy metal band. As a human born in the year 1094AD, he would always wonder what the brew tasted like. He hoped it would be as heavenly as the aroma permeating the store, sweet, earthy, and pungent. He inhaled deeply and exhaled slowly, feeling a little bit like an addict.

Yes, he knew all about that word, as well as need and cravings, the likes of which a human could never understand. There was the blood, and there could only ever be the blood, even when he tried to enjoy something as simple as a coffee shop.

What the hell is wrong with me?

Would there ever be a time when he could step up to a cash register and pay for a bag of Arabica that he'd give away, without thinking about the river of life? Maybe he'd be better off thinking of the rogues, the out of control vampires that he'd had to kill too often lately.

Frowning, he turned, left the store, and stepped out onto the sidewalk. Mayhem assailed with a cacophony of sound. The blare of a car horn, the rumble of a truck over uneven pavement, to the thoughts of the hundreds of people he didn't want to listen to. He tried to block out the sounds, to no avail. He stepped right into the path of three lovely women who parted like the Red Sea then came back together again as they passed. One, the blonde with the ponytail, looked back over her shoulder.

Chaz stilled. Her round face could've used more chin and less cheekbone. She had dark brows and even darker rimmed glasses. But, there was something about the beautiful eyes behind the lenses. Bright, the color of a midday sky, filled with energy and curiosity and such life. God, he could drown in that gaze, never surface, and remain happy forever.

Except for the blood.

She turned to her friends, and the moment died the way moments like this do, except he heard her say, "Oh my God. I just saw the most gorgeous guy."

"What?" asked the tallest of the three. "Stacy? Stacy Ann Morgan? The geek-cop? Noticing—oh-my-goodness—" She placed a hand against her chest. "—a man?" Her tone oozed attitude.

"Ease up, Kels."

Stacy. He liked that name. Curiosity piqued, and the irrational need to see those eyes again had Chaz wanting to hear more. He turned and followed them at a safe distance.

"No way. This is simply too delicious. Maybe Stace'll try and dissect him first. Wait. No. She'll run a two-week background check on him right down to his seventh cousin's middle name."

"Low blow, Kels," the woman on her right said. Her shoulders drooped a little, then her back straightened. "You do realize she carries a gun, don't you?"

"Ladies...stop! I'm right here you know."

Yes, indeed, he thought.

She walked with a long determined stride and had a trim, athletic body. She seemed to assess everyone and everything around her as she walked. Was that out of curiosity or protectiveness? By blocking out the myriad of voices around him, he also blocked out hers, so he'd have to find out.

"Of course you are," continued the one they called Kels. "But we know all about you quiet ones, don't we? You may act shy around the opposite sex, but still, waters run deep and all, right?"

They walked a few steps into *Adrian's.* Chaz continued down the block. Sometimes prudence really was better. But then he pivoted, turning back. This time, not for the blood but for the want of simple human contact. Stopping in front of the steps, he hesitated again. There would only be one winner tonight, the blood, and for a moment that made him sad. He shook that off and walked through the door. They were standing in front of the bar like they were waiting for a table to the restaurant.

He walked over and ordered a glass of Cabernet and leaned on the wood as he took a small sip. He watched Stacy's gaze soften as she leaned toward the sad woman.

"How are you holding up, Tori?"

A woman wearing expensive-smelling perfume approached him, and he tore his gaze away. Every pore on her face was filled with artifice, and he shook his head, making it clear he didn't want to be picked up. Her lips thinned at the rebuff, but she turned around and went back to her friends while he focused on the conversation he wanted to hear.

"They say time heals. Some days it's almost bearable. Some aren't."

He watched Stacy reach out and hug her friend, wishing he had someone that deeply invested in his well-being, someone close. Vampires were singular and very territorial. They had to be to survive.

While Stacy and the one she called Tori spoke together, the

woman they called Kels turned to stare at him. Her brow lifted, her hips shifted so that the line of her leg drew his gaze. He palmed his chest and mouthed, "Who, me?"

She nodded, offering a sly, knowing smile. He took his time pushing off the wood of the bar and sauntered up to her, already feeling her claws dig deep. She entwined her arm with his, but Chaz had no interest and extricated himself with deft precision. He ignored her pout and flashed them all a huge grin.

"Good evening, ladies. I know this is incredibly forward of me, but might I buy you all a round while you wait? Charles Tower at your service." He bowed, gracing them with the manners which had been proper in his time, and they hemmed and hawed, all except *her*. Stacy simply stared at him, assessing, head slightly cocked as she made her judgment. Funny, for the first time in just over a century, he didn't want to be found lacking.

You can service me anytime.

How…unexpected. He nearly grinned. Then he heard, *Where the hell did that come from?* He wanted to ask the same question. Too bad this night was about need and not pleasure.

Kels, the dark-haired one who was all talk licked her lips like he was some kind of treat. She turned him off, much too full of herself to be inviting. Tori, the sad one, frowned and eyed him up and down a couple of times, her gaze filled with mistrust. He let her see what she wanted to see, someone normal, someone human, and she nodded slightly. Then he claimed the prize, sinking into that incredible crystalline blue gaze once more, made even more delectable by the doubts she expressed.

"Sir? What can I get you?"

He started and looked up, indicating that the ladies each give their order to the bartender. "Put it on my tab."

Kels refused to give up, wedging her body into the tight space between the other women so that she separated him from her friends. Chaz steeled his features, daring her to touch him again. Her human instinct warned her, and she stepped back, allowing him to reach out and move Stacy away from getting stepped on. He trailed a light finger across Stacy's skin as he let go, pleased to see her skin bead from his touch.

"Do you come here often?" She winced, and he held up his hand, feeling a touch of dismay. "I know. Lousy pick-up line, right?"

He cocked his head, gave her a rueful lift of the corner of his mouth, and let the truth ring through his words. "But I've been so overwhelmed by your presence that I don't know what to say."

She didn't answer.

"Okay, that came out a bit too much, didn't it?"

She nodded, and he drowned in her killer blues, which was hard to do for one already dead. "Shall I rephrase?"

She stared, disbelief filling her gaze as she shouted her thoughts. *Make that more than once.*

Outwardly determined and in control, that was very evident. But inside? How fascinating. "Perhaps I should start over?"

She still didn't answer.

"You don't talk very much, do you?"

Her gaze flitted from her hands to his chest and then after a deep breath, made eye contact. But at that moment, her shoulders squared and she gazed at him openly.

Her cheeks bloomed pink. "I work in a lab." She half laughed. "The extent of my conversations run from who took an evidence bag to why the damned mass spec is down again."

She tightened her fingers around her glass and stared down at her drink again. *Is this really happening?*

Now he couldn't help himself as he grinned.

Look at the simple curl of his lip—the arch of his brow.

"Perhaps we could start with your name?"

Her heart sped up, and he could hear the rush of her blood in her veins. His mouth watered. Chaz swallowed, hating his reaction to her. She seemed nice, too nice to simply be used.

"Sorry." Again, twin spots of pink tinged her cheeks. "Stacy. Stacy Morgan." *Nice going, dumb head. Probably thinks I'm sixteen now.*

Actually, Chaz found the combination of her boldness and insecurity intriguing and decided to reassure her.

"I'm a bit rusty in the world of social gatherings myself," he said.

She certainly made for an interesting combination. Supposedly she was some kind of scientist, her friends called her a cop, but she carried an innocence about her he hadn't encountered in a very long time.

The bright light in her gaze dimmed with uncertainty. Chaz might be considered more human than his fellow vampires, but make no mistake, this moment was all about the blood and only could be about the blood.

"Me too. Umm, let me introduce you. This is Kelly." Chaz wondered if his message had been clear enough. She shook his hand and let go quickly. "And this is Tori." Her sad friend was much more reserved and much less trusting.

"Ladies? A pleasure to meet you both." He inclined his head with a slight smile and leaned against the bar again. He picked up his glass, his gaze studying them over the rim. "This place is really busy tonight."

Kelly agreed. "More than usual."

Tori didn't answer.

He turned his attention back to Stacy. "I gather you're here to celebrate? Special occasion?"

"No," she answered. "We try to meet up when we can."

"Then I wouldn't be tearing you away from your friends if I asked."

Her nose scrunched up, making her glasses fall. She pushed them up with her finger. "Asked what?"

"Would you like to get out of here? Grab a bite?"

She gulped a deep draught of her drink then put her glass on the bar. He followed with his glass, still holding onto the bag of coffee. She seemed caught as she hesitated.

"Somewhere quieter? I can hardly hear myself think."

Her heart began to flutter. "I'd like that."

With a nod, the bartender came over, and he handed the young man a hundred-dollar bill. "For the tab and anything else they want."

"Ladies? Again, a pleasure to meet you. I've given the bartender enough to cover your drinks and perhaps more. Stacy's agreed to have dinner with me. So if you'll excuse us?"

Are you kidding me? For real? Kelly practically shouted.

Tori was much more skeptical and cautious. She threw Stacy a look. He couldn't help but hear her shout. *If I don't get a text from the restaurant, I'm calling the cavalry.*

She had good friends. "Stacy, you won't forget to send a text, will you? To let everyone know you're safe?"

"Of course," she answered, nodding, looking ready to roll her eyes, so Chaz led the way outside, blowing out a deep breath before he gave her a smile.

"Much quieter."

She didn't answer.

"You have some very good friends."

"Sometimes they forget I can take care of myself." A wisp of hair had loosened from her ponytail to frame her face. She blew it off her cheek with a sideways breath.

"I'm sure you can, but they also care about you."

"A little too much, but I guess I shouldn't complain. Certainly not to someone I've just met."

He dipped his head, lifted a brow, and smiled. "Let's make this a special occasion then. Our first meeting. The Chart House?"

She shifted her pocketbook strap on her shoulder, and some of the tension in her shoulders eased. "I've been there. That would be lovely."

He inclined his head but drew his brows together as if he had a problem. "I have a favor to ask. Would you mind driving? My car is in the garage of my building. We'd have to walk a ways to get it. Or Uber."

"Sure." She turned, and Chaz followed, admiring the view before falling into step next to her. That long stride of hers nearly matched his. "You had everyone going, you know."

"Excuse me?"

"My friends. They're not exactly subtle."

He lifted his eyebrows, hoping he appeared ignorant or innocent, but she didn't seem to buy it.

"Come on. You mean you didn't see the drool all over the floor? Kelly tried to chain you to her."

"That's why I stood next to you. I'm not interested in the obvious."

"Okay. So if I'm not obvious?" she asked, heading down another block. "What exactly am I?" She stopped next to a beat-up Jeep.

A word popped into his head, and he hated it immediately. "Intelligent. Strong. Beautiful."

She tipped her chin, head tilted, eyes widened, and huffed. "Really?"

"Really," he repeated. He climbed in the passenger side while she got in behind the steering wheel. As she put the key in the ignition, he covered her hand with his. Her gaze lifted, filled with confusion, anticipation, and a bit of curiosity. He leaned in and breathed in her scent, a heady mixture of expensive perfume and hormones. Her skin pebbled as he blew lightly on her cheek. Chaz heard the distinct rhythm of her heart as it hammered in her chest, which rose and fell with short rapid breaths.

His incisors grew, and he swiped a taste of her neck. Perfect.

She moaned as he bit down. *God, she tasted sweet.* Much more like dessert than a meal. He sucked and swallowed, sucked and swallowed, and her heart slowed, pounding in his ears to the same rhythm as the city.

Chaz.

He reared back away from her neck. Had he taken too much? Horror filled his gut. No, her flesh was still warm, pulse low and steady, eyes closed.

Thank God.

He leaned over again and bit down, but this time it was to give her the Lethe, the drug that would make her forget he ever existed. He admired her beauty one last time, then reached in her purse and found her driver's license, committing her address to memory. *Shouldn't have done that, Charles.* He climbed out of the car and placed the bag of coffee in the crook of her arm. She would wake up in about an hour or so and not remember a thing.

Damn. That sucked.

CHAZ WALKED HOME DEEP IN THOUGHT. HE COULDN'T GET STACY out of his head. He replayed every moment they spent together, and then he remembered a small detail he must have disregarded. She was a scientist *and* a cop? What if she could help him understand what was happening to his people, why there were more rogues now than he'd seen in the last three hundred years? The idea tantalized. Then his stomach hollowed. He'd be putting her in grave danger. The Council would never allow a human to know about them.

But she was strong. A police officer. She'd be able to stand up to The Council.

And if they decided to end her life anyway?

Chaz shuddered. Then his cell phone buzzed. He stared at the number and smiled. "Pitch?"

"Charles Tower, as I live and breathe."

"You don't."

"Semantics."

"Captain Pritchard. To what do I owe this pleasure?"

"I'm at your place. Apparently, you're not."

Chaz smiled. "I will be in two or three minutes. It's been a long time. You slumming?"

"Uh, no." Pitch hesitated.

"What's going on?"

"When you get here, Chaz. When you get here."

Pitch wanted to talk in private? His stomach clenched. He walked as fast as he dared without attracting too much attention and made it home in two minutes.

With the sun having set, a chill breeze picked up, adding to his unease. A police siren sounded in the distance, reminding him of his duty to protect, making him wonder if there was another rogue they needed to put down. Pitch pushed off the wall and stepped out of the shadows when he arrived at his building. Black hair pulled into a knot at the nape of his neck, slight of build, but with a wiry strength and determination that just wouldn't quit, Pitch was the one vampire Chaz would always want guarding his back.

He clapped his friend on the shoulder, gave him a quick hug, and opened the door. "Smells like you just fed."

Her address was a burned tattoo inside his brain. "I did. Do you need to go out and come back?"

"Nah. If I leave, I'm not planning on coming back. You feel me, bro?"

Chaz winced. There was something out and out wrong about a Colonial Army Captain trying to mimic modern slang. He stepped into the elevator, and Pitch followed. Still curious and out of sorts from wishing he was with Stacy and not Pitch, he didn't say anything. He opened the door to his loft and walked up to a credenza, opened a drawer, and pulled out a key, which he threw to his friend. "In case you need a place to crash."

"Thanks."

Turning, he pinned his friend with a stern stare. "Okay. So what's going on?"

Pitch rubbed the back of his neck and started to pace. "You're gonna think I'm crazy, but I'm worried about Mick."

Chaz snorted then let out the laughter he tried to hold in.

"I know. I know," Pitch answered. "I'm crazy, right? But I'm really worried about him." Pitch stopped pacing, and his brows drew together and two creases furrowed his forehead. "I've been trying to get a hold of him for two weeks. He's not answering my calls or texts. So I went by his place. Doesn't look like he's been there in a while."

"He's been off the grid before."

"Yeah, but if I'm a real pain in the ass, he'll answer. Eventually. Not only have I tried him like three or four times a night, I even checked out his cottage up in Vermont. No sign of him."

A chill crept down Chaz's neck. He dismissed it immediately, as the idea of the three laws and that robot movie filled his head. Vampires had their three laws also.

Vampire rule number one stated a vampire may drink but were forbidden to drain a human to death. Rule two: humans must never know vampires exist, and every human must be given Lethe, so they never remember anything after a vampire has fed. Included in this rule was an edict that, unless a vampire was willing to put his life on the line to defend his actions, he dared not turn a human into a vampire. A long time ago, Chaz figured that was because there weren't that many humans walking the earth. Now he figured this was to continue to safeguard their anonymity.

The final rule, the most important, Chaz believed, was that a vampire should not drink from another vampire. *Ever.* Drinking from another vampire created a connection for as long as their eternity lasted. Before Pitch was born, Chaz and Mick had been forced to drink from each other to stay alive. Chaz would've known if Mick was in trouble.

A chill settled on the back of his neck anyway. "Mick is a big boy. He's been taking care of himself way longer than we've been around."

Pitch waved his hand, dismissing Chaz's explanation. "I know. But this…this feels different."

"What do you mean, different?"

"Well, for one," he paused, glancing at the bottles of wine in the rack. "You gonna offer me a drink?"

Chaz walked over to his bar and poured them both a small glass of wine. Pitch chugged his. That chill on his neck turned ice cold. "The last time I talked to Mick, he sounded, well, I know you're not going to believe it, but he sounded concerned. Anxious, even. And we both know that's just not Mick."

What? How was that possible? Why didn't he know? Oh shit. What the hell was going on? Chaz sipped on his wine to cover his angst. "Did he say why?"

Pitch stared down at his glass like he wanted ten more. Chaz knew what kind of pain that caused. "Got mad and told me to quit bugging him, that I'd know what was going on when I needed to."

Chaz nodded. "Well, that sounds like Mick, doesn't it?"

"Yeah. Except that was the last time I talked to him. Over two weeks ago."

When Chaz clapped his friend on the shoulder, Pitch looked up. His gaze was filled with worry. "Listen. You need to feed. I'll check around. Try and find him, although we both know if Mick doesn't want to be found…"

Pitch nodded.

"Let's touch base tomorrow night, okay?"

"Hey, look," Pitch said. "Maybe I'm just being paranoid. But he's like a father to me."

"To us all."

He walked Pitch to the front door and gave his friend a quick hug. "He's probably doing it on purpose 'cause you've been bugging him."

"God, I hope so." He punched Chaz in the shoulder and straightened as if the weight on his back lessened. "Thanks, man."

"And not a word to Ozzie or the others yet."

Pitch nodded. "No need worrying them."

"Agreed." Chaz smiled. "Next time, let's go hunting together. Like the old days."

"I'd like that."

"Good. I'm glad you stopped by." But as Chaz shut the door, he knew he was lying. Mick had sent him a file a couple of days ago that made no sense. Pictures of an abandoned estate up in New York. No message. Just the pictures.

What the hell are you doing, Mick? And why aren't you talking to me?

A few hours later, Chaz was still trying to figure out what was going on when his phone buzzed. He read the number, and relief flooded his veins. "What the hell, Mick? You've had Pitch going crazy. Even had me worried."

Silence. Then a voice whispered. "Help me."

Chapter Two

CHAZ

WHAT THE DEVIL? "MICK?" IT DIDN'T SOUND LIKE HIM. "FOR THE love of God, Mick. Talk to me. Please."

Silence.

Chaz stopped his fist just in time before he shattered the laptop on his desk. He waited. And waited. And finally, dead air, and the tell-tale beep-beep that said the call had disconnected.

Vampires never experience nausea, but right at this moment, he could swear his stomach churned. He went back to the pictures, trying to glean any kind of information from them. His thoughts shouted in his brain.

Call me back, Mick. Talk to me. Please.

Again. Silence.

He paced, raking his hand through his hair, hating their connection. With Mick, it tended to be all one-sided. His. And yet he couldn't get away from the awful feeling that Mick was in terrible trouble and there wasn't a damned thing he could do about it.

He'd met Nicholai Alexander Mikhail Kirilenko in the kingdom of Poland in 1223 AD. Chaz had been a vampire for over one hundred years, and truth be told, not very good at it. Mick explained in his singular dry humor that draining people even though he didn't kill them, was very counterproductive to their existence, and that Chaz could manage the hunger if he tried. Mick said he'd learned some things from the people in China, things like meditation that could help with the thirst. Chaz couldn't fathom it until they journeyed to Asia sixty years later.

Chaz threw himself back in his chair. He rubbed his face. He stared at his hands, long fingers, pale skin, the hands of a killer, the hands of a Paladin.

They were all Paladins, the protectors who kept rogue vampires from killing anyone or anything carrying blood, each unique in his or her own way. It wasn't like Mick was taciturn, like Ozzie. Or mean spirited, the way Vanessa made herself seem sometimes. Mick simply didn't talk much unless he was teaching. He was a quiet man, thoughtful, intelligent, and yes, irascible. But there wasn't a Paladin among them that didn't love the old man deep inside their hearts.

Mick? Where are you?

A picture flashed in his head. A long blonde ponytail. The curve of a hip he'd never forget. What? Wait a minute.

Mick. What the hell?

Mick laughed, and the hairs lifted on the back of his neck. Chaz had no idea what was going on but he had never been able to see Mick's thoughts before, only hear them, and Mick never laughed like that. His mentor sounded like he'd lost his mind. If so, then Stacy was in danger.

I don't understand. But whatever is going on with you, please don't hurt her. Don't do this.

Vignettes flashed through his brain, randomly scattered pieces of the past. Some he recognized. Some he didn't. He grabbed his keys and threw on a jacket, not for the cold, but for the hidden tools of his profession—the extract, a long silver-handled knife with an edge so sharp it could cut through bone, a steel stake with a vicious point at the end. And then he realized. Chaz had no idea where to go.

He ran down to his car anyway. *One hundred and thirty-eight.* Confused, Chaz didn't understand. All of his instincts screamed at him to throw the car in drive to go somewhere, anywhere. Instead, he centered his being and let the world fall away.

Tell me more, Mick.

One hundred and thirty-five.

Chaz pounded his fist on the steering wheel. A loud crack brought him back to reality. He stared at the leather-covered plastic and was grateful it wasn't hanging in pieces.

What the hell was Mick trying to tell him? He was counting out, oh shit, of course. Numbers.

Chaz punched the ignition button, and the engine roared to life. His tires screeched and his nose wrinkled at the smell of burnt rubber as his car sped out of the garage.

He headed onto 78W and then got on the Garden State Parkway heading south. Mick was reading road signs.

Come on, old friend. You're stronger than this. Whatever it is, you need to fight it. Let me help you fight it.

Sweeeeeet....taaaassssttte.

Chaz didn't have to ask who; he already knew. His fingers trembled. Mick had always had secrets, but he'd never been coy about them. Belligerent? Unbearably so. So his behavior didn't make sense. Normally Mick would've told him to go fuck off by now. And the only true vibe he'd gotten from his friend was about blood.

"A rogue loses all capacity to reason as the fever progresses. Remember that, my young friend," Mick had told him decades ago. "The need becomes all-consuming. And if a rogue vampire marks a human, he'll stop at nothing to drain that human dry. He'll travel to the end of the earth to taste that blood. For that will be the last blood he drinks before death."

Please no. Don't let it be true.

Chaz gripped the steering wheel even tighter. He shifted in his seat. The miles sped by. Red Bank. Seaside. All of a sudden, his heart dropped. He knew where Mick was going. Her address filled his vision. His foot stomped down on the gas pedal. Finally, he pulled off at exit fifty-nine and, following his nav system, drove as fast as he dared to her house. There was no sign of her car or Mick. Then he picked up an image—a bar by the bay.

His tires kicked gravel everywhere as he wheeled the car around. He sped down the road, following the familiar thick and dank scent of the bay. Up ahead, he spied the semi-lit billboard of O'Reilly's Bar. His tires screeched to a halt as he slammed on his brakes. He threw open the car door and scrambled out.

A different scent filled his nostrils, one he knew all too well. For a human, death has no smell until the body begins to fester. But for a vampire, the end of life was decay, piece by piece, bit by bit, until all that was left was the rotted remains. Mick wasn't Mick anymore. His hair lay matted, and greasy flaky tendrils hung limply to his shoulders. Flesh, unable to keep its composure, sloughed off in raw patches from his face making his mentor barely recognizable. Chaz recoiled at the putrid stench; Mick was decomposing right before his eyes.

Chaz had never seen any vampire this far gone rogue and still left stand standing.

"Put your hands up where I can see them, and don't move!" Stacy commanded. She stood, feet braced, arms extended, the handle of her gun firmly gripped in both hands, ready to fire.

"Whatever you do," Chaz warned. "Please, do not fire your weapon."

She hesitated.

"Mikhail," he said. "Listen to me. You're better than this. Try to remember who you are. You're a Paladin. You know what you have to do." He paused, having no idea how this was all going to go down. "Please. I beg of you. Don't give in to the madness."

Stacy's gaze followed the creature's every move. *Creature?* To call the one man he named his father a creature? He watched her make sure the muzzle of her gun never wavered from his heart—Mick's heart. Only Mick wasn't a man anymore. He was…oh God…a thing. And the thing Chaz chose to call a man shifted from foot to foot, and crouched like an animal waiting to strike.

He tried to move slowly so that his body came between Mick and Stacy. Only, Stacy kept circling to keep her gun trained on Mick.

"What the hell is going on here? Is this some kind of horror movie?"

He didn't answer. Instead, he spoke to…it. "Mick. You need to go to Sanctuary. Please."

"Charlessss," the thing hissed.

Like fingernails on a blackboard, the long talons sprouting from Mick's hands scraped against the macadam. Droplets of what looked like old blood, dark and brown, splattered the fabric of what was left cf his shirt.

"Mick. Please. If you have any humanity left inside, stop this insanity. Go to the caves. Don't make me kill you."

Man? Sunken cheeks, lips drawn back in a grotesque caricature, were proof that whatever-it-was in front of him, it certainly was not a man. "Mikhail. Friend. Mentor." Each word filled the air with heart-wrenching anguish.

The creature lifted its head. The words found their mark. "You taught me how to accept my life," Chaz continued. The agony in his belly dug deep. "You taught me there was integrity in what I'd become. Don't make me erase that goodness. Please."

With the ocean not far away, a foggy night thickened with clammy cold air. Chaz shivered as a gust of wind brought a fresh wave of salty decay to his nostrils. A murky haze seemed to settle around them, making everything slow down.

Short, staccato breaths left Stacy's mouth in rapid succession. "Wait a minute. You know this...*thing?*" For a split second, her gaze flew to his. "What *are* you?"

"The only *thing* keeping you alive."

"Comforting."

He dismissed her with a wave of his hand. "Mick, if you want to die on your own terms, then let her go. No collateral damage."

"Collateral damage? Really?"

Chaz watched Stacy stiffen, arms steady as she took aim. Her fingers tightened around the butt of her gun, and she inhaled. In the time it took her to release that breath, Chaz turned, sprinting over to the corner of the bar, pulled a vent pipe off the building and then charged, using the pipe like a baseball bat, swinging so hard he thought the muscles in his neck would break from the strain.

Mick staggered and fell, screaming in pain.

"Stacy. Run!"

"Not on your life," she cried, holding her ground.

Mick shook his head and lifted into a crouch. A wave of foul decay filled his nostrils, dank, and putrid. Stacy coughed and choked just as affected.

"Get out of here now!"

"No!"

"You don't understand," Chaz said. "A terrible craving is tearing at his insides. Mick can hear your heart race, feel your blood pump. You're the one he wants. Not me."

"Feel my blood pump?"

Mick balanced on all fours ready to spring. His lips drew back in a feral snarl. Long sharp incisors hung over his bottom lip, unable to retract anymore. He stalked towards her.

"What the hell?"

Time to get her out of here. Only there was a huge problem. Mick stood between her and her car. She could run into the bar, but that would only put the two humans inside in danger. "Run! Run into the complex."

Suddenly, Mick stopped moving. Dank, filthy tendrils of hair swung as he whipped his head around. The click of the handle sounded at the same time. A door opened and closed with a bang.

"Stacy. Shoot. Shoot now!"

She hesitated. Mick twisted, first towards the sound, and then towards her. And then it hit him—the sound of another human heart. Still beating normally as the person it belonged to had no idea the danger they were in.

"For the love of God, Stacy. Fire!"

She pulled the trigger, and her revolver exploded. Three shots in rapid succession, yet Mick still half-stood there even though his left shoulder flew backward with the force of her bullets. All three. Straight into its heart. If he had one left.

Just as a tiger can lie placid on the grass so it can leap and kill its prey in mere seconds, so could Mick. Or whatever Mick had become. He gathered and bunched and vaulted for Stacy. So did Chaz, landing on his back. Rooted to the spot, he realized Stacy could only stare as Chaz pulled back Mick's head, yanked open his mouth, and tried to pour the extract inside.

Mick wasn't having any of that and threw Chaz off him with a mighty swipe of his arm. The guard, hearing the commotion, came charging into the parking lot. Chaz scrambled to his feet. "Get back!" he yelled to the guard. "Get away from here! Run!"

Mick couldn't make up his mind. Two human hearts thundered. Chaz ran to protect Stacy as the guard tried to scramble away. Stacy raised her revolver again. Before she could get off another shot, Mick lunged, tackled the guard, grabbed his collar, and tried to run. Chaz bolted after Mick and jumped on his back. He wrapped his arm around Mick's neck to pour more extract, but Mick swiped his arm away. Mick threw him off his back, dropped the man, and sprinted away.

Chaz ran back to the guard and knelt down. Blood began pouring out of a wound in the guard's neck. How fitting that Mick would use the last of his humanity to put him between a rock and a hard place. For he was going to have to try to save the guard while Stacy watched.

And he was going to have to try not to drain the man dry.

———

CHAZ LAPPED AT THE WOUND, HOPING HE COULD SEAL IT. BUT IT was pretty deep and very close to the man's carotid artery. Funny that even at a time like this, he could notice the subtle difference in taste. Stacy's blood was brighter, cleaner. This man's was deeper, earthier. He couldn't imagine what she must be thinking at the moment, all he could hear were words and phrases jumbled together. Even as he tried to get the wound to close, he drank, hating himself for his weakness.

There was a chance this man might die. Sometimes, in order to save a life, a Paladin had to take a life. That was his duty. Even though he felt remorse, his feelings didn't matter. Mick was so far gone rogue, he could kill hundreds before Chaz was able to stop him.

He heard Stacy approach with hesitant steps. He didn't want to look up, didn't want to see the horror in her gaze, the fear, the realization that he was a monster and not a man. He did anyway and found he was right, except there was still that underlying curiosity in her gaze that gave him hope, hope that she might believe he was still a man.

She fell to her knees beside the guard. Her thoughts raged through his skull with the precision of fine cut steel. She couldn't comprehend what just happened and couldn't equate that to what he was. She wanted to help the man lying on the ground, but more than that, she wanted to get him far away from the guard.

Chaz didn't have time for human fear. He had a rogue to follow. He rose and scanned the parking lot. The trail wasn't hard to find. Drops of blood like the breadcrumbs in a fairy tale dotted the pavement. He became a bloodhound, half walking, half- running as he followed. And then he realized, Mick had circled back. He was going after Stacy.

In the time it took for him to reach the bar parking lot, he found them both. Stacy didn't have time to even draw a breath as she turned. Mick lifted her up off her knees by the neck to bring her flesh to his mouth. Chaz didn't think. He leaped and pulled out his knife, slashing at the hand that held her. She fell to the pavement coughing and gasping for air, the sounds music to his ears. She was still alive, for a grip like that could've snapped her neck in two.

Mick howled in agony. Chaz crouched as they circled one another. He feinted with one hand and threw the knife into the other and lunged. Mick knew the trick. He sidestepped and swiped at Chaz, long talons tearing at the flesh of his stomach.

Chaz groaned with the pain but never let his focus wander. His left arm now cradled his belly, but his right still held the knife. Mick lifted his own wrist to his mouth and sucked and sucked then lapped at the wound.

How did he know to do that? Could there still be some of Mick inside? Somewhere? "Charlessss,"

"Let me make it quick. One stroke of the blade, and you can be at peace. Think, man, think. You don't want to hurt people. You spent your life protecting them."

Chaz lunged again. He missed Mick's heart but caught him in the shoulder, feeling flesh and muscle tear as he yanked the knife free.

Mick screamed this time. Chaz choked on the decay. But that split second of lost focus gave Mick the chance to charge Stacy. Chaz didn't think, didn't hesitate. He threw himself between them just as

Stacy fired her weapon. He felt the bullet pierce his shoulder first, before the burning tear of his flesh, then the crunch of landing on the ground. Air whooshed from his lungs, his head spun, his midsection curled in upon itself for protection.

Mick faltered. Whatever humanity was left inside, the vampire stopped him from finishing Chaz off. Mick froze. Perhaps it was the shock of trying to kill Chaz; perhaps it was the last of the principles he held so dear. No matter the reason, Mick turned and ran off, disappearing—once again—into the darkness.

Heavens above, the pain.

She ran over and fell to her knees beside him. How wonderful the human spirit. "Oh, no. Oh, no. I just shot you." Her hands fluttered over his body. "Oh God, I'm sorry. You got in the way. Why did you do that? You shouldn't have gotten in the way. I had him. Dead to rights. I wouldn't have let him hurt you."

Amazing. Even now, she called Mick a *him* instead of an *it.*

A wave of searing hot agony as painful as his own misery spread from his side to his middle then rolled back again. He moaned. "Listen to me. Please."

She stilled. "Yes. Yes. What?"

"Too late."

"Pat! Mike! Over here!"

She called them Pat and Mike. They came running out of the bar. "Stacy. We heard something like a—holy shit. It was gunshots."

"He's hurt. Badly. Got in the way. Call an ambulance. NOW!"

"NO!"

She whipped her head around and stared at him. "But I shot you...the security guard."

A terrible sadness filled him. With his injuries, he couldn't possibly move fast enough so that she wouldn't have a ringside seat to watch what he was about to do. He rose to his knees, gulping air, and used her shoulder like a brace to stand. He targeted the older man first as he wouldn't be as strong.

He grabbed the man's arm and pulled his wrist to his mouth. Humans have an incredible instinct for survival that he'd always marveled at. The older man brought his free fist down to punch

Chaz's back and pull away. Using his own free hand, Chaz stopped the man and held him still.

Blood, warm and sweet, filled his body. The man weakened as he sucked and swallowed. In the remaining few seconds before the younger man dove at them, Chaz gave the older man the Lethe. He tore away but not before Stacy got a good look at what he truly was.

He really hated that look on her face.

With fresh blood in his system, energy zipped through his body. That energy enabled him to pin the younger man up against the wall of the bar. A wave of pure need buckled his knees as he sank his incisors into the man's neck.

Blood. Always the blood. Every time he fed, he faced the question of whether to kill or not to kill, and he always answered the same. Chaz reared back. He repeated his vow as he had thousands and thousands of times before.

I will not kill again.

He gave the younger man the drug, lapped at his wounds to seal them, and stepped back.

Turning, he found that Stacy had already pulled out her cell phone. He plucked the phone out of her hand and put it in his pocket. Her mouth opened in surprise. So many thoughts were racing through her mind; it was like the flow of a swift-moving stream. In a way, he was glad. He didn't want to have to explain anything at the moment.

Brushing past her, he went back to the young man and lifted him in his arms. The best place to leave both of them now was the bar.

Pain laced through his shoulder. A gunshot was harder to heal than other wounds, even with the fresh blood zinging through his system. He put the younger one on top of the bar and stepped out into the parking lot again. Her feet were braced. Her gun pointed right at his heart.

And she stood over the body of the elder gentleman ready to protect until her dying breath.

"Who are you?"

"Charles Tower." He started to laugh at the absurdity of his next action. He bowed as he would have during his day. "At your service."

"What are you?"

Now that was harder to answer. What did they call them these days? "Your worst nightmare."

"I got that already. What did you do to Mike?" Her chin lifted, so he realized that would be the young man on the bar.

"He's on the bar. When he awakens, he'll be absolutely fine."

She looked down at the man lying at her feet. "And Pat?"

"The same."

But she didn't lose focus. *How…police-like of her.* She kept the gun trained on him every time he moved. "What did you just do to them?"

"Do you really want to know?"

His question seemed to catch her by surprise. The thoughts and words inside her that kept cascading down that streambed began to slow. She hesitated, wiping her chin against her shoulder. He felt her pain, which surprised him. She winced, and he moved closer, but she shook her head. "Uh-uh. I wouldn't do that if I were you."

Then her mind kicked into gear. "You need to give me my cell back so I can call an ambulance for that man over there." She pointed to the guard.

"I'm sorry, but I can't do that." Chaz listened carefully. He barely registered a heartbeat.

"Do it now!" She started circling him, trying to get closer to the guard.

"You don't understand. I can't." This was one night he was going to regret for a millennium.

"Or won't?"

"Both." The heartbeat grew fainter. "Look. Keeping me talking isn't going to help the situation. Nor is calling an ambulance. They won't be in time. He's dying, I'm afraid. He must be bleeding internally."

"I'm only going to ask one more time. Then I'm going to shoot you for real."

The guard's heart stopped beating. Chaz stepped back and allowed her access. She ran to the guard and knelt, feeling for a pulse for quite some time before she sat back on her heels in defeat.

"I'm sorry," Chaz said.

"You're sorry? I just put three bullets into the heart of a nightmare, an innocent man is dead, you wouldn't let me help him, and you're sorry?"

"I don't normally regret my actions, but it seems I involved you in something you should never have been involved in. For that, I am truly sorry."

She rose. "An apology isn't going to bring that man back to life."

"An apology isn't going to bring Mick back either," he exploded. "But I was able to save your life. And theirs. Barely."

"Not the security guard."

Chaz sighed. "Collateral damage."

She huffed. "Collateral damage?" she asked. "How cold of you." She swallowed. "One last time. Give me my cell phone."

"You're going to call the police. I can't allow that to happen."

Chaz shook his head. He watched her finger close around the trigger. Not wanting to get shot again, he snatched the gun out of her grip. He threw the offending weapon down towards the complex where it skittered against the macadam, finally sliding to a halt hundreds of yards away.

Relentless. Dangerous. Beautiful. Chaz hauled her up against his body. He had no other way to stop her without doing possible damage. So he pulled back her head, exposed her neck, sank his incisors into her sweet flesh, and drank until she passed out. He gave her the Lethe, but this time, he had no idea if it would take or not. He'd never done it twice in one night.

Laying her gently on the ground, Chaz pulled out his cell and hit speed dial. "Pitch?"

"Did you find him?"

"I'm afraid so. And you're not going to like it."

Chapter Three

STACY

STACY NEEDED A DRINK. NO, MAKE THAT A BAR FILLED WITH drinks. She looked around. Well, at the very least, she was exactly where she needed to be. She was in O'Reilly's, sitting in a corner, propped up by the back of a booth. Strange. She remembered driving here. She remembered a bag of coffee and wondering where she'd gotten it from. But it smelled really good when she'd opened the flap so she figured she'd picked it up and forgotten she did.

She looked down to find the remnants of a meal she didn't recall eating. God, what the hell did Pat give her? Supercharged cabernet? One minute, her head seemed straight, the next, it seemed to float somewhere between Venus and Mars.

She tried to sit up, and the entire room spun. Damn. Drunk? Maybe she didn't need those drinks after all. Was that possible? Oh hell. She could swear she only had half a glass. She lifted up real slow and looked around. No Pat. No Mike.

"Hey, Pat? What the hell? Did you spike my drink?"

No answer. That was strange. Maybe they were in the back or downstairs and couldn't hear her. "Yo! Pat! Mike! Where are you?"

Concern filled her but from a place very far away. Everything seemed to move in slow-motion. She tried to shake the murkiness from her head, but that turned out to be a bad move. Her stomach rolled over.

Okay, so maybe it was time to go easy and work her way over to the doorway. Of course, walking turned out to be harder than she thought, but she was finally able to get her wobbly sea-legs under her and wove her way toward the back room and downstairs.

"Hey, Mike? Pat? Somebody?"

Still no answer. And she didn't see anyone. So she made her way to the front door. And that was when she heard voices coming from the parking lot.

"Took you long enough to get here."

"I came as fast as I could. I didn't want to deal with a state trooper or a cop."

"I know."

Voice number one let out a huge sigh. "It was Mick. He's gone rogue."

"Rogue, as in dying rogue?"

"'Fraid so. Can't you smell it?"

Voice number two exhaled hard. "Yeah, I can smell it." Was that pain in voice number two? "I can't...no, I don't want to believe it's true. He wasn't old enough."

"It is, Pitch. And you're right. So we're going to have some digging to do. But right now, we've got a lot to cover up. There's a security guard over there that's dead."

"Oh great," voice number two muttered.

"And three humans, one's inside the bar, that I had to drug."

Drug?

"Was one of them a woman?"

"Yeah. Why?"

"I found this over there." Dead silence. Then three words filled with horror. "Oh. God. No."

"He has her scent, Chaz." Chaz? Why was that name familiar to her? "He'll come after her, won't he?"

"His last human. Yes, he won't rest until he gets her."

Last human? What the hell was this, some kind of horror movie?

"Chaz, it's Mick. Do you really think after all that he's done to protect humans, he'll try to kill her?"

"Yes." Voice number one sounded determined. "But I'll stop him first."

Voice number two let out an agonizing wail, and a shiver coasted down her back.

"Pitch, listen to me. You have to screw your head back on. You can grieve tomorrow. Right now, we have until dawn to clean this mess up. I need your help." A crash-thud rocked the entire building. "Including fixing the hole you just put in the wall."

A hole in the building?

Stacy closed her eyes. She needed to screw her head back on too. None of this made any sense at all. She dug her fingers into the wood of the doorjamb and forced herself upright. Taking a deep breath, she opened the door and walked out into the parking lot.

Reaching down, she went to pull out her gun. And that was when she realized she no longer had it in her possession, but one of the men she faced did.

"WHAT DO YOU THINK YOU'RE DOING?"

Both men started. The one with her pistol reminded her of a young Sean Connery but with light brown hair and less intense eyes. The one without her pistol reminded her of Collin Farrell but with a rounder face and thinner eyebrows. Both were gorgeous, but there was also something deadly about them. Without her weapon, Stacy was simply going to have to brazen this one out if she could.

"That's...impossible," the dark one muttered.

"Twice in one night. Maybe not so impossible as you'd think."

Was he talking to his compatriot or her? "Twice in one night...what?"

The dark-haired one shook his head. "You're right. I've never seen an evening go so wrong in all my life. Tell you what, I'll deal with the guard. You deal with her, okay? I'll notify Ozzie and the rest of the

Paladin about Mick. Do you think we should tell Sam what went down?"

Paladin? What was a Paladin? And who was Sam?

The lighter-haired one considered the question a moment. "No. Not yet. Besides, this is Hunter's territory. He should be notified first. If we need to. You take care of the security guard. And I'll…I'll…I'm not sure what I'm going to do yet," he said, turning and glaring her way. "But I'll figure it out."

The darker-haired one nodded. "Good luck with that. And don't bother trying to find me later on tonight. Depending on how I feel, maybe I'll find you."

"I understand." They clasped hands and clapped backs, then the dark-haired one simply walked off down towards the complex.

"What the hell is going on here?"

He held out his arm to guide her back into the bar. "I'll explain inside."

"No, you'll explain now. And you'll give me back my gun." He certainly looked skeptical about doing that. Then she turned her head. There was a fist-sized hole gouged out of the brick. *Who the hell could do that with a bare hand?*

"Or what?"

"Excuse me?" She shook her head again, and the world tilted. She lost her balance, and he grabbed her elbow to steady her. But being near him allowed an idea. She reached out and grabbed her gun, backing away as fast as she could. The asphalt rolled like she was in a wave machine. He took the pistol back, but this time held it with two fingers, barrel facing down.

"I promise I won't hurt you. Please let me get you inside so you can sit down. I don't want you to fall and crack your head."

Her mind felt as convoluted as the moving floor. "Where's Pat? And Mike?"

"I took them home, so they'd be more comfortable when they woke up."

She narrowed her gaze at him. When that didn't work, she tried closing her eyes. She couldn't focus. Okay, this had to be a dream. And a bad one at that.

He grabbed her elbow again, this time not letting
break away, then she tried to snatch her gun again. "W₁
stop?" he exploded. "I'm not going to hurt you." He drew .
breath and expelled the air in a heartfelt hiss. "Technically, ı
your life just now."

"Saved my life?" The earth beneath her feet rolled, and his fingers
tightened. "What are you talking about?"

Stacy moaned, more from confusion than misery, but he seemed
to mistake her intent, for he picked her up in one fluid movement and
carried her back into O'Reilly's. As he walked, Stacy caught a whiff
of a familiar cologne and wondered how that was possible. The only
men's cologne she'd had the pleasure of not enjoying was her co-
worker Dan's, and he reeked of it. But better that than the alternative.

"Put me down, please."

He complied, placing her down in the same booth where she'd
awakened.

"Who are you? What are you doing here? Why'd you have to take
Pat and Mike home? Why is there a hole in the bricks of the building
about the size of my fist? Who's Pitch? Who's Mick? And for the love
of Pete, what happened here?"

He pulled out a chair from the table next to him, swung it around,
sat down backward, and folded his arms on the back. "How do you
want your reality? Small bites or large doses?"

"Is this some kind of joke or prank or something? Did Pat and
Mike put you up to this?"

His features turned grave, and his shoulders slumped. "Trust me,
no joke. No prank."

Her hand fluttered to her brow, and concern filled his soft brown
gaze.

"Are you all right?"

"I could swear I've been drugged, but I have no idea how that
would be possible."

He rose and walked behind the bar, returning with a glass of cold
water. "Thank you." Stacy gulped half the glass before she stopped.
Her stomach rolled a couple of times then stilled.

"My name is Charles Tower. You were attacked. Pat and Mike

came out to help. They got a little beat up trying to defend you. Neither one wanted to go to the hospital, so I told them I'd keep an eye on you and on the bar until you woke up. You hit the pavement pretty hard, but I don't think you have a concussion. They said you would be able to lock up?"

"Yeah, I can. Did you say something about a security guard being dead? Or was I just dreaming that? Because if that was the case, and I got attacked and someone got killed, this place should be swarming with cops."

"It is, in a manner of speaking. Or it will be soon."

What? "Sorry. I don't understand. Who are you? FBI or something?"

"Or something," he muttered. "You're very lucky you're not dead. But I'm afraid I'm not."

"How's that?"

He held up a glove. Her glove. "Hey, where'd you get that?"

"You dropped them in the scuffle."

"Where's the other one?"

"In the possession of the man who tried to kill you."

"Kill me?" Stacy rubbed her face with her hands, trying to get the world to solidify. "What the hell are you talking about? Why would someone want to kill me?"

No matter how gorgeous or incredible the man across from her looked, he could get real serious in a hurry. His body snapped to attention, back ramrod straight, brows drawing together to become a straight line. "Because I involved you in something I shouldn't have involved you in. Not your fault or mine, just bad luck."

Bad luck? That was one way of putting things when your life was supposedly on the line. Which she wasn't sure she believed. Still, he didn't seem like he was trying to hide anything from her.

"Involved in something," she repeated. "Would you mind telling me what?" Stacy looked down at her watch, then back up at him. "Because as sure as I am that the sun is going to rise in a few hours, I *know* Pat would never leave this bar unattended unless he was on his deathbed, or if Mike was here. So you'd better start talking and fast."

He opened his mouth then snapped it shut. He cocked his head, seeming to judge her. "Okay. You want the truth? Here it is. You were attacked by a rogue because I drank from you. This rogue is the only real father I've ever known. He picked up one of your gloves in the parking lot, and he's marked you as his last. He has your scent, and won't stop until he gets you."

Was she missing something here? Because not one word he said made sense. "Rogue? Drank? What the hell are you talking about?"

He drew in a breath that seemed almost painful. "Before I answer, I'm going to do something I shouldn't." He lifted her gun out of the waistband of his pants and placed it on the table. Stacy noted the safety was on, but that problem could be easily remedied. "You should know that a bullet, even two or three, will hurt me but not kill me. And should you decide upon that route, I won't appreciate being hurt. Not at all."

Oh, man. This guy really believes what he's saying. Maybe I should play along.

"There's no need to play along. And yes, I'm completely sincere."

"What the hell? How did you know what I was thinking?"

He didn't skip a beat, just kept talking like they were having an every-day conversation. "I can hear your thoughts within short distances. Most of the time, I don't want to. Too many human thoughts are like a discordant symphony, they grate on my nerves."

"Right." *Hear thoughts? The next thing that's going to happen is that Robert Pattinson is going to walk into the bar, followed by none other than Kristen Stewart.*

"You're not that far off," he muttered.

"Excuse me?"

He seemed to be fighting with himself, shifting in his chair like he wanted to get up then sit down. His fingers alternately clenched the wood of the back of the chair then let go, and each time that happened, his knuckles turned white from the strain. Or were they always that pale?

"A rogue is an out of control vampire."

Stacy couldn't help herself. Boiled up laughter spilled out. She picked up the gun and flipped the safety. "An out of control vampire," she repeated. "Really?" She caught what looked like hurt in his gaze before his face shuttered completely.

"Not a joke."

"Sorry." Stacy pushed her hair off her face with her free hand. "Not every day you get told a vampire wants to kill you. So I need to know. Who set this up?"

He frowned. "Fine. Don't take me seriously. But you need to understand that this rogue has marked you. He has your scent, and he won't stop chasing you until he drains you dry."

"Wow." She sat back and grinned. "You really are awesome. I mean, you should be on Broadway. The big screen. Damn."

"I'm not acting." He jumped up from the chair, raking his hand through his hair. "And I'm not joking."

"C'mon," she said. "I gotta know. Who put you up to this? Who paid you? Kelly?"

"You mean the brunette with the attitude?" Chaz asked.

"I knew it! I knew it! Wait until I get my hands on her." Stacy lowered the gun and flipped the safety back on.

When she looked up, Stacy found his shoulders slumped, and his body deflated like a dying balloon.

"How the hell am I going to make you understand? I'm not kidding."

Her phone rang. He pulled her cell out of his jacket and handed it to her. Her brain clicked back into gear, and she began to assess. Too nicely dressed to be in a bar like O'Reilly's, and Boss cologne had no place in a world of brine.

Her finger hit the button. Tori.

"Stace?" Tori said. "Hi!"

"Hi, yourself."

"I thought you were going to text me."

"Sorry," Stacy said. "I lost track of time."

"So how's the date going?"

"Date?"

"Yeah. With that guy. Said his name was….Charles. That's it. Charles Tower."

Stacy started to grin. Ahh, so it wasn't Kelly, it was Tori. Or maybe both of them. "He's right here with me. We're at O'Reilly's"

"You know," Tori continued. "I was kind of concerned, what with him flashing around hundred-dollar bills and all and getting you to leave us in like five seconds flat."

Because you paid him to? "But it seems like you used your head if you're at O'Reilly's."

Then again, if Tori and Kelly had done that, Tori would've given up the joke by now. She couldn't pull a prank to save her life.

"Give Pat and Mike a hug for me," Tori said.

First thought crashed. Second thought crashed.

"And don't do anything I wouldn't do."

It was coming back. Jersey City. *Adrian's.* Kelly drooling.

"Be careful," Tori continued. "And use precautions. Doctor's orders."

Stacy lifted her gaze. His head tilted, caution filling his gaze. "Of course."

"You can tell me all about it tomorrow. Smooches."

The phone beeped. Tori hung up. Stacy stared down at the screen, a hollow forming in the pit of her belly. She fought with herself. *Adrian's.* A man. Way out of her league. Talking about drool. An invitation to the Chart House. Walking to her car.

She looked up. *Impossible.* But was it? Who the hell knew? So she asked because she had to. "Did you give me a bag of coffee?"

"As a matter of fact, I did."

Chapter Four

CHAZ

THE FUNNY THING ABOUT BEING A VAMPIRE WAS THE MEMORIES. He watched her go into shock, knowing exactly how each moment felt—the spread of fear that locked every muscle in the body, the fade from pale to white, and that last complete blank before passing out.

"Whoa! Wait a minute. Don't—"

He reached out. Stacy's eyes widened. Her shoulders stiffened. Instead of fainting, she skittered back against the booth's cushion, but she knew enough not to forget the pistol. The safety clicked off and she had it pointed straight at him faster than he ever expected.

He reared back, hands up in the air, palms facing her. "Sorry. I just didn't want you to hurt yourself. You were about to faint."

She nodded, very carefully, and very deliberately. She looked completely sober. "So you're a vampire."

"Yes." *Did she really believe him?* "May I lower my hands?"

She nodded.

"I'm not going to hurt you. I swear."

She looked down at the pistol in her hand, no longer accepting its ability to protect her. "You said bullets don't kill you."

"No. But they make holes that hurt a lot. And I bleed profusely for a while. They don't kill until you use a lot of them, and I can't…replenish."

"Replenish?"

"Yes. Blood. I can bleed out."

Her head moved up and down in slow motion. Yeah. She was in shock. But he had to admit, she was handling things better than he expected.

"And you can hear my thoughts so any plan I try to devise to get away, you'll know it, won't you?"

"Yes." His secret was out, and Chaz wasn't sure how he felt about that. Black and white had gone awful gray awful fast. Still, most of this was his fault. "I'm sorry."

Her brows lifted. "Sorry?"

"I don't like invading a human's privacy. And you're not supposed to know I exist. I gave you the drug twice tonight. I dare not try a third time."

"Drug? You drugged me?"

"To make you forget that I drank your blood and what just happened."

She pursed her lips then bit her lower lip, deep in thought, but her sharp gaze never left him, nor did the pistol pointed at his chest. "You want me to forget that I discharged my firearm, put three bullets into someone, and ignore that a man whose name I think is Jim, just died?"

Chaz scowled. "I have no choice."

"Well, I do." She settled the gun back into her palm, and her fingers tightened around the grip, making him angry. He wasn't the enemy. "And *that's* not going to happen."

"Look," he growled, stepping to the table next to them. He pressed his palms into the wood so he wouldn't do something stupid. He stared as if sheer will could make her understand. "You're not listening, and I'm running out of moonlight here. I have friends coming back here who need to believe you're out cold. Besides, I already know you're dead on your feet."

"Very funny."

"Not meant as a joke. You're exhausted, and I'm going to fall asleep soon. Can we maybe go back to your house? I'll explain more when we get there."

"And make me walk away from a crime scene?"

"There is no crime scene," he exploded. "The guard is lying in his bed in his home as we speak. His family will believe he had a heart attack and died very peacefully in his bed. We'll have washed away the blood in the parking lot by morning. The hole in the brick wall will be repaired and a thought given to Pat that a truck backed into it by accident. Shall I continue?"

She took each statement as a blow. Her body flinched, but she never moved to block or parry. "Why are you doing this?"

"Because you're not supposed to know I exist. I mean, humans aren't." Chaz found he didn't like hurting her. "Being invisible has allowed us to survive for millennia. You tend to shoot first and ask questions later."

"So you're just going to simply cover up a murder?"

God, she could be one-track. "It's not like that." But it was. And he knew it. More importantly, she knew it. "He already had clogged arteries. He was a walking time bomb waiting to explode."

"Wait a minute. How do you know that? And how does that justify what you've done?"

"It doesn't. I could hear the blood flow through his blood vessels. He was a heart attack waiting to happen."

"He was a man. A simple man. Probably thinking about nothing more important than grabbing a bite because his shift was done."

One hand left the pistol and picked up her phone. She began to dial. *Damn it!* "Why can't you simply accept what I am and what happened for now?"

Because he had no choice, Chaz flashed over to her and plucked the cell out of her grasp, then regained his previous position all in the time it took for her to blink. He closed the call. "I can't let you call anyone. I'm sorry."

She stared at him like he was some kind of freak. Then her brows drew together, and her lips thinned. "You're sorry? Did it ever occur to you that maybe he had a family? Children? That he might have a soccer game to go to or a baseball game or a movie that he promised to attend?"

"Yes." Hurt seeped through him, but he couldn't change the past, only protect the future. So he lifted his chin and answered, "I've been protecting humans for the last seven hundred and fifty years."

"Well, you sucked at it tonight."

"You think I don't know I failed in my duty?" All the anger and frustration of the night boiled over. He took the chair in front of him and threw it across the room, where it broke into pieces. "Mick was like me. A Paladin. He spent thousands of years protecting humans. I would never, could never, have foreseen this happening. You have to believe me."

Chaz turned and stared at the broken pieces of wood on the floor, His heart hammered in his chest like an out of control piston. He turned back, clenching his fists, his gaze pleading that she try to understand. "Someone or something caused Mick to go rogue. I need to find out who and why. You need my protection. So I'm asking. Do you think you can hold onto your duty for just a little while? All I can promise is that none of what transpired tonight was taken lightly. The guard was treated with the utmost respect. His family will be taken care of. There will be an insurance policy they never knew about."

"Won't bring him back."

"I know."

"And my gun?"

"Pitch is a firearms expert. It's a hobby of his. He'll replace the bullets, clean and oil, whatever it takes to make your gun brand new. No one needs to know."

"And me? I'll know."

"For now? Yes, you will."

CHAZ HAD A HARD TIME CONVINCING STACY TO GO HOME. Eventually, when she saw that he hadn't lied, that the building and the parking lot looked as he said it would, that the silent man who took her gun did so with grim anguish, she accepted what he told her. He followed her back to her home and listened as she thought about locking him out of the house; he simply stared and waited. She didn't live far away from the bar. Her small shore home was a perfect retreat. Stacy lived on a lagoon at the end of a block in a small town called Tuckerton. He could tell she'd made some recent renovations to her home by adding another floor, for he could still make out the scent of fresh-cut wood from up above.

"I have a weapon in my bedroom gun safe. Touch my bedroom door, and I'll empty the entire chamber into you. Do you read me?"

Chaz nodded. The door slammed shut. He walked over to the sliding glass door in the kitchen and waited for the sun to rise, agonizing over every moment of what happened and asking if there was anything else he could have done, could have changed. There wasn't.

Not too long ago, the first hint of the sun would have him yawning. But lately, he'd been able to see almost a full sunrise before needing to lie down. This morning, though, the sun became a round orb in the sky before he even yawned. A testament to a night he'd rather forget.

A knock sounded on the door. He opened the portal to find Pitch standing on the deck. It seems, he too was so upset the rising of the sun had less effect. Pitch didn't say anything; he simply handed Chaz Stacy's gun. "You should probably stay here."

Pitch shook his head. "I checked into a little dive motel about two minutes away."

"I understand."

Pitch nodded and hurried down the steps. Strange, a strong emotion such as grief could forestall the inevitable. The gun was wrapped in a soft cloth, cleaned with loving hands that would never hug their father again. He placed the firearm on the table.

My fault. My fault.

God, he could hear Mick screaming at him. *Not your fault. You did what you had to do to survive.* But someone or something was at fault. Because Mick didn't go rogue on his own. In fact, Chaz was certain. The thought of it would've made him put a gun to his heart and pull the trigger. Mick's family was killed by a rogue. Mick was the only one to survive. He should've died. Instead, he became a Paladin.

Chaz looked at her closed door then back at the couch in the living room. Her soft breathing told him she was finally asleep. He figured there'd be no harm in sleeping on a soft mattress. He didn't touch the door exactly just the knob and shouldered it open, surprised to find it unlocked.

What a shame. Stacy didn't know her own beauty. He imprinted her on his mind hoping she could stave off the nightmares he was sure to endure. He didn't dream often. When he did, he had a tendency to remember them. He lay down beside her, wishing he could comfort her. But nothing would comfort him.

Dawn would break soon. Too soon, Charles thought as he continued to follow the scent of old blood and decay through the forest. Normally, he would have enjoyed running across the countryside, his heart pounding with the sheer freedom of movement. But this night was no ordinary night. His quarry no ordinary quarry.

He knew something was wrong as soon as he entered the inn. He'd found no stable boy asleep in the hay, no innkeeper came at his entry, shuffling and yawning to take his coin. A half-empty mug sat upon a wood plank table.

All of which caused an icy ball to form in the pit of his belly.

But worse than these signs? The smell of fresh blood. He followed the scent, his anxiety growing—a slipper resting haphazardly under a bush. A stocking cap caught upon the branch of a tree.

Charles shivered, knowing now what he would find. He followed the trail to a small clearing by a stream and found his answer. Three dead—the innkeeper, his wife, and a young girl barely come of age. His breath caught as he cried out in agony. When his kind turned rogue, they could feel it coming, and when it happened, they were supposed to go to the caves. They were supposed to let Samira perform the ritual. They were supposed to die.

Sometimes they ran. When they did, Charles's job was to stop them.

He hesitated, caught between want and need. He wanted to keep tracking the rogue. He needed to take care of the dead.

Very quickly, Charles placed a drop of rosary pea extract on each hole in each neck. He said a quick prayer, not sure what the ceremony would do now. They were already gone.

So unnecessary. These poor people should never have died.

His jaw clenched. He would have to return and bury them later. If there was a later.

Charles sped over to the edge of the clearing. A winding path threaded through the trees. The crackle of dead leaves mixed with the wind as he tried to listen. There. A faint drag-scrape, drag-scrape. Barely discernible.

He scanned the path. Footprints. Charles followed them as fast as he dared, tasting the air to make sure he wouldn't make a mistake. Wait. The trail simply stopped. He doubled back and found the last print.

Lifting his head, Charles scanned the woods for a sign. His heart began to pound. God, help him, had he lost the rogue? Then he spied a broken branch in the distance. He inhaled deeply. He could still smell that sickening, rancid, bitter mockery of life.

Coward.

His hand fisted, crushing the branch. He ran through the tangle of twisted vines and brush. Branches slapped at his face. He ignored the pain. But not the rage.

Such a waste.

He sped through the trees, knowing he gained on his prey. The hunter was now the hunted. A moment later, a terrified scream ratcheted down his spine. The rogue stopped to feed.

The small cottage sat in a clearing. A man lay unconscious on the ground, his ax next to him. The body of a young woman was draped over the rogue's arm. The creature seemed to pause, just about to sink his incisors into the girl's flesh, and Charles swore he saw it grin. He launched his body into both of them, rolling across the ground and onto his feet before the rogue could snatch the girl and sprint away.

They circled each other, predator against predator. "Do you think you can ssstop me?"

As they circled, he realized the rogue refused to travel far from his meal. "You had no right to kill these people. You should have gone to the caves."

Charles kept charging, trying to distract the beast from its prize. "I am immortal. I have the power. They are fodder. I shall not die."

"Yes, you will," Charles replied, circling the rogue. And then the fiend made a

fatal mistake. It tripped over the girl's leg and fell, giving Charles the opportunity he'd been seeking. With all of his might, he threw the rogue on its back and drove his fist into what used to be a face. Again and again, he punched the creature senseless.

From inside his coat, he withdrew the extract and poured it down the rogue's throat, watching it thrash and writhe until the creature was unconscious. Panting from his efforts, Charles sat back on his heels, and he stared straight into damnation.

The girl had watched him take down the rogue but not kill the beast.

Charles curled in upon himself as self-loathing tore him to pieces. Because there was more. He withdrew a wicked-looking knife from his coat and severed the head of the rogue from its body. She would watch.

In a moment, however, he was going to make her forget. Everything. But Charles would always remember—there would be no solace of sweet forgetfulness. He would carry the chains of his memories.

And the blood.

Chapter Five

STACY

DAMN, DAMN, DAMN, STACY MORGAN THOUGHT, HER HEAD pounding inside her skull. She needed to stop drinking so much on the weekend. Then she realized she wasn't alone.

So beautiful. The man lying next to her reminded her of a model —high cheekbones, squarish chin, thin nose, and strong brow. Straight, silky blonde/brown hair framed his face. She reached out to move an errant strand off his cheek.

He stirred, opened one eye, and peered around, and then he let his head fall back onto the pillow. That was when reality slammed into her.

Chaz.

Talk about nightmares. Stacy wasn't sure if she'd be better off laughing or crying. "It wasn't a dream, was it?"

He looked as if he didn't know how to answer. "No."

"You're a vampire."

"Yes."

"The bar? The guard?"

He frowned. "Yes."

She put her head in her hands and tried to stop the pounding in her ears. Then, he was massaging her neck and making the pain go away. She wanted to shout at him not to touch her, but even the light pressure of his fingers mesmerized, making it easy to drown in sensation.

"I thought I wasn't supposed to remember anything."

He let go. She sat up and rolled her neck. As she turned, he watched her. "Oversight."

"I thought I told you not to touch my bedroom door."

"I didn't, exactly."

He leaned back on one elbow, looking perfectly at home in her bed. A lock of hair fell onto his forehead, and she forgot the events of the past evening in favor of simply savoring the picture he made. He destroyed that by saying, "Your gun is in the kitchen if that makes you feel better." Pain filled his gaze.

Her stomach soured. Seemed reality sucked for both of them. He swung his legs over the bed, and his head hung between his lowered shoulders, hands cradling each side until a long shudder rippled through his body. When he looked up, their gazes caught and held for an awkward moment.

"We have to talk."

She nodded, and that was when she realized she was barely half-dressed. "You have me at a complete disadvantage. So, you'll have to wait. I'm not about to have any kind of a serious conversation without some clothes on."

His gaze raked her body then skittered away like she was some kind of forbidden fruit.

"And not without some coffee in my system," she continued.

He nodded. "Fine. Go ahead."

Stacy showered as quickly as she could and got dressed. When she came out of the bathroom, she found him shrugging into his shirt. The front had a tear in it, and the shoulder was stained with blood.

"Here," she told him, rummaging in the closet then throwing a flannel shirt at him. "This should fit."

"Ex-boyfriend?"

Did he sound a little jealous, or was that just her imagination? "No. Mike's." She scrunched up her face. "He stayed here for a while before he found his own place." She half-laughed. "He and Pat were having a bit of an issue. Sometimes it's tough working with your Dad. Mike was military police. Pat can be a bit of a hard-head."

"Tough job."

She paused. "Yes." She shrugged, feeling that familiar surge, scared and proud all at the same time. "Mike's like a brother. We grew up together. Helped me get over my first heartbreak in high school." She pushed back the emotion that welled inside her. "Besides, although he gets it, he isn't thrilled with my profession either."

"The cop part?"

"Not exactly anymore. After my parents died, I got tired of the city. Maybe I got tired of my life altogether. I don't know. I quit working in the blood center and went back to school, majored in forensics, and got my Masters. Then I went to the Police Academy. When I applied to the Ocean County Sherriff's department, they couldn't wait to hire me. Doesn't have all the bells and whistles, but it's home."

Stacy walked into the kitchen, and Chaz followed behind her. She started the coffee and watched in amazement as he took the open bag from her after she was through. He inhaled, held his breath for several seconds, and then let the air out.

"I don't eat. Obviously, but I have an incredible sense of smell. Sometimes I buy a bag of freshly ground just so I can do this. But then I have to give it away or throw it out."

Stacy didn't know how to answer. "You really *are* a vampire."

"Yeah."

She shook her head. "You're a figment of my imagination."

"I'm supposed to be."

"In spite of all the hype? I mean, that television series made you all celebrities, no? The movies even more so."

"Hide in plain sight," he answered with a shrug. "I wouldn't say I did a real good job of that last night, would you? You're in the middle of this fiasco now whether you want to be there or not."

"Fiasco? Damn right, this is a fiasco."

He nodded. He looked out her kitchen slider at the last rays of the sun glinting off the lagoon. He lifted his shoulders and let them fall, air rushing out in a heartfelt sigh. Or was that her own emotions projecting on him? "Yes. And we have some problems we can't solve."

Stacy didn't like any of what happened. A hole burned in her stomach at the thought of covering up a murder. Still, informed was better than floundering in a world she didn't understand. "Enlighten me."

"You," he said.

"Me?"

"Yeah, you. The rogue has your scent."

"The rogue. That thing that attacked me?"

"Yes. You dropped your gloves." His voice was sharp, but not cold. "He has one, and as sure as the sun is going down right now, he's going to come after you."

Not sure how she should answer, she asked, "Is that supposed to frighten me?"

He inhaled as if he were dealing with a small child. Of course, she was behaving that way because she had no idea how to handle any of this at all.

"You bet your sweet ass it is. You have no way of standing up to a vampire. Certainly not a rogue."

"I don't?" she asked softly, and then Stacy countered. "I stood up to you pretty well."

"With a gun?" He scoffed. "You do remember what I said last night, don't you?"

She nodded, feeling like a little kid getting a reprimand. "You got lucky you didn't shoot me more than once."

"Lucky?"

A streak of sadness flashed across his face. "I am what I am, Stacy. And you'd better start accepting that."

"Not fair."

"No, and you'd better get it through that thick freaking head of yours—you don't know what you're dealing with here."

His voice was sharper now and cut with a coldness that might have frightened her if she hadn't seen everything she had the night before. The threat was there, but Stacy wasn't scared.

"You're vulnerable. You're going to make a mistake that will cost you your life."

"What do you mean?"

His shoulders slumped. "Do you remember what I told you? That you're not supposed to know about me?"

"Yes."

"I was supposed to give you Lethe and make you forget all about me. But I can't. I need your help."

"Need my help?"

He walked over to lift his jacket off the back of a chair and fingered the tear in the material. "I've gotten you involved in something way over your head, put you in unnecessary danger. That security guard died because I met you. I'm sorry about that. I didn't mean to involve you, but you're in this up to your eyeballs. I need you to promise me that you'll follow my instructions to the letter so I can protect you."

Stacy turned to pour a cup of coffee so she could gather her thoughts. When she finally sat down at the kitchen table, he didn't follow. He watched her closely, and something in his expression made him seem more than worried. Unsure.

"All right, I promise."

He cocked his head, as though he listened for something beyond her words.

"I don't care how, but you need to stop reading my mind. I have a right to my privacy."

"I'm trying."

She shook her head. "No, just now, you wanted to make sure I was telling the truth. Do that again, and all bets are off. Are we clear?"

He looked affronted. He opened his mouth like he was ready to say something, but Stacy glared. She shot him a look she knew told him there was no way of arguing.

Chaz stared for a moment. "Crystal," he said.

"Good. Now we may differ about how much protection I may or may not need, but three bullets to the heart has my attention. So, keep going. You haven't tried to drug me yet for a reason."

"I need your expertise."

"Expertise?" she asked. "What do you mean?" Why would a very self-sufficient vampire with some very powerful vampire friends need her help?

"Well, I discovered what you just told me. That you were not only a forensic chemist but that you had a special master's in blood banking."

"Continue."

"A rogue vampire is a very rare occurrence. The first rule we learn is that when we feel it coming, we go to a place to die—a safe place. So we don't hurt anyone. But like everyone else, vampires can get scared. Some run."

Stacy took a sip of coffee and pondered. That made sense. Sort of. "All right, but what has that got to do with me?"

He hesitated as though debating what he wanted to reveal.

"Trust goes both ways, you know," she added.

"This isn't the first rogue we've had to eliminate in this area." His words tumbled out, spilling out on top of one another. "It's the third in the last six months. And all of them except Mick were way too young to go rogue."

Wow.

"No one knows what I've done yet. That you still know who and what I am. I'm not sure of the consequences of that," he continued, the fear in his gaze real and terrifying. "But I need your help. Maybe you could figure out why these vampires are going rogue. You're a scientist. A Specialist in Blood Bank. A blood banker and a forensic chemist."

A huge two-hundred-and-forty-watt light bulb went on inside her head. She sat back in her chair and breathed. "You need my science."

"Yes. I'm afraid we've never really taken a medical interest in our existence."

"Then you need my friend Tori, not me," Stacy said, sure of her answer. "She's a pathologist."

"No, I need you. As a forensic chemist, you're also a cop. You know what it means to catch the bad guys. You understand the need to protect your race. The same way I need to protect mine."

Without conscious thought, she played with the rim of her mug. "I guess I do. I'm also guessing there's more behind the request." She stared at him. "I think you'd better explain."

"The rogue that has your scent, the one searching for you, was my adopted father. His name is—sorry was—Mikhail. And he was way too young to begin turning rogue, just like the others. My guess is that something made him turn. Some kind of poison, some kind of manipulation to the blood he consumed."

"And you want me to find out what that is?"

"In return, I'll keep you alive. For the few days it takes."

She laughed. "You're right. You really don't know anything about science. It may take a whole lot longer than a few days."

He winced. "Then, it takes what it takes."

Stacy heard the sincerity in his voice and realized he meant business. "And in the meantime? Am I allowed to go out?"

"As long as it's daylight, yes. The rogue won't risk being seen and will have to wait until dark to feed again."

That was reassuring. "And you?"

"I'll be waiting right here when you return," he smiled.

His smile, part hopeful, part reverent, part plain old hot, reached deep inside to the place of need she tried never to let out. For if she did, she'd have to acknowledge the complete, utter, loneliness of her life.

"And if I don't return?"

He leaned forward, wrapping his hands around the top of a chair as if to keep them from breaking something. "You're dead, and that's all there is to it."

"Comforting," she replied without an ounce of emotion in her voice.

"It was meant to be." There was no humor in his tone either.

"And if I survive?" Here comes the kicker, ladies and gentlemen. "Are you just going to make me forget you again?"

He hung his head between his shoulders.

Stacy drew in a harsh breath. "Thanks."

"That's the way it has to be, Stacy."

At least, he sighed.

"What are my chances?"

"Of surviving?"

She nodded.

"Me. I'm your only hope. You saw what those three bullets didn't do."

"Not a damned thing." A rock formed in her belly and fell to her knees. "And if you fail?"

"Then we're both dead, I'm afraid."

Chapter Six

STACY

DEAD. LIVING DEAD.

Stacy reached up to touch the scrapes on her neck. Because these were real, she took her coffee down to the bulkhead and sat, trying to make sense of the rest. Chaz followed but not too close, standing guard on the deck above her. She glanced back. His feet were planted shoulder length apart as he stood guard. His posture seemed natural, and it made her wonder.

He could hear her thoughts unless he blocked them. She forced a picture into her mind where her bullets did kill the rogue and turned to watch his reaction. He hid his feelings well.

"I wouldn't play that game if I were you. Some of my compatriots are quick to anger and not prone to remorse."

"Then, get out of my head and stay out."

"Stop shouting your thoughts, and I will."

Shouting them? Suddenly she realized that thoughts and emotions were intertwined. The more upset she got, the louder she 'shouted.' So, Stacy stared at the water lapping at the wood planks of the bulkhead and tried to apply reason to the last twenty-four hours.

Vampires don't exist. Vampires do exist.

All right, time to use the scientific method. Vampires don't exist.

Therefore, this is simply a nightmare. Stacy pinched the skin on her arm. "Owww."

No dream. Therefore, vampires do exist, and one was standing on her deck. Footsteps crunched against the gravel behind her. Stacy whirled around, and Chaz was gone.

"Captain Jeremy Pritchard, Third Continental Regiment, at your service." He bowed. "Please call me Pitch."

Ahhh. The man from last night. "Where's Chaz?"

He stepped closer, lifting his brow, a sardonic smile growing on his face. "You know where."

"Huh." A picture entered her mind of the thing that tried to bite her, patches of skin sloughing off, long teeth hanging over its bottom lip.

"Stop. Please. Don't do that," Pitch strangled out. "He was my father."

Surprise stayed any remorse she might have felt. "You could see the picture I made?"

He shook his head. "No. I didn't need to. Your description…" His voice trailed off. "He's not a monster."

Stacy frowned and turned back to the water, drawing both knees up to her chin. "He is now."

"I wish you could've known him. You'd understand why this is so hard for all of us to comprehend."

"Any harder than for me to comprehend your reality—who and what you are?"

He snorted. "I suppose not."

Stacy played with some stones then brushed the sand off her hands. "I don't want to thank you, but thank you for cleaning my gun."

"I didn't mind. Kept me from having to pay for trashing a dive hotel room."

"Rinkleman's? We used to call it Rinky's for rinky-dinky-do. You know. For— they charge by the hour."

"I understand." Was his tone just a bit lighter? "I slept in the chair."

"Copy that." She shifted to keep him within her eye line, letting her legs fall over the edge of the wood. "Would you like to sit?"

He opened his mouth, his jaw hanging, and lifted his eyebrows until they were nearly in his forehead. "I'm not used to having this kind of conversation with a human."

For a moment, Stacy wondered what kind of conversations he did have. Then she shook her head. "Look, Chaz already told me that I have no real way to protect myself, so I'm going to have to go on faith that what he said was true. You don't want to harm me."

He bowed. "Thank you for your offer, but I haven't fed yet. It's better that I don't."

Whoa! "All right then." Stacy decided to change the subject. "Continental Army, eh? Did you serve with General Washington?"

"Actually, no. I served under Colonel James Reed. You see, as a vampire, I've had to train myself to only take what was necessary to survive. The blood of a battlefield? Not a great place to be, especially for someone so young. The smell." He shook his head and stepped up to the bulkhead so she wouldn't have to twist to talk to him. "Just like this water. Very fishy."

"Chaz told me you have an incredible sense of smell."

"When men die on a battlefield, that's one you don't forget."

Stacy was used to crime scenes, not carnage. "I can't imagine."

"So now you know why I wasn't in the infantry. Actually, I was a spy."

Somehow that made sense. "The water is from the bay. Kind of just sits."

Throughout their entire conversation, Stacy had the feeling they were speaking on more than one level. So she addressed the underlying thread.

"Chaz said there was nothing either of you could do. I can only equate what I saw, and what attacked me, to a rabid animal. There's no reasoning with it. A rabid animal is a danger to all, people and animals." She paused to think about it. "And I even suppose other vampires. It needs to be put down for everyone's safety."

"I know," he said, his words coming out strangled.

"Chaz said someone or something caused your friend, sorry father, to go rogue."

A crunch on the stones had them both turning. Chaz frowned at her.

"Did he now?" Pitch asked.

"Pitch, listen." Chaz reached out to Pitch, but his friend simply stared. "I didn't tell you because I don't want you to go off half-cocked."

Stacy watched them carefully.

"So you knew Mick was in trouble?"

"No. Of course not. He sent me some pictures of an abandoned estate. I still don't know if there's a connection. What I do know, and so do you, is that he's going to come back for her. And that we'd have a better shot at stopping him at my place, not here."

"Yeah. Too open." Pitch bowed his head. "Ma'am." Then he walked over to Chaz. "I have your back. As always."

Chaz hugged him and clapped him on the back. "Thank you."

The sound of stones mashing together sounded as Pitch left. "Is he going to feed?"

"Yes."

Chaz looked at odds with himself. One minute he seemed to know exactly what he wanted to do, then he didn't.

"Something's wrong. What is it?"

"I need to give you Lethe. You can't know about any of this."

"I thought you said you needed my help."

"I know what I said!" He stood next to her before she could even blink. "I can't put you in that kind of danger. You'll be better off acting normally. Pitch and I will be with you every step of the way. We'll get Mick. You'll get your life back."

"That's very kind of you, but you need my help. I'm a big girl. I can make my own decisions."

"I can't let you do that."

Stacy picked up a particularly large stone and hurled it, where it crashed against the opposite bulkhead then plunked into the water. The sound echoed down the lagoon. "You can, and you will."

He shook his head.

"I'm still a police officer sworn to public safety. My duty is to protect. I use my knowledge, my brains, and my expertise to catch criminals so they can't harm anyone else. Sound familiar?"

He rubbed the back of his neck. "I can't let you put your life on the line. My job is to protect also."

"The needs of the many outweigh the needs of the few or the one," she answered, quoting one of her favorite characters in one of her favorite sci-fi series.

"Good line. No longer applicable."

Stacy slammed her hand down on the bulkhead. "Don't you understand? I have to make amends somehow. I have to do something —anything—so that Jim didn't die in vain. You won't let me tell the truth, at least give me this chance to redeem myself."

He looked ready to reach out and shake her. "So you can die too?"

"If that's my fate."

He barked out a bitter laugh as his arms fell to his sides. "You know nothing about fate."

"And you do?"

"After nearly eight hundred years of being a Paladin? Yes, I do. Fate sucks. Fate isn't kind. Fate isn't predictable. The moment you think you know what's going to happen, bam! Fate's a fickle bitch and definitely not to be trusted."

Stacy sat back and stared up at him, surprised by his answer. "Wow. You haven't been very happy as a vampire, have you?"

"My happiness or lack thereof is not the issue here. I'm beginning to think you have a death wish."

He looked like he wanted to start pacing, but the edge of a bulkhead wasn't the place for that kind of exploit.

"Far from it. But I do have a duty. I can't change what happened, and by putting together that cover-up, I can't tell anyone the truth. No one would believe me." Stacy sucked in a deep breath, letting the air out slowly and stood. "But I *can* do everything in my power to make sure no one else dies."

"Duty," he said. "I have a duty, too, to protect my race. We have a Council of Elders. They may decide you're a liability. If they do, I won't be able to stop them from killing you. Now, do you understand?"

Stacy twisted to stare at the water again. "I believe that what I've done with my life was for a reason. If so, it sure makes sense now. I mean, c'mon. Don't you think it's a little odd that I gave up blood banking to become a forensic chemist? And a cop? Kinda surprised me too. But it all felt right—every moment. So please don't take this moment away. Give me the chance to do what I'm meant to do. Fate simply dictates an outcome. Destiny reaches an outcome with purpose. Let me fulfill my destiny."

"And if I can't protect you?"

"Then buy me some time, so I can help you. Let what time I have left have meaning."

"What time you have left? Are you crazy? How can you accept what I've said, what I've done, what I am, so easily?"

Was that what she was doing? Simply accepting her fate? Stacy wondered. "When I was a little kid, the whole world spread out in front of me. I thought I could do anything. A drunk driver changed that." Stacy couldn't help the images flooding her mind.

"I'm sorry," Chaz choked out.

"So don't think for a second that I don't know what fate is." She swung around and looked straight into his eyes. "You took what I said wrong. What I meant was until I have to forget you. Which I don't think will happen now. But then again, I'm entitled to my own opinion. Can you guess why?"

Heat flared, lighting up the soft brown of his gaze. She didn't have to hear his thoughts to know what he was thinking. His head dipped. Her heart started to hammer. Their breaths mingled. Stacy closed her eyes.

A moment later, he was gone, a slight slough of wind brushing her face. She opened her eyes to find him about ten feet away. Funny, she didn't even hear the stones move.

"No. You. Me. Bad idea."

The corner of her mouth quirked. "Gotcha." *Then again, maybe not such a bad idea at all.*

Chapter Seven

CHAZ

TIME. TIME WAS AN ENTITY HE KNEW ALL ABOUT. SO WERE mistakes. He'd misjudged her, fallen into her trap, and let her know he cared. And Chaz dared not care about anyone. For nearly a thousand years, Chaz had been alone yet not alone at all. The memory of what he'd done to his wife still haunted him. He'd drained Mary to the brink of death, and only her will allowed her to live. Mick tried to tell him it wasn't his fault. But he knew the truth. He stayed nearby, hunting in the area, so terrified of hurting another human that he barely fed. And he watched from a distance as his wife died, bit by bit. He watched her waste away and succumb to the fever a few short months later.

The knowledge that he was responsible for Mary's death would never leave him. But it was the loss of control that haunted him the most. The understanding that the need for blood could overtake even *him*.

How arrogant and yet he knew no better. Once he found his purpose, and he watched what blood fever could do to a man. He understood. One day he would go rogue. A comforting thought, that. Would he run?

Chaz vowed each and every time he fed, he wouldn't be the

cause of another death. So there couldn't be more than what he called a bite and a bang. Which left him cold inside. And so very alone.

Now a beautiful woman stood within ten feet of him ready, willing, and able. Damn.

Stacy left and went into the house. He followed her into the kitchen a few minutes later. Her cell rang. "Hi, Tori. Did you get that info for me? Uh-huh. I see. Yeah. Thanks for letting me know. I'll be in and out of my lab tonight. Good. Later." She hit the end button on her screen.

He watched her features fall, knowing he felt the same remorse.

"I called my friend, Tori."

"We met. At Adrian's."

"She's a pathologist at the hospital. They took Jim to the morgue. I wanted to get some details."

His stomach fell through what he believed to be shared regret. "You shouldn't have done that. We were lucky last night that we were able to cover up what happened."

"Lucky? A man died. Does that even mean anything to you?" Stacy yanked on the coffee pot cord.

"Of course, it does."

"Really?" Both her hands banged down onto the counter. "You could've fooled me. You certainly didn't act like you cared. Then or now."

"That wasn't my intention."

She drew in a huge breath, shuddering with the effort to control her temper. "Then what was?"

He raked his hand through his hair, jaw clenched. The question deserved too many answers. Or none at all.

"Don't you see? It's eating away at me. I didn't save him." Chaz closed his eyes then opened them. "Again, I'm sorry. I've been alive long enough to see…too much death."

"*Alive* too long," she repeated. She nodded as if she understood what he was trying to tell her.

"I had no choice."

"So you're simply ready to move on?"

His gaze darkened, and his body locked. He could feel the muscle above his jaw twitch. "That's not fair and you know it."

"I'm not so sure. Everything you've done since we met has been calculated, with purpose. You asked me to help you. To do that, I need to understand where you're coming from."

"I did what I had to do to survive."

"And that makes everything all right, Chaz? You tell me."

He didn't answer. Couldn't. He was what he was. But Stacy was different. So he listened and found her fighting with herself because she wanted to believe *he* was different. She needed him to be.

"Do you care?"

"Of course, I care."

"Do you?" she asked. "Then cry. Feel. Something. Anything. Because an innocent man whose only crime was to go to work, just died."

"I'm trying, Stacy. I really am. But you have to understand that's not the way of my existence. And hasn't been for over nine hundred years."

She picked up her coffee and sat down. "Wow. Nine hundred years. Nearly a millennia. I can't comprehend that. But I can ask. Does time lessen the value of life?"

He still didn't answer.

"You've seen so many things, new and wonderful things. To learn history through books is one thing, to actually live it? What must that have been like?"

"When I was human, people used pitchforks and wagons. A horse was transportation. Then I watched men harness electricity, build skyscrapers, and invent machines to ease their labor." He shook his head. "You seem to think my lack of guilt stems from living too long? God knows I've seen and done it all, so nothing can surprise me anymore. But I don't think time lessens the value of life."

"Action is always better than intention."

"Yes. And for some, being a vampire means not being able to care. But I'm a Paladin. I'm different. So yes, I feel. I hurt. I care." Chaz knew that from the way she'd looked at him, the way her gaze turned liquid not so long ago. How the bright shiny marble of her eyes turned to ocean blue. He just didn't want to admit that yet.

Their gazes met. Then he tore his away. Thank goodness her thoughts were jumbled. He would be selfish if they weren't.

He watched her lean forward on the table, wrap her hands around her mug, and stare at the milk swirling around inside her coffee. Two emotions rang true. The guilt and shame were still there.

Chaz frowned, pulled out a chair, and sat down across from her. "This isn't your fight."

Her gaze stayed locked on her coffee as if she didn't want to look at him. "I was the one who should have died last night. My scent. Like you said."

"Yes. A rogue knows no bound. It has no limits, no humanity, nothing. There's nothing but the blood."

"Instead of yelling," she continued, obviously intent on beating herself up. "I should have fired my gun, found a way to distract it. It should've come after me."

"So you could be dead, too?"

And she didn't seem to want to stop. "Yes. That's my job. That's what I was trained for."

He leaned forward, removed her hands from around the mug, and wrapped them in his. "And I could have lured it away somehow. And—" He stopped, raising a brow to make his point. "You want to keep going?"

"Yes. *No.* You don't understand. I'm supposed to protect innocent people, and I failed."

He shook his head. God, she was magnificent. "You don't need to carry that kind of guilt. How many times do I have to tell you that? If you'd met Mick, when he was Mick, you'd understand. He was the most honorable man I've ever known."

"You mean, vampire, don't you?"

"No, I mean man. He would never hurt a human being on purpose. Ever. So you need to understand once and for all—a rogue is a rogue. A rogue knows nothing but the need for blood. Now he wants yours. Maybe for one split second, he recognized your soul. We'll never know. When I called him Father, he recognized mine. You saw how fast that disappeared. All I can tell you is that his insides are churning with need. One hundred times worse than your worst addiction. My fear right now is that he won't stop until he kills a whole lot of people and then kills you."

Stacy stared at him for a long time. "Well, if that's the way you feel, then put me out as bait."

"Wait a minute, what?"

"You heard me."

There was that need to be a cop again. "You're serious, aren't you?"

"Very. That's the only way to draw it out, isn't it?"

He didn't answer. He didn't have to. She was right. They both seemed to know it. Chaz hated that more than anything. All the more reason to do what he had to do. He tugged gently on her hands to draw her forward. She resisted, so he leaned close to nuzzle her neck. She shivered. He made to brush up against her cheek, and her body relaxed. How he wanted to kiss her. Instead, he moved faster than she could comprehend, letting his incisors plunge into the soft skin of her neck. He sipped a little then gave her the one thing he could to save her life.

Chapter Eight

STACY

STACY'S EYES WIDENED AS SHE STARED AT HER SURROUNDINGS without recognition. The modern, masculine décor chilled her, as did the blackout shades on the windows. Only a single lamp lit the room, casting an unflattering glow.

She rolled onto her back, her head completely out of sync with her body. Questions flooded her brain. What time was it? What day? Most of all, where the hell was she?

Reality began as would a wave with the water sucking back then building with power, growing taller and more forceful with each passing second. Heaven above, it was true. All true.

Sitting slowly, Stacy remembered everything. Their first meeting, the attack, the cover-up, and the drug. At least this time she didn't feel like the inside of a lava lamp. With a sharp huff, she decided she'd have to tell him about the do's and don'ts of using said forget-me-not.

She looked around, frowning. No phone. Indeed, no clocks either. She wondered if it was on purpose or simply because vampires didn't care about time.

Vampires. No one would believe her. No one. Hell, they'd probably put her on administrative leave if she tried to explain and force her to see Dr. Redmond twice a week for a month, if not more. And Redmond was a whack job.

All right, time to assess. Prisoner or partner? Both, perhaps? Neither, she realized. He'd given her the what did he call it again, that's right, Lethe, to protect her so he'd expect her not to know a thing. While her heart warmed at his intentions, she simply didn't know how to make him understand she was a big girl and could take care of herself.

Okay, not entirely true. With his help. So now that he believed she didn't know anything, how would he play his next move? Ahhh. The pick-up. What else would he be able to pull off with a woman in his apartment? Well then, guess what? Two could play that game.

Stacy rose. Time to assess. No electronics. She turned to her left and found the side of the bedroom opened into a bathroom with a sliding door. She walked around the bed to her right. The room ended with a doorless closet. Several of her outfits hung there and in a set of shelves undergarments, shoes, the jeans she'd been wearing, and wait a minute. She looked down to find herself wearing a pair of pajamas. *Great. Just great.*

She walked back around the bed and into the bathroom. Half of her toiletries sat on the vanity and shelves—even her hairdryer. Guess he expected her to remain here for a while.

Arrangements can be made. Arrangements can always be made.

Double great.

Time to plan. Stacy climbed in the shower, where she did her best thinking. An hour or so later, she thought, Stacy opened the bedroom door and stepped into a dark hallway. She made her way into a large room and finally found a light switch, pleasantly surprised to find an open concept kitchen, dining room, and living room.

At least he'd been busy. The refrigerator was stocked with milk, fruit, vegetables, and cheese. A bag of coffee sat next to a brand-new coffee maker. Muffins and a large crusty loaf of whole-grain bread graced the counter. She found she was starving and tore off a hunk of bread to munch on while she made coffee.

She recalled what he said about his sense of smell, and she wondered about his physiology for a moment. No marks or scars graced what she had seen of his skin, and he was cool, not quite cold, to the touch. His face was usually pale but had flushed red after drinking from Pat. He'd been able to fight even after she'd shot him so he must heal quickly.

He would make a formidable enemy.

"Mornin' darlin'.

Stacy whirled. She blanked out everything but the thought of joy at seeing him, then she hesitated with what she hoped was just the right amount of shyness. "Good morning? How do you know? I can't tell anything. The shades, you know? And I can't find a clock anywhere. Have you seen my cell?"

He turned and walked over to a panel by the front door. He hit a button, and the shades began to drop. Low afternoon light filtered into the room.

Chaz had a watch on his wrist. "It's nearly five-thirty. But seriously, darlin'. Who needs to know what time it is?"

He approached with debonair flair, with just the right amount of sway to his hips and enough grin to sidetrack a bloodhound hot on a trail. Damn. "I guess I don't."

Her heart began a slow pound inside her chest as he inched closer and closer. He leaned in but only to tease. "Looks like you started without me."

"I was—hungry."

"Just as well," he shrugged. "My appetite isn't for food at the moment."

Fire flooded her veins and pooled between her legs. He had on a tight long-sleeved tee and low-slung pants. She traced a lazy finger down his chest and sighed, "Please tell me it's still the weekend."

A flash of concern filled his gaze before he answered, smooth as silk. "It's the weekend for as long as you want it to be."

"Oh, good," she breathed. His gaze turned to brown velvet. "I was hoping you'd say that."

"Your wish is my command," he whispered, nuzzling the shell of her ear.

"Goodness," she stammered, her voice breaking ever so slightly. She drew in rapid breaths that seemed to never be enough. Visions of their bodies entwined, a tangle of arms and legs, touching and tasting, filled her head.

He grinned, just that uptick of the corner of his mouth that she'd come to know. He leaned closer, grazing the sensitive skin just below her jawbone with his lips. She gripped his shoulders, drawing him closer, his muscles quivering beneath her touch.

"Down boy, down. You promised to take me to Room 84." Seemed her plan was working. He thought she only remembered meeting at Adrian's.

He nipped his way down her cheek, over her nose, and across her eyelids. "Did I? I don't remember that."

Short staccato breaths blew out through his nose. Stacy drew back and pouted. "I want to party."

"We can have our own party here."

"What fun is that?" she countered. "I want to show you off to all my friends and make them really jealous. I mean, I can't wait to see the look on Kelly's face." Stacy turned and looked around. "Damn. Do you know where I left my phone?"

"No, I'm not sure."

"God, can you just imagine?" she crowed with glee. "Kelly's going to sooo hate my guts. I'll bet Tori'll even be a little jealous." Stacy looped her arms around his neck. "Mine. All mine."

"That I am, gorgeous. That I am. So why even bother going out? Why don't we stay here? Have our own party?"

"We can," she answered, shooting him a sly look. "But I really want to go out. I'll make it worthwhile when we get back."

He hesitated. She leaned closer, rubbing her hips against his. Heat flared in his gaze, and for a split second, Stacy let herself be seduced. After all, she was only human.

"Make it worth my while, eh?" he whispered, then traced her lips with his tongue. Stacy shivered. He grew bolder, nipping her skin, then biting down and sucking the area into his mouth.

Stacy gulped air. "You're dangerous."

"Am I?"

He leaned back and grinned as he slid his fingers into her shirt and popped open one button.

"Really."

"I don't take no for an answer."

Stacy reared back, her tone made up of icicles meant to pierce. "No, you just take."

Startled, he tried to backtrack. "Hey. If you want to go party, we'll go party."

"Truly?"

"Of course." He leaned back and frowned. "What's the matter?"

Stacy filled her mind with images from the last twenty-four hours. "Arrangements can be made. Arrangements can always be made. Right?"

He froze. Stacy laughed, the sound cold even to her ears. "You'd have gone through with it, wouldn't you?" He didn't answer. "Wouldn't you?"

She lifted her arm, primed to swing. Then she realized he wasn't worth the effort.

He didn't try to excuse his actions, didn't even try to apologize. "How long have you known?"

"Since I woke up. Seems your drug no longer works on me."

"Outstanding."

Chapter Nine

CHAZ

HOW THE HELL DID SHE FOOL HIM?

Easy enough when you get caught up in your own libido.

Her door slammed. There were no locks, but Chaz owed her what privacy he could give. Except for the shouting in his brain. "Wait a minute. You need to listen to me."

"No, I don't."

He flashed to her door. "I know I have no right, but you feel so damned good in my arms."

"We'll discuss that part in a moment. You're aware the word is called kidnapping, correct?"

"Yes. But only to keep you safe." Okay. He screwed up. He figured he'd ask. "Are we talking?"

"Maybe." She paused. "You'd have had me flat on my back in three seconds."

"I won't lie to you. You're damned straight, I would. And you'd have reveled in every moment."

He didn't need to read her thoughts to know that wasn't the best thing to say. "Thanks for throwing that up in my face."

"Damn it, Stacy. That wasn't what I meant." His fists clenched, and he had to keep himself from barging through the door. "Don't you understand? I get all caught up when I touch you. I can't help wanting you any more than I can help wanting to protect you."

"And you expect what? For me to simply puddle at your feet? Oh, my goodness. The great and all-powerful vampire. Thank you for showing me how much integrity you have left."

Chaz whirled. He heard footsteps approaching his front door. Damn. Pitch. He'd given him a key. "Look. Pitch is here. I need to go out."

"Say it!"

"Okay! I need to feed. I'll take you to dinner when I return."

"My choice. We'll go to Luigi's."

He knew better than to argue. He turned, grabbed his jacket, and brushed past Pitch as he was coming in without saying a word. He didn't take long. A woman in a bar, a young man in a vestibule, a taxi driver asleep in his car. When he returned, Pitch sat on his couch, looking sad and morose, and Stacy stood in the kitchen, drumming her fingers on the countertop. "Let's go."

She didn't answer, simply swept past him. He got the message. So before she walked out the door, he pulled her cell out of his jacket pocket.

"Your friend, Tori texted. She was checking to make sure you were all right."

"What do you mean, so she'd know I was all right? Give me my phone. Now!"

Not until he had her promise. "Do I have your word that you won't tell her the truth about me?"

Thunder started brewing on her brow. "I'm not your prisoner. What I do is my choice."

"I know. Making you a prisoner is the last thing I want to do. And we all have the right to choose. But you'll put her in grave danger if you tell her the truth."

"Give me my phone now." Chaz handed her the cell slowly. "Oh my god, Tori called work, and they told her I called in sick with a stomach bug. Did you do that?"

"I had no choice. Hide in plain sight, remember?"

"How the hell did you…?" She didn't finish the question.

He watched her dial her friend wondering if he was doing the right thing. "Tori? Hey." There was a bit of silence, then Stacy continued. "No. I felt fine when we got to O'Reilly's. Maybe that last glass of wine. It could've been something I ate too. No, I've been drinking tea. Yes, and lots of water." More silence. "I might try some toast later. No, no fever." And then a strangled laugh. "No, I don't need you to come over, I'll be fine. Yes, love you too."

When she hung up, Chaz released the breath he hadn't known he was holding. "Thank you." He didn't know how else to answer.

"You have no right to invade my life like this."

"I didn't mean to. Didn't want to."

"Damn your arrangements."

"Yes." He jammed his finger into the elevator button. "Look. The only way I can make it up to you is to keep you alive. Can we call a truce while I do that?"

She didn't answer. But she did follow him into the elevator. A step in the right direction?

He followed her once they were out on the street, feeling guilty. He hadn't answered to anyone, not any human, in a very long time.

"I'm sorry."

"You've said that before. When I told you to put me out as bait, I didn't think you'd treat me like a worm."

He winced. "That bad, eh?"

She nodded.

So he stopped. "Perhaps we can start over. Charles Tower at your service."

"We've done this before."

"Yes, I know. And you said…"

She groaned. "I know what I said."

"I won't lie. That hasn't changed. But for now, I'll accept you keeping your gun holstered."

She laughed. "No promises."

Harmony somewhat restored, Chaz followed Stacy. She stopped walking in front of a small pizza parlor called Luigi's. Not a place he would've noticed.

"This restaurant is my favorite," she said.

He nodded and motioned for her to go inside. The smell of garlic assailed as she opened the door, and he wrinkled his nose. She threw him a look to ask if that bothered him. He shrugged.

"Luigi. How are you?" Stacy asked as they walked in. Luigi stood behind the counter and beamed, his white apron not so white, his bald head shining under the artificial light, and a bushy mustache highlighting his dark, swarthy features. "This is Chaz."

Luigi bowed. "Nice to meet you." Then the man turned to her. "You too thin, Stacy. I keep telling you. *Mangiare*. Eat."

Stacy laughed, and he was glad, hoping she was beginning to calm down. "Luigi, you know I drive up here once a week for your pizza, not the girls."

They sat at a table near the window. "Once a week?"

"Our sorority is headquartered here in Hoboken. I'm good at organizing. We run the annual ball. I know it's just as easy to Face-Time, but it's an excuse to see my friends."

"Thank you."

"For what?"

"Talking to me."

She made a face, and he shrugged, hoping she'd remember their truce.

"I'm afraid nine hundred years of habit can be hard to shake." He tried a peace offer. "Think you could trust me? Even though I don't?" He didn't have to add the word. She knew he meant 'eat.'

She nodded, throwing him a look that said pizza yes, the rest no.

"Your house special. For two. And you look like a man who makes his own, yes?"

Luigi nodded.

"Then, let's have a bottle of the homemade."

"Just between us, eh?" Luigi cautioned. "Bring your own."

"Luigi's wine is some of the best I've ever had. How did you know?"

He lifted a brow. "Oh. Right. His head's not sacred either." She frowned. "You can drink wine?"

He smiled, only one side of his mouth lifting and that touch of sadness inside filling his gaze. "No more than a small glass. Anything more and well, think of your worst hangover times ten."

"By all means, drink away."

He deserved that. Then again, maybe he didn't. "Right reasons, wrong execution."

Her shoulders slumped a little, and her stony demeanor softened. "Apology accepted. Sort of. I'm not fond of having an offer of putting my life on the line thrown back in my face."

"You're right. And I would've played out the whole scenario." Chaz figured he had nothing to lose. "You'd have enjoyed it."

She tried to continue to be angry, but he watched as her lips twitched then parted in a smile. "You're incorrigible."

"And impressed that you hid your thoughts from me so well."

Luigi brought an old family pasta dish and two plates to the table. Chaz leaned in. "If he doesn't serve me, people get suspicious. You can take the leftovers home."

She took one bite and sighed with pleasure. "Damn straight, I will."

"I hope you get a chance to eat them."

Her face fell, and she stopped chewing for a moment. Then she dug back into her food. "I'm pretty hard to get rid of."

Chaz made the motion of eating. "I'm glad."

A short while later, he watched Stacy push back from the table with a satisfied smile. Then she frowned. "You know, if Tori ever finds out I was here, she'll know I was lying to her."

"We'll have to hope she doesn't." He motioned to Luigi for a check, gave him an enormous tip, and watched Stacy hold onto the bag with the leftovers like they were gold.

When they left the restaurant and began walking down Kennedy Blvd, Chaz remembered when he used to do this regularly. For a time, Chaz lived in New York City. He would let go and just enjoy, becoming one of the crowd, and reveling in the sights and sounds of a place with people. And though the city wasn't New York, and there weren't crowds out, there was a nice flow, a vibe, that he always appreciated.

As they walked, he thought about how long it had been since he'd simply enjoyed someone's company. He looked over at Stacy to find a shaft of light from a streetlamp catch a few golden strands in her hair.

God, she was beautiful. Her bright blue gaze that could shine with joy, cloud with confusion, smoke with heat. On the outside, she seemed like a simple woman, but like Luigi's wine, she was so much more complex. She was also human and as forbidden to him as his own kind. She had a mess-with-me-at-your-peril set of her shoulders. Where the women of his time were strong because they had to fight to survive, Stacy was strong because she wanted to be strong.

Damn it. She was human. He couldn't have her, but she made him feel alive. The soft curve of her breast, the sexy swing of her hips. What he saw inside her. Like sunlight. Like compassion. What he would die again to have. Like love.

Maybe that was why he wanted her to live.

"How did you end up this way, Chaz?"

He sighed. He guessed he owed her that truth, at least. "My real name is Charles, of the first guard of the Tower of London. I was a soldier and a blacksmith. One day, a very dangerous prisoner was due to be executed. I'm not sure what made the commander request extra guards, only that I was one of them. Maybe he had a hunch something terrible was about to happen. I don't know."

Chaz remembered the horror, the paralyzing fear as he watched the poor jailer's throat torn open. "You see, there was nothing unusual about escorting prisoners in those days, only I was never usually one to be requested. My skills were in honing blades, not using them."

"Did you ever kill a man? I mean, in battle?"

He simply stared at her. "Of course. Just because I was a blacksmith, that didn't mean I wasn't a soldier. But I can relate to how you felt last night. I know what it's like to become paralyzed by fear. A human can starve for weeks. Not a vampire."

Chaz closed his eyes to blot out the worst parts of a scene that would never leave him. "The vampire inside the cell had what we call blood fever. Imagine your worst craving and multiply by one hundred. He kept raving about how he'd been double-crossed and that he'd made his payment. The day before, the jailer showed me a silver cross.

Very ornate, one only a wealthy noble could own. He asked if I could change the design."

Chaz opened his eyes. "The vampire tore open the jailer's throat so viciously, you could see his spine. Drained him dry in seconds flat. Then it jumped to another soldier and did the same. The rest of the men tried to flee. Two had their necks snapped. The other, he simply lifted into the air and broke in half. I'd never seen such cruelty before."

He watched her shudder, not needing to hear her thoughts as her face paled. "My god, what you must have been thinking."

"Thinking?" He gave her a sad smile. "All I could think of was that it was going to drain me too. You see, I never found out this vampire's name, but I understood anger. Obviously, the vampire had bribed the jailer with that silver cross to set him free, and the jailer reneged on the bargain."

"That's terrible."

"Terrible? Worse than that. You see, my fear kept me there. I couldn't move, and in all my worldly life, I'd never been afraid. He sank his incisors into my neck just as I have with you, so don't think I don't know how that feels either."

She nodded in commiseration.

"But you only know a moment, Stacy. In that short space of time, while he drained me dry, I begged and pleaded for my life like a coward."

"A human reaction, no?"

Chaz shrugged. "When he was finished with me, he threw me away like a piece of garbage and left me to die. Only I didn't die. I wanted to, but I didn't. And to this day I don't know why. I became a vampire, but I never turned. I never became a vampire willingly. Which made me a vampire yet not a vampire."

"I don't quite follow," she replied, her tone perplexed.

"I know. It's a hard concept to equate. Hell, even I had a hard time with it at first. As I told you before, when a vampire is made, their human body is drained of blood. But just as death occurs, there seems to be a moment of truth. The essence is transmitted. It takes, or it doesn't. Some vampires become vampires to become immortal.

Some out of revenge. Others because they believe they have no choice.

"But I wanted to die. I fully embraced the fact that I would die. To this day, I don't know why I didn't. And that makes me, well…There are others around the world who've suffered a similar fate—so that makes *us* different. It makes us a little more human. It sets us apart. We take advantage of that. We police our own kind."

"I think I understand. You retained your compassion?"

Chaz smiled. God, she was smart.

"I know." She held up her hand to forestall his answer, creases forming above her nose as her brows drew together, and her lips pursed. "Some of you don't."

"Mikhail was my friend. I met him when I was fairly young. He was like me. We safeguarded the world from our own kind. He became my mentor and taught me what I needed to know."

"You loved him."

Chaz nodded, a familiar sense of loss welling inside. "Yes. There haven't been that many instances of a rogue that I know of in the last nine hundred years. Only a couple dozen. At least until six months ago."

"It's your job."

"Mick told me it was why we were here, to keep all living beings safe from those who would destroy them. I don't know why I was chosen or when I'll be released from this duty. But it is my duty, and I'll perform that duty to the best of my ability."

She nodded. "I feel the same way."

"I know. I wish I'd never gotten you involved, Stacy."

"I'm glad you did. You need my help."

"But you also must understand that as things stand right now, you're in danger from every vampire in this city. And you're on *his* hit list."

She threw him a look. "Haven't we been all over this already? I really can take care of myself."

Chaz stopped walking for a moment to catch her gaze with his. "Not when it comes to vampires."

She frowned. "I can handle it."

Chaz shook his head. God, he hated this situation. "I have no doubt that you can. But you also have to understand that if we do, by some miracle, manage to figure out what's going on, not only am I going to have to let you go, Stacy, I'm going to have to make you forget you ever met me."

"Did it ever occur to you that I would die before revealing your secret?"

He frowned. "Yes, but you can't keep that secret."

"Your Lethe didn't work on me again. It may be a secret I'll have to keep."

"Drug or no, once this is over, I can never see you again."

Stacy whipped her head around and stared up at him with a strange gaze. Warm yet guarded. At first, he couldn't understand what she was trying to tell him. Her gaze cleared and opened. Then he realized she'd told him this once before; she was willing to put it all on the line for him.

No one had ever offered to put anything on the line for him before.

Not even Mary.

Standing there, staring down into her eyes, Chaz felt his inhuman heart swell. He wanted to tell her how much her caring meant to him, but the words got stuck in the back of his throat. And he knew why. Because he couldn't tell her. He didn't dare tell her for her own sake.

He grazed his thumb across her cheek, and she closed her eyes.

God. Nine hundred years was an awfully long time to be alone. He might deny it with every breath he took, but it was true. He *was* alone and had been even before his death. It'd taken hundreds of years to acknowledge that he'd loved Mary and yet not known what love really was. Now he would never know, and his heart broke into little pieces, not only because of the danger he was putting Stacy in, but because he knew he could never really have her.

"So you just want to let me go? Up and walk away without so much as a by-your-leave? Bang. Done. It was fun while it lasted. See ya?"

Chaz wanted to put his fist through a wall, stand on a mountain top, and howl in frustration. "I don't have a choice!" he exploded. "If I don't, they'll kill you."

"Kill me?"

He simply stared at her trying to make her see the truth. Then the hairs on the back of his neck rose. He whirled to see a black limousine following them. Chaz was freaking mad at himself for getting lost in her gaze and not paying attention to his surroundings. Otherwise, he might have been able to get them away. Instead, he could only put his arm around her shoulders and wait.

Stacy was about to get her wish and find out if his fellow vampires would let her live.

HIGH UP ON THE CLIFFS OF THE PALISADES OVERLOOKING THE Hudson River, the mansion sat behind a tall stone wall with iron gates. Chiseled stone pieces fit into each other with seamless perfection, the detail of the work indicating how much it truly cost. With tall windows and lacquered wooden beams between them, the mansion gave an air of modern and ancient all at the same time. No one would think that a cell of vampires lived in a very affluent suburb of New York City. Why would they? The property looked like any other gated property in the area.

Which was the point.

Long ago, vampires realized they needed to be invisible to society. Why? First, creating new vampires was forbidden. If someone turned a human being, there'd better be a damned good reason. So there were a whole lot more humans than vampires walking the earth. Second, fear made humans dangerous. Yes, vampires were stronger and faster, but vampires kept to themselves, strangers created suspicion, and mobs turned ugly with little provocation and had throughout time.

Chaz laughed to himself. Hiding in plain sight hadn't always been easy, and his usual modus operandi for feeding was a lady's bed. But jealous husbands could be just as dangerous as rogues at times.

Rogues. Only one vampire that he knew, Samira Anai Se-Bat or

Sam for short, was exempt from that fate. She was a high priestess of Ancient Egypt, turned with the blood of the ancients. Sam was of pure blood and the oldest of their race.

The limousine pulled into a driveway, and the gates opened automatically. No visible security was necessary for the mansion. The vampires inside would know if the visitor trying to enter had been invited or not.

Chaz got out and walked up the steps trying to dispel a feeling of absolute dread, and when their guards took Stacy away from him, his stomach went south. She turned her chin over her shoulder as she struggled, but to her credit, the look she gave him was one of trust. He nodded, knowing he was going to have the devil of a time living up to that look.

Chaz walked into the room and noted the lack of windows. The room reminiscent of an older age with its vaulted ceiling, but there were no paintings on the walls, no sconces to light, no crystal to shine. Simple. Austere. Much like his host.

Close cropped black hair, long aquiline chin, Hunter Pierce was one of the oldest vampire leaders and a member of The Council. The New York cell was his cell.

Hunter entered the reception hall, shoulders back, and head held high. "You really blew it this time, Charles."

"Did I?" he replied, not really appreciating Hunter's use of his given name.

Cold gray eyes stared back at him without emotion. Their gazes fenced for a few tense moments. As one of the oldest vampire leaders left, Hunter didn't waste time with amenities. Or wasted emotions. Hunter's brow lifted ever so slowly in answer. While on this property, Chaz and especially Stacy, were at the mercy of Hunter's decisions. Chaz tamped down on his fear and reined in his thoughts. "You're as disturbed by this rogue as I am," he answered. "And you know it."

Hunter tented his fingers and tapped the first two against his chin as he leaned back in his chair. No other furniture graced the room. Which was meant to intimidate.

He figured Hunter knew he was successful at it.

"Yes, but I'm not sure which is bothering me more. A human

knowing we exist or another rogue vampire running loose in the area."

"Hunter." He paused and swallowed. "It's one of us. The Paladins."

If Hunter was shocked, he certainly didn't show it. "Not anymore."

Pain knifed his guts. "I have to stop him. You know I do."

"And the woman?"

"She's the least of our problems right now."

"Our problems?" the vampire leader asked, his tone a bit incredulous.

"Look. She's my responsibility," Chaz tried to reassure him. He didn't want Hunter to find out he'd enlisted Stacy's help. That might turn out to be a disaster. "She won't betray us," he insisted.

"So you say." He cocked his head, the stare growing harder. "And why is that, Charles? Why hasn't she been enthralled?"

"Because she might not live long enough to be a threat. The rogue has her scent."

He watched Hunter's gaze fill with surprise at his statement. "Indeed."

"I wouldn't have allowed you to bring me here if I wasn't sure, Hunter. The rogue will come after her. We thwarted its will once. You know there won't be a second time."

The vampire leader frowned but answered without emotion. "Yes, I do."

"Hunter." He paused. Chaz hadn't said before, but now he needed to make the man understand. "It's…it's Mikhail."

Hunter's eyes widened but the vampire did nothing more to acknowledge what that meant. Stoic described Hunter the best.

"But that's nothing compared to our growing problem," he told him, bothered by Hunter's lack of emotion.

Vampires made great soldiers, they knew how to fight, how to protect, but not how to be great friends. Making him wonder. Would being alone always be the curse of his kind?

"I know," came Hunter's cool reply. "I believe this makes three in the last six months."

"Then, you might also want to know something else."

"And that is?"

"Before I found the rogue, I met a couple of young vampires. Not newly made, but pretty young."

Hunter waved his hand for Chaz to get on with it. "They were sanctioned."

"Were they? By whom?"

Hunter frowned. "Not your concern."

"Really? Now that's interesting. Because I followed them, and I told Mick. And when I talked to Pitch, he said Mick had gone off-grid, like he was investigating something. I think that's how Mick ended up…" But the creature wasn't Mick anymore. "A rogue."

"Coincidence?"

"My gut tells me no."

Hunter didn't answer right away. "Agreed. Any idea's why?"

"Something very dangerous. What if someone was creating rogues and trying to control them?"

"A rogue army?" Hunter whispered in disbelief. "Impossible." But once said, the idea wouldn't disappear; it bloomed, thrived. "I'll speak with Sam and warn her that there's trouble brewing."

"Right under your own nose."

That brow went up again as if to ask if Chaz was impertinent enough to suggest Hunter didn't know what was going on in his own cell. "Thank you for letting me know."

Sarcasm. Politely cold. Just what Chaz needed, even if he did deserve a dope slap. "Let us go, Hunter."

"And your friend?"

"Like I said, let us go. We'll both be dead if I don't get her somewhere safe before the sun goes down."

"My home is about as safe as it gets," Hunter replied, his tone dry.

"Maybe, but are you willing to risk that danger? Aside from the stuff I can't quite prove how many of your people do you want to lose before we destroy it?" He paused before adding, "*If* we destroy it?"

They eyed each other for a long, tense moment before Chaz continued. "Look. One human knowing we exist is meaningless compared to the shit that's going on here. You know that, and I know that, but if it makes you feel better, I give you my word. I'll make sure she doesn't talk. All right?"

Hunter didn't reply. Chaz frowned. Obviously, Hunter didn't like putting control into the hands of other vampires.

"I'll make sure she stays safe, then I'll find…" He'd been about to say Mick again. "Your rogue for you, and I'll destroy it because it's my job."

"Your job?" Hunter asked with disdain. "I don't give a good goddamn about your job. Rogues are uncontrollable, no matter what either one of us thinks. They enjoy killing."

This time Chaz didn't answer. A statement like that, and Mick would never equate.

The vampire leader shuddered lightly. "You know as well as I do, going rogue is every vampire's deepest fear. When will the change start? When will my vampire life start coming to an end? I'm one of the oldest now, Charles."

Chaz gave the man a sad smile. "I think it has to do with what's left of the soul."

"Do you now?" Hunter deadpanned. "Cheeky bastard."

Chaz didn't want to go anywhere near there, but he asked anyway. "Am I?"

Hunter leaned back in the chair. "You're right. This is the wrong time to get into a philosophical discussion."

He seemed to be weighing every option. Chaz figured he had to. Otherwise, Hunter wouldn't rule this cell for long.

"Are you certain you don't want to stay here?"

"No. I think this is one fight that should be waged outside of your cell." Relief washed through him. It seemed that, for the moment, Hunter was going to let Stacy live. "By the way, thanks."

"Right now, I'm not sure gratitude is in order."

Tell me something I don't already know. "I may need some help besides Pitch. And I'm going to reach out to Ozzie. Some of your best soldiers? Just in case?"

The vampire rose and nodded. "Agreed."

Any and all back up would be greatly appreciated. Chaz watched Hunter flick his wrist, and a door opened. "Against my better judgment, you may both leave." He stepped toward the door. "Do you need sustenance?"

"I'd be grateful."

"It will be provided."

Chaz inclined his head. "Thank you."

Up close, Hunter Pierce seemed even more intimidating than from far away, but Chaz knew better. Deep inside, Hunter had something no other vampire had–a heart.

"I'm not sure gratitude is in order," Hunter replied. "Mikhail knew every cell and every defense we have. If there's any vestige left of him inside, we may all end up very dead."

Chapter Ten

STACY

A PLAIN ROOM. NOT QUITE AUSTERE. A BED. A DRESSER. A CHAIR. Plain white linens. Stacy was certain she'd go mad if she had to wait a second longer for Chaz to rescue her. Then the door opened, and Stacy sprang to her feet. "You have no right to keep me here."

The man who entered had close-cropped black hair and a look that took dead aim, a no-nonsense guy; he wasn't going to mess around.

"Rights are non-existent in this house, Ms. Morgan."

She wasn't surprised that these vampires knew who she was or that they operated the way they did. And she dared not let them see she was frightened. So she lifted her chin and said, "A lot of people will ask questions if I go missing."

He laughed. "Indeed, they will, and I'm sure Charles has already explained, we prize anonymity above all else."

"He may have mentioned it."

The vampire continued to smile. And that seemed to surprise him. "Which puts me in an interesting Catch-22."

Indeed it did. Stacy studied him for a long moment. The man standing before her was huge. Tall, well over six feet and stacked, kind of like a tight end. His suit jacket stretched across his shoulders, and his hands looked like they could wrap around a tree trunk without effort. He had cropped black hair and icy gray eyes.

"And you are?"

"Hunter Pierce, at your service." The man, no vampire she reminded herself, gave her a gracious bow.

"Well, I'm glad you figured that out at least." Her haughty tone hid so much more than he would ever know.

A flash of surprise ran across his face, removing his smile. But he didn't respond.

"So, where is he? Where's Chaz?"

"Downstairs, getting something to eat."

"You mean drink, don't you?"

He inclined his head, his lips twitching to keep from smiling again. "Of course."

She frowned. Was it bad form to discuss dining habits with a vampire? Then she decided what the hell? She was a scientist. Besides, Chaz had already decided to enlist her help. All she had to do was be careful. She didn't want Hunter Pierce to know she was on a fact-finding mission. "I'm curious. He went out and fed not too long ago. How much do you have to replenish? How often?"

"An interesting term, 'replenish.'" There was an underlying thread of humor riding his tone. "Very delicate and very astute. So I'll be honest. As I'm sure you're aware, someone of my size would carry around six quarts of blood."

Stacy took a moment to estimate his height and weight. At a height of over six feet and a weight of probably more than two hundred pounds, the vampire in front of her would require a bit more. "I'd estimate at least seven."

"Humans lose about two ounces a day. We lose about two pints."

Shocked, she answered, "Wow. That's a lot."

"However, the fluid volume isn't our issue. It's nourishment. The effects of the blood we drink only last for so long."

"Now, I understand."

He smiled. "I doubt you do. However, it does make dining often a necessity. And since there are rules about how much we can take, it makes us, shall we say, territorial."

Now that was interesting. Survival seemed to be a term that crossed both worlds. "And this is your territory?"

"It is."

"So, you're the guy I have to convince."

"Convince?" He seemed startled by the term.

"Of course. That I'm worth more to you alive than dead."

"Yes." He peered at her and cocked his head as if trying to judge her. "But not to me, I think."

Stacy wondered how Hunter knew she had a connection with Chaz. She thought she'd gotten good at hiding her thoughts. Then she shrugged. She was finding that all bets were off when it came to these people. "You stand a better chance of getting your rogue if I do."

The vampire laughed. "Indeed."

"But then, I become a threat to your anonymity."

The laughter left his face. "Indeed, you do."

"Quite a conundrum."

"On the surface. However, there is one thing you need to know. Human life means nothing to me."

Stacy lifted her chin. "Sorry to hear that. Your feelings mean nothing to me. We're talking logic here and the best situation for all involved."

He stared at her, surprised by her attitude. "We are."

"So, I'm free to go?" she asked, knowing the question bore so much more depth than an immediate answer.

The vampire leader held up his hand. "Yes, but before you leave, answer one question." Hunter's gaze seared right into her. "What would you do if you had to choose?"

Stacy grimaced. "Between what?" She had a bad feeling she already knew the question. "Or should I say whom?"

"Charles and my people."

"Not a fair question."

The vampire leader nodded in understanding. "I know."

"Chaz," she answered without hesitation.

The man smiled with genuine warmth. "If you'd lied, I'd have drained you dry on the spot."

Stacy shivered. She didn't think he was kidding. "I'll remember that. Thanks for the hospitality, Hunter."

The man's mouth quirked in sardonic amusement. "The pleasure was all mine." Stacy held out her hand, surprised when he shook it. "Nice to meet you," he said. "I look forward to future discussions."

"I do too."

She met Chaz in the house's foyer, his shoulders lowering, and the tension around his mouth easing when he spotted her. She guessed he was as grateful they were leaving the mansion unscathed as she was.

They climbed into the limousine that picked them up. "Do you really think your Council wants to kill me?"

Chaz looked uncomfortable, fidgeting in his seat. *The driver can hear you.*

"I'm assuming he was chosen for his discretion." She leaned up against the seat in front of her. "Weren't you?"

The vampire driver didn't answer, and Stacy made a face at the back of his head. She turned to watch Chaz fight not to smile. *You really are amazing.* "Killing you would certainly be the easiest course of action, but they're not stupid. Hunter saw the advantage of keeping you alive. So will The Council."

"I'd like to be more than a means to an end, you know."

He lifted his hand and turned her face towards him. "Stacy, listen to me. I admire you. True courage is rare to find in anyone, but you stood up to Hunter without thinking anything of it."

"I guess he admired that."

He grimaced. "Which was pretty amazing, Stace," Chaz began, shortening her name in a familiar way that she found she didn't mind. "Hunter, although a slave, was revered in his day."

"A slave?"

"Yes, a gladiator."

She shook her head. "Wow. This is all difficult to take in. Makes me feel like I'm just a mere human."

Chaz really smiled at her this time. "Mere? I don't think so. You had the courage to go toe-to-toe with a rogue. You've also offered to help us by using your skills despite being a target."

The limousine pulled up to the curb in front of the apartment building Chaz lived in. They got out of the vehicle, rode the elevator up, and walked into his loft. He walked over to the bar and poured her a glass of wine that she didn't refuse. "Stacy. Listen. You need to try to understand some things if we're going to get through this mess. Vampires have gone through more than you'll ever imagine during your human history. We've had to fight and scrape to survive. Many of the myths are true." Stacy watched an old pain enter his gaze. "I— I've done things. Terrible things. Simply to continue existing."

Stacy tried to think back through history. She realized they called the Dark Ages dark for a reason.

"I guess you have."

"I think, well, I think that when you become a vampire, you carry a piece of your humanity with you. Not all vampires want to hurt humans, and not just from a practical standpoint." He sighed. "But many of us have had to do—things. To stay alive. As a result, we've been hated, shunned, even hunted. If we seem hard or uncaring, maybe it's because we've had no choice."

Stacy wondered how many wars had been fought during the millennia Chaz had walked this earth? How many eras? Societies? And there would always be a class structure no matter how it was defined, by society or by economics. Because of people. Because of humans.

"I understand."

"I don't think you do." Was he warning her? "Though some of us might still show feelings towards humans, there's no love lost between our races. We're still predators."

"I said, I understand."

He grinned. "Good."

"Okay. So now that that's out of the way for the moment, what's next?"

"It's dark. That's one problem, and we have our other issue to deal with."

"Ahh yes," she answered slowly. "Your encounter with those young vampires a couple days ago. You said there was something strange going on. Strange? In what way?"

"They weren't frightened of me."

"Frightened? As in big bad Paladin frightened?"

"Yeah. It was weird. Other vampires don't like me. I'm a necessity they don't like having around. You know how people are leery of you because you're a cop? Same with me. The other vampires, too. In the end, I'm the guy who'll put them down if they can't do it themselves. And yet, these vampires could've cared less that I was following them."

Stacy got the unpopularity part but not the importance. "Hang on a minute. Aren't you being just a little paranoid?"

Chaz frowned. "I'd like to say yes, but I don't think so."

"Okay then. So you need me as bait for the rogue, but you also want to use me as bait for these vampires that are acting weird to see if they're connected. But what you really need is for me to work in my lab, right?"

He grimaced, raking his hand through his hair. He seemed to really hate everything Stacy said. "Yes," he bit out.

An idea flooded her brain. "You know, if you were to catch one of these young vampires, I could maybe test their blood. The sooner I find out what's causing vampires to go rogue, the sooner I can help you stop this mess."

"Bad idea. No. I don't like this idea one bit."

"Obviously," she said, rolling her eyes. "You'd be killing two birds with one stone, you know."

"How?"

Stacy swallowed hard but squared her shoulders. "By going back to O'Reilly's and capturing one of these vampires that care less about you."

"Capture?" Chaz asked in disbelief.

"Well. You seem to think they're acting weird, right? And you seem to believe someone is using something to turn vampires rogue. If something's going on biochemically, I'm the one who can test their blood to find out. Let me help you, Chaz. Let me feel like I can make up for what happened to Jim by not letting it happen to anyone else."

He didn't answer.

"I'm sure your friend Hunter would tell you the best way to use bait is to tantalize your prey. If you want to get a snake to come out from between some rocks, you tease it out. I can do that on both counts. If I hang out in the bar and draw them outside, you can grab one."

"No. I refuse to put you in that kind of danger."

"Any more than I'm in already? Do you just want to sit back and let your friend get his claws in me first?"

"He's not my friend!" Chaz exploded, and Stacy felt something warm open inside her. "Not anymore." *Ah. He cared. He really did.* "And no, I don't want that."

"We can use other things. Like…like stuff out of my pocketbook or whatever. Why not let this rogue think he's found me? Why not entice him? He might just make a mistake and fall into a well-set trap."

Even though Chaz paled, which was hard to do as a vampire, he agreed. "That might work. If I can get some help."

"Pitch can help. Maybe one of your other Paladins."

"I already thought of that. I'm going to contact Ozzie." He rubbed his chin. "It might work."

"Thought you might see things my way."

Chaz didn't look like he even wanted to think about her suggestion, let alone answer.

"I don't have too many options at the moment, and I don't think you do either. But don't get cocky, okay? The minute you do, you're dead."

"I don't do cocky," she shot back.

His shoulders tensed. He walked over to her bar, picked up a glass then put it down. Contemplating another drink despite the consequences? "Stacy," he said, turning. "I don't think you really understand."

"I don't?" She stared hard at him. "I'm putting my life in your hands. End of discussion."

Chaz opened his mouth to protest, then snapped his jaw shut.

"I don't plan on dying," she continued.

Stacy watched as his brows drew together, and his jaw clenched. "The young vampires are going to be bad enough. But the rogue?"

She watched him shudder. "In all likelihood, by the time we're able to catch him, you'll be dead."

The truth shivered down her spine, and Stacy took a deep breath, letting the air out slowly. She swallowed hard. "Well, then, what are we waiting for? Let's get to work."

UNEXPECTED, STACY THOUGHT. THE LOOK ON HIS FACE TOLD HER she mattered.

"I can't believe you. Your courage, your fortitude. Damn. You refuse to acknowledge the possibility of failure."

She watched him pace, part guilty, part terrified.

"There has to be a way to do this without putting you in so much danger. I can't let you offer yourself up on a platter like this, Stacy." Fear was evident in his tone. "I was wrong. It's suicidal."

"I don't seem to have much a choice, now do I?" She wasn't happy about the situation either. She was counting on him being able to capture a wayward vampire and then kill a rogue. Talk about a worst nightmare. Neither would be easy.

"Yes, you do," he said. "Stay here. Don't go back to your house. I have the best security system money can buy. Give me time. Capturing wayward vamps is one thing, but you've never seen the aftermath I've seen. Let me see if I can corner this thing on my own first."

"I'd love to be able to do that, but you don't really have any more time, Chaz. If I stay here, I can't work in my lab. Besides, if I do stay here, it'll only follow. You said that yourself."

"I can't let you die," he whispered.

"Die? I have no intention of dying. You'll do what has to be done. I know you will."

"Easier said than done. You know what Mick is now."

"Yes, I do," she answered with a shudder. "Don't forget, I've seen the son of a bitch in action. But I also know you'll be able to stop it before it gets to me. I believe in you."

Turning white seemed hard for a vampire to do. Chaz paled, his throat working, and his chest moving like an out of control engine.

"I trust you," Stacy said.

God, if the situation had been any less grave, she'd have started laughing at the look of utter disbelief on his face. He walked up to her until they were almost touching. Good lord, he was beautiful. Trust filled her gaze. She memorized the strength in his face and tucked it deep inside.

He feathered his fingertips down her cheek. Her eyes closed, and she leaned her head into his palm. Her entire being centered on his touch.

She'd never wanted to melt inside anyone before.

When her eyes opened again, Stacy smiled. He leaned his forehead against hers. "I'm standing on my farm in the middle of my garden surrounded by color, surrounded by life. I'm walking through the city to go watch a play. I'm gazing at the pieces in a museum where I'm telling you the truth about those artifacts in their cases. And I know what this is. It's a dream. Because a dream can only last so long before reality intrudes. You've decided to place your life in my hands. And the truth is, I've never been frightened in my immortal life, until now. I don't want anything to happen to you."

He wrapped her in his arms and crushed her to his chest, bending to rest his cheek against her hair. She didn't need to hear his thoughts to know he wanted to make love to her, but now was not the time. He let go slowly and stared down into her eyes. "Stacy, I—"

She shook her head. She lifted her chin, and that was all the invitation he needed. He bent down and kissed her lips. Her mouth parted, opening to him. He fenced with her tongue but only to taste.

She tightened her arms around his back as he kneaded her shoulder blades. There was only one connection between them, and that was caring. Well, caring and trust.

Stacy didn't want to let go, but she had to.

"You've become a light in a very dark existence, Stacy. I don't want to lose that." He raked his fingers through his hair. "You made the suggestion out of desperation, and I'm grateful. But I can't, no I won't, put you at risk."

"You don't have a choice," she insisted again.

"Stacy, listen to me, please. There's strength, then there's stupidity." He pulled her close one last time. "There's a necessity. I won't put you in danger. I won't let you be a hero."

He nuzzled her ear, her neck, her forehead, and down her cheek. She didn't reply, she simply wrapped her arms around his waist and laid her head ever so slowly back down on his chest.

"Oh, Stacy."

She didn't want to let go. She wanted to drown in the moment and never come up for air. Never before, not ever, had she shared a moment like this.

She lifted her head and gazed up at him, profoundly unshakable in her belief. She knew he wouldn't let anything happen to her.

"It'll be all right, Chaz."

He nodded. "God, I hope so."

EVERY TIME THE DOOR TO THE BAR OPENED, STACY JUMPED. SHE couldn't help it. She sensed Chaz nearby but had thought he'd stay with her. Instead, he'd insisted on being able to move freely. So, he'd faded into the shadows, leaving her alone. Being the cheese in a trap sucked.

Two young men came in very quiet and unassuming, not at all like guys looking to enjoy a beer and a game on the television.

Neither one spoke; they took out their wallets to prove they were legal and ordered a couple of bottles, moving to one of the free tables. They didn't really talk to each other, they barely touched their drinks, and they certainly weren't watching the game.

Were these the two young vampires Chaz had mentioned before?

The minutes dragged by like hours. Being they were strangers, Pat wiped down the bar for the tenth time. His son Mike brought up a third set of glasses that were then slid into wooden racks above his head. Bottles were dusted. Peanuts poured. Stacy thought for sure she'd go mad with waiting.

Then, the two young men stood, their expressions never changing.

Stacy's heart started to hammer in her chest as they approached her table. Neither one sat down. They seemed to realize standing and staring down at her would be intimidating as hell.

Stacy hated to admit it was working. "Something wrong?"

"Yeah," the first one answered. With the hood of his sweatshirt thrown back, she noted his straight brown hair could use a wash, and there was a peculiar smell coming from him. It took her a moment to place the scent—kind of like the first time you walked into the morgue—a bit antiseptic but also old and dead. "You don't have any company. You look a little lonely. Ain't that right, Nick?"

"Sure is, Donnie."

Nick let her see just a hint of incisor before he covered his smile. He'd opted for the bald look, which seemed all the rage now. And though he didn't smell quite as bad as the one he called Donnie, there was an intensity inside that made her realize he was probably older and far more dangerous.

"You both left your drinks on your table. Why don't you go get them and bring them over here?"

And while you do, I'll bolt for the door.

They didn't listen to her suggestion. Indeed, they inched closer to her. "That's not the kind of drink we were talkin' about, lovie," Nick answered, his fingers trailing down her hair.

Stacy tried to hide a shudder. Her arm tightened involuntarily against her holster, reminding her she had her gun with her despite what Chaz told her.

"Yeah," Donnie chimed in. "We had something a bit—warmer—in mind."

Nick seemed to think that was funny. He laughed, seeming not to care if she knew what he was or not. That frightened her even more. Chaz. Hunter. They both stressed the merits of anonymity, to the nth degree.

"I think you'd both better leave right now. I'm a police officer, and I don't think you want any trouble with a cop."

Nick laughed even harder. "Let me go find a pair of boots to shake in, pulleesse."

"Go on, Nick. Get over yourself already," Donnie chided his

friend. "The lady doesn't seem to want our attention. Now, what do we normally do when that happens?"

Nick tapped a long index finger against his chin as if deep in thought. "Coax her over to our way of thinking."

"Coax? Now that's a new one. But I like your thought process, my friend."

Nick pulled out a chair and sat down, so his knees nearly touched hers. His gaze turned to ice then got colder. But they'd underestimated her strength and her stamina. She'd be damned if she'd show them one ounce of fear. If Nick wanted a staring match, well then, he was going to get one.

Not sure how much time went by, Stacy started when Pat called out. "Hey, Stacy, you having trouble with these young—gentlemen?"

She dared not get Pat involved. "Nothing I can't handle, Pat."

And since Pat knew what she was, he backed off. For the moment. "All right, guys. Fun's over," she told them, swiveling around to play with the bottle of beer she hadn't touched yet. "Go back to your drinks. I'm not interested in company tonight."

"But we are," Nick answered, his face turning deadly serious.

Where the hell was Chaz?

"Look. I don't want any trouble. Pat is a good guy. He has a decent place. Tearing up the furniture isn't nice."

Donnie roared. "She wants to fight us, Nick. Can you believe that? *She* wants to fight *us*."

Nick laughed harder and louder. Stacy glanced up and saw Pat's fist curl around his dishrag. Then she saw Mike start to reach under the bar for his baseball bat. She didn't have any more time to soothe the situation.

"Damn, Donnie. Now that's a new one on me. Ain't never fought with my supper before."

Stacy knew she had one shot at getting out of this in one piece. To take it out into the parking lot where Chaz was waiting—somewhere. She hoped.

She swiveled off her seat and rose. Turning her back on them, she headed for the door as fast as she could without running. For a moment, she didn't feel them follow. Probably surprised the hell out of them. Then they were next to her, surrounding her.

Nick reached out to grab her arm. She tried to break his grip but couldn't. They seemed to agree with her decision to leave the bar. For that, she was grateful.

Once they got outside, however, their veneer of civility fled. They threw her up against the wall, letting go of any restraint they'd shown in the bar. Her head hit the concrete, stunning her for a moment.

Pat came running out of the bar brandishing a sawed-off wood handle. Mike raised his baseball bat, following right on his heels.

"No. Go back inside,"

Donnie charged and plucked the wood out of Pat's hand. He back-handed Pat, knocking the bar owner unconscious. Mike took a swing but missed. Donnie spun him around and landed a right hook. Mike went down in a heap too. But it looked like they were both still alive. Thank God. Stacy pulled the piece out of her holster and flipped the safety.

"Back off. Now."

They circled her, their grins showing their enjoyment. "This is fun, Donnie."

"Yeah, Nick. She's a feisty one."

"Gonna taste real sweet. I can hear her heart going a mile a minute."

"Yeah. Then those two over there are gonna be dessert."

A white-hot shard of fear sliced through her, but Stacy kept her focus on both of them. *Chaz! Where the hell are you?*

The next thing she knew, Donnie yanked the gun out of her grip and threw it into the middle of the parking lot.

Then each of them grabbed an arm, pinning her against the wall. Donnie pressed his body up against hers as his tongue snaked out to rasp against her skin. "Tastes real nice, Nick."

Nick grinned. "One at a time or together?"

"I get her neck."

"Damn, I wanted her neck."

"You got the neck the last time."

"No, I didn't."

"Yes, you did."

Stacy had heard enough. She brought her knee up between Donnie's legs, and he grunted in pain. And that amazed Stacy. Then she remembered Chaz telling her about vampire lessons. She broke his grip and twisted away from Nick, who took one look at Donnie, and any amusement he felt at his compatriot's incapacitation fled. His face tightened into a hard knot of hate.

"You're mine now, little girlie."

Stacy bolted for her car. Nick moved so fast he seemed to disappear and reappear in front of her, forcing her to skid to a halt. She turned and tried to run back into the bar. Nick moved the same way, kind of like flashing, to stop in front of her again.

Stacy tried to zig-zag a path to freedom. An ugly laugh greeted her attempts. Then Nick grabbed her arm again, twisting it until she thought her shoulder socket would explode.

White stars danced in front of her eyes, but he'd left her feet free. She stomped down with her shoe heel onto his foot with all her might. Nick cried out in pain as he let go of her. And her resistance only made him angrier.

She started to run, but he stopped in front of her, and this time she couldn't halt her momentum. With pure pleasure written all over Nick's features, he lashed out and backhanded her across her cheek. Stunned, Stacy didn't even have time to feel pain as Nick yanked her head up by her hair. He pulled until she thought a clump would come out in his fist. Then she realized his intent. He had her bent over backward, and her neck open to a pair of very sharp incisors.

"You're gonna taste right nice, and then I'm gonna let Donnie have the rest. And when we're finished, I'm gonna fuck you until you beg to die."

Stacy had thought the rogue would be her demise, not some young punk vampire. "Do your worst. You'll get yours in the end."

Nick roared. "Really? I think you got that wrong, little girlie. I'm gonna get mine right now."

Suddenly, Nick let her go and spun around.

"I don't think so," came a soft-spoken reply.

Chapter Eleven

CHAZ

CHAZ HELD THE OTHER YOUNG VAMPIRE OFF THE GROUND BY THE scruff of his neck, who hung like a limp rag doll, since he'd knocked him out cold. "Let her go. Now."

"But she—" Nick protested.

His guts swirled with fear for Stacy. One wrong move and this vampire could throw her hard enough to break her in two, bend her into a pretzel if he wanted, or drain her three-quarters dry before Chaz could stop him. He willed his body to relax, slowed his heartbeat so the young vampire would believe he was in complete control.

Yeah, right.

Thank God he'd decided some extra help would be a good idea. Besides, Sam needed to see firsthand what was going on around here.

"I'm not going to tell you again. Let her go now. If you do, I'll play nice and give you back your friend in one piece."

"Don't care about him."

Chaz wasn't surprised. "All right. Let her go and you get to live. How's that?"

The young vampire licked his lips.

"I don't have all night." Chaz growled, seeing the bruise begin to well on Stacy's cheek. A sear of pure anger surged through him. He shook the vampire in his hand like a rag doll. Suddenly, two more young vampires emerged from the shadows. *What the hell?*

Chaz threw the vampire in his grasp up against the wall as hard as he could to make sure at least this one wouldn't get back up for a while. That left his hands free. His next thought was to get Stacy out of this mess.

But even as he assessed the situation, Chaz realized there was more going on here than even he understood. Vampires didn't make war on The Paladin. Ever. They were their only protection against rogues.

"Look. You're all young. I get that and maybe you didn't have someone teach you the rules. The first rule—you don't mess around with the police. Got that?"

No one answered.

"And I'll even go so far as to say that maybe you didn't know who I am. Because if you did, that would be against the law, so to speak."

While Chaz spoke, he continued to figure out options. If he went after the one holding Stacy, the other two would try to grab him from behind. He'd have to be quick.

"You're going to take your medicine like a good child, and I won't kill you," he told the one holding Stacy. "All right. Any of you. But Hunter's gonna have to hear about this. There are rules you don't break. I'm one of them."

"No rules anymore, grandpa," the one that stood next to Stacy cried out.

"You sure about that? There's a rogue loose. And he knows this place. I don't think you want to be anywhere within ten miles of here."

"Rogues don't scare me," the young vampire insisted. Chaz twisted his head to see the others nod in agreement.

"They should." But even as Chaz said the words, he realized the young vamp wasn't lying. He wasn't frightened of him or of a rogue. None of them were, and that terrified Chaz.

Chaz decided surprise was his best plan and ran full speed, stopping right next to the vampire holding Stacy. The next thing he knew, he was surrounded by all three. He drop-kicked vampire number one and grabbed Stacy's arm, yanking her away from him.

"Run."

Stacy scrambled to get away. The other two hesitated, not sure if they wanted to go after her or him. This created enough space for him to escape. He hit the afterburners and ran over to the fire escape so he could climb up onto the roof of the bar.

"You're gonna have to try harder than that, gentlemen," he called, staring down at them.

One vamp followed and dismissed the ladder in favor of jumping up after him. Chaz swung his leg out and tripped him as he landed, causing the man to fall off the roof. "Ouch."

The other two started to spread wide, knowing Chaz couldn't keep track of both without turning his head because of his vantage point. They'd use that split second to gang up on him—bad idea.

Chaz ran across the roof to the back of the building. He jumped down and rolled, refusing to acknowledge any pain. He came to his feet and ducked behind a dumpster looking for a weapon. He found a pretty large rock off to the side and picked it up. Then he rose from behind the dumpster, keeping his hand shielded by the metal.

One of his attackers tried to come at him using the lid of the dumpster. Just as the vamp flipped the lid over to bring the metal—full-force—down on his head, Chaz sidestepped, twisted and smashed the rock down on his back.

"Double ouch."

The other two weren't so stupid, and Chaz remembered the dinosaur movie and how Raptors hunted. Two would draw their prey out into the open while the third— a gunshot exploded in the night. Stacy had followed the fourth vampire who'd circled from behind. God bless the woman and her courage, but that also put her into terrible danger. A wounded vampire wouldn't stop to talk. Or listen to reason.

He had to hurry. He didn't have time to mess around. Fear seared through his guts. He took a syringe of rosary pea extract out of his pocket. It had been for the rogue, but now he was going to have to use it on the unconscious vampire. He plunged the needle into its heart.

That would slow the vamp down should he awaken while Chaz was busy with the others.

He withdrew the needle and flashed over to the third vampire in less than a few seconds. This vampire seemed a little sluggish and clearly had no real fighting skills. Chaz took advantage by throwing a right hook with all his might. He felt the crunch of bone beneath his fist. The vampire twisted away with the force of the blow and went down in a heap. The vamp moaned and tried to lift up. Chaz swung his leg upwards and caught him just under the chin. "Do yourself a favor. Stay down."

Chaz could feel the fourth vampire approaching.

Hey, Sam? I could use a little help over here.

In moments, Sam appeared. She took one look at the scene and froze the rest of his attackers. "*What* is going on here?" she asked.

"You tell me, Sam," he yelled back, running towards Stacy. "Oh God, are you all right?" he asked her, terror sending little spikes into his belly.

She nodded. She stared down at the gun then at him and shook her head as she holstered her weapon—just another thing he'd have to make right.

She stared up at him, steadfast, fear, and relief swirling in her gaze. But that was Stacy, wasn't it? Standing her ground in spite of her fear? His guts tightened into a cold knot as his fingertips grazed the bruise on her cheek. His arms wound around her, and he knew he never wanted to let go.

"They decided they wanted to have me for dinner," Stacy told him. "I had other ideas."

Chaz didn't just hug her, he enveloped her in his arms. She held on for dear life. Over her head, he caught Sam's gaze.

"They were trying to kill Stacy," he told her. "And me."

From the looks of things, Sam had just been about to let them go when she stopped dead. "They were *what?*"

"They were trying to kill me."

Astonishment filled Sam's features. "Why would anyone in their right mind do that?"

"I have no idea. You tell me. Because none of tonight makes sense."

Stacy let go of him and caught his gaze with hers. He stared down at her for a long time before he let his arms fall to his sides.

"Sorry about the vampire lessons, but you needed the diversion. There were too many of them."

"Thank you." She hesitated. "Sam." Then she looked over at Pat and Mike, both still unconscious. She ran to them, bending down to see how they were. Chaz moved to follow.

Until they heard a scream.

Chaz whirled in the direction of the noise. "*Pitch.*"

SAM ARRIVED WAY AHEAD OF HIM. HER INDRAWN BREATH WAS ALL he needed to hear. But he had to see for himself. If for no other reason than he abandoned the one friend he had in this other existence.

Pitch lay crumpled on the ground. Right where he'd been thrown. The smell of dead blood mixed with the unique scent of rogue vampire blood. A regrettable combination he'd smelled before.

Oh, God. Pitch.

Mick had been his mentor and friend, father figure, but the elder vampire had been stern and had held a piece of himself in reserve. As if he'd been afraid to get close to Chaz. Or maybe because of the bond they shared that no one knew about. Or because Mick had known one of them might die saving the other. Pitch had been closer to his age, and because of his nature, much easier to approach. They'd become friends.

Chaz remembered Pitch's laughter, deep and hearty. And his first question when Chaz told him he was purchasing the loft in Hoboken. "You're not gonna steal any of my women on me, are you?"

His heart broke. He remembered Pitch's easy smile, easier manner, and he remembered his comrade in arms, his brother.

Sam started chanting in her native tongue. A prayer for the soul of the dead. He'd heard her chant this before, but Pitch wasn't dead yet, and Chaz wasn't sure how he was going to get through the next few moments.

Sam stopped praying and squeezed his shoulder. "We have to be quick, Chaz. If he begins to heal, he'll go rogue."

He nodded, his insides hollow, and his heart broke. "I don't have any extract. I used it to save Stacy."

"You won't need it. I will keep him immobile. As I am with the others."

Dead yet not dead. Drained yet not drained. Chaz couldn't imagine a worse way to end his vampiric life. To come awake to nothing but the blood.

"We need to take his head. But with what? I have no sword. No knife."

Sam opened her jacket to reveal a very long, very wicked-looking dagger sitting in a leather holster. "This comes from a time when becoming a vampire was an honor," she said, handing the dagger to him. "Pitch would have wanted to go out in style."

Chaz nodded. His eyes burned and dried as no tears came. They laid Pitch out with reverence, and then Chaz knelt beside his friend. There wasn't much left of his neck anyway.

Sam began chanting again and, with a sad smile, nodded that he should get it over with. A single stroke, that was all he needed, and Chaz severed his head. Then he brought the knife down straight into Pitch's heart. A moment later, Pitch began bleeding out.

What the hell was I thinking? Stacy…

Her face filled his vision. Stacy. The thought of her name hollowed his insides. *Oh, my God. Stacy!*

"Sam?" he strangled out.

She breathed deeply. "I don't sense him, and the stench seems to be dissipating." Her hand clenched his shoulder. "You must finish here. Besides, I'm faster, and I still have a hold on the others. She will be safe with me."

She sped off, and after the way the night unfolded, Chaz asked himself why too many times to count.

All of a sudden he heard someone crashing through the brush. He rose, ready to take on the rogue, but it wasn't Mick. Ozzie came running into the clearing, his chest heaving, and skidded to a halt next to Pitch. Chaz stared. Ozzie fell to his knees beside the body. He rocked back and forth, his arm curling around his stomach as he moaned. Chaz waited until Ozzie stilled.

"Too late," the vampire whispered. "I called to Pitch to warn him. He didn't answer."

"It's okay, Ozzie."

"No, it isn't. I lost the trail. Damned, wily, son-of-a-bitch. He doubled back on me."

"It isn't your fault. We all made the mistake of underestimating him."

Ozzie shuddered and rose. They waited and it didn't take long until there was no blood left inside the body. Then he poured a scented oil on Pitch's body, and Chaz lit the match. Chaz reached out but Ozzie fled, unable to watch Pitch burn.

For a moment Chaz wanted to die too. Then he looked down. Inside the pool of blood on the ground, he found a silver cross, right where Pitch's hand had been. And he knew exactly who the cross belonged to.

Chapter Twelve

STACY

STANDING IN FRONT OF THE BAR, STACY HAD NO IDEA HOW SHE would explain she'd ended up using her gun. Again. Five bullets.

Toasted. Plain old toasted. Boogeymen and myths.

Speaking of the Boogeymen, Chaz and the woman he called Sam vanished, leaving Stacy alone with a bunch of vampire statues, creeping her out to the max. Her cheek throbbed with fire, and she *so* wanted to go over and do more damage to Donnie's privates. But she'd always been taught not to kick a man when he was down.

Then again, she thought, her tongue licking her lips, he wasn't a man.

A reaction set in, and Stacy shivered. She helped Pat sit up against the outside wall of the bar. Pat's cheek was already red but not too swollen, thank goodness. Mike groaned, so she shifted to see how he was doing. He had a large knot growing on the side of his jaw that was going to turn all kinds of colors and hurt like a bitch.

A sigh rustled through the trees, sort of like a last breath. She shivered again. Then the most beautiful woman she'd ever seen flashed back next to her, her face filled with anger. Sam.

"Are they all right?"

"I think so."

"I'm going to have to give them each a little of the Lethe. Then I'll put them inside."

Stacy nodded. "I don't think either of them has a concussion. Being a little high right now might help with the pain."

The vampiress nodded, picked Pat up like he was a child, and took him inside the bar. She came out a minute later and did the same for Mike. When she returned, she nodded to let Stacy know they were all right.

"I drained some of the swelling on their wounds."

"Thank you."

The woman's jaw clenched, and she stared at the frozen vampires looking like she wanted to dope slap each one of them. She began pacing, stopped and stared brows drawing together.

"I thought about going after his nuts again," Stacy explained. "But I wasn't sure, given his current state, if he'd feel it or not."

The woman lifted her head, features clearing. "Not a bad idea. They can hear, see, and feel." She turned away, muttering to herself in a language Stacy didn't understand as she surveyed the area, then she shrugged. "Be my guest."

Stacy started walking towards Donnie when Chaz reappeared and caught her elbow.

"What are you doing?"

Stacy pointed at her compatriot. "She said I could kick Donnie in the balls again." When Chaz didn't grin, Stacy realized something was terribly wrong. "Chaz? What's going on?"

Dread filled her at the grief in his gaze. "Pitch is dead. We had to take his head."

"What?"

"I've never met a more genuine soul," the woman lamented. "He had a zest for life I've only encountered a few times before. Never will again now."

Chaz nodded, grief etched in his features. He shared a look with the woman, a look Stacy knew she could never be a part of. They'd shared hundreds of years together that she could only guess at.

"Oh, God, no. Not Pitch." She tried to snare his gaze. "I'm sorry.

So, so sorry. I liked him. He told me who he was when he was human."

Chaz looked like he wanted to scream. Instead, he ran over to a plastic garbage can and threw it, so it bounced into a fence with a slam. He whirled back towards her, chest heaving, fists balled. He looked like he wanted to fight the world.

"Damn it all!" Chaz exploded. "Pitch was one of the good guys, and we weren't with him when we should have been. And because we weren't, he had to try to destroy the rogue by himself."

"It wasn't your fault, Chaz," Sam told him.

"Yes, it was. I should have been there. The rogue was more important."

That hurt. But Chaz was right. In his world, he had his priorities.

"You couldn't be in two places, nor could I," Sam added.

Besides, this was her fault. She was the one who pushed to be the bait. "I'm grateful you came to my rescue," she said to Sam.

Chaz didn't seem to realize how terrible she really felt, and Stacy tried to understand. He was grieving. "Shouldn't we be interrogating Donnie and his friends?"

"That's not for you to do," Chaz fired at her.

"Got it," she blasted back, turning to hide her tears.

She headed for her car. "Stacy, wait!"

"No," she called back, waving over her shoulder. "It's fine." She hurried to the car, trying to keep the stupid hurt she felt from bubbling over. Logically, she knew Chaz was in pain. He'd lost someone important to him. He needed to prioritize.

Stacy needed some space from the night, from this new reality she'd found herself in and the man she knew she was quickly falling for.

"I need some sleep," she told him, not looking back as she tried to keep hurt from her tone. "And you need to figure out what's going on. You have your priorities, and I have mine." She shrugged, glancing once over her shoulder, affecting an even expression, half-understanding, half-hysterical worry she was sure he'd never buy. "Go take care of your vampires, Chaz. You, too, Sam. I'm going to try to find a way to explain why I discharged my firearm to my boss without getting fired," she added, a sharp pain gutting her as she remembered the care Pitch'd taken to restore her firearm the first time she'd used it.

Stacy shut the door of her car, feeling ridiculous and helplessly alone. Neither one of them followed. She understood, though the truth of the matter still stung. In their world, Pitch was a loss they might never get over, and she was expendable.

He flashed over to her car. "The rogue is still out there. You're still in danger."

Stacy ignored him, started the car, and spun the tires to get away.

As she drove home, Stacy tried hard not to let their exclusivity hurt her. She'd never really experienced any kind of prejudice before, but she likened the feeling to when she was a child and never got invited into the 'popular' circle. They were telling her she would never be part of their circle. She was human. They weren't.

Fair enough. She could handle that except for one small detail —Chaz.

What the hell was she going to do? Just accept that they were from two different worlds? And then what? Die? That was a lovely thought. Let him drug her into sweet forgetfulness? Now that was even lovelier.

Welcome to the wonderful world of vampires.

Stacy pulled into her driveway, knowing she'd better come up with a plan and soon. Because sooner than later, she wouldn't be able to extricate herself from the situation she was in, and neither would they.

Chapter Thirteen

CHAZ

Chaz wanted to go after Stacy, but he hesitated.

"Go after her," Sam said.

"I'm not sure I should."

"Why? Does she frighten you?"

He laughed softly despite the grief tearing at his guts. "More than you do."

Sam laughed with him. "Time heals, my friend. Of that, we are both certain. So go after her. Let what time you have together help you heal."

"I don't know, Sam. I really don't know if I should."

"Why not?" Sam asked, her tone surprised.

"She's human."

Sam shook her head at him, making him feel like a child. "She is. And yet, I wonder. She's done nothing but try to help us." Sam lifted her shoulders, but Chaz sensed no apology. "She was shouting her thoughts, and it seems we've done nothing but kick her in the teeth for her efforts."

"Not exactly fair, is it?"

"Not exactly nice either," she added, her tone filled with respect. "Are we really that different?" Sam chided, her tone gently berating them both for their prejudice. "Are we all not beings with infinite possibilities?"

"You can ask that after what just happened? Pitch is dead. We tried to set a trap, and we got trapped instead. Doesn't that bother you? Even a little?"

"Yes, but we didn't have a great deal of time to plan."

He shook his head. "I don't think any plan would have worked. I think we were set up."

Sam stared at him, her gaze turning to deep thought. "By humans? I think not."

Chaz shook his head. "That's not what I meant. No, someone smart is behind all this."

"A plot?"

Chaz nodded. "I believe so. Don't you?"

She didn't answer right away. "To what purpose?"

He shrugged. He didn't know. Not really, but a bad feeling had snaked its way from his spine to his guts, telling him they were in for trouble.

And then there was the cross. He decided not to tell Sam about that just yet. "I have no idea, but vampires fear going rogue worse than death. In nearly a thousand years, there have only been a couple dozen. Now there's the three in six months? I don't believe in coincidence."

"Agreed."

"So, the question becomes, is a person, or maybe a group of people, using these vampires to create mayhem? And is there a possibility that these vampires and the increase in rogues are related?" He watched Sam frown as she considered his questions. "Shouldn't we ask them?"

"In a minute," she answered, her brow furrowing. "If your logic is correct, someone is creating and playing with some very dangerous toys."

"I know. So we need to find out who and then why."

Sam seemed to agree. "My first guess would be that this person or people are after Hunter's cell."

"Maybe," Chaz agreed. "But we've always been a straightforward bunch. If someone wanted Hunter's cell or Jason's or any of the leaders, they'd make war. They always have in the past."

Sam frowned and glanced over at the young vampires in her mental grip. He had the feeling she wanted to do more than just hold them, and he understood her anger. There was nothing honorable about the way they were going about their 'business.'

"True," Sam replied. "But times change. Just as Stacy has reminded me that humans are constantly growing and gaining knowledge, so are vampires. This may be a new way to make war."

Which left them both with a very important question. "Who would be powerful enough to control vampires this way?" he asked.

Sam shook her head. "I don't know, but somehow, I don't think this is purely mind control. Even I couldn't do something like that. And as you know, I've tried many techniques at Sanctuary."

Chaz nodded. "What I don't get is the danger. This is like playing with an atom bomb. Rogues cannot be contained. One wrong move and…why take that risk?"

Sam seemed to agree. "Because of the reward. We've been talking about single cells. What if this person, or more than one person, wants more. Perhaps, by creating enough chaos, they think they can take over all vampires."

"All vampires?" Chaz stepped back to examine the possibility. One ruler? A vampire empire? The idea seemed beyond the realm of reality. Vampires were loners, singular; they only came together in cells for the right to feed. "That's a major stretch, Sam."

"I know."

"And if anyone were powerful enough to do that, it'd be you."

She threw him a look but agreed. "Only pureblood would make it possible."

He frowned. "I've got another question for you. Why now, Sam? Why not twenty years ago? Or forty years from now? Or one hundred? Time is the one commodity we can use to our advantage."

"I'm not sure. However, this is the age of technology. Human science has gone to great lengths to understand their own biology, but, in the end, it all boils down to power."

She said the last word with such vehemence that Chaz asked, "How can you be so certain?"

Sam turned to him and gave him a look he'd never forget. Sam had been part of a race of vampires who were proud and honorable. Mixed deep inside her anger, he read sadness. Only a coward would use beings to further a goal. "The lust for power destroyed my people."

It was a story he'd never fully heard. Only bits and pieces. Someday, Chaz thought, he'd like to know more.

She frowned and fell silent for a long moment. "All right," she continued with a long sigh. "What we've discussed is certainly plausible. I'll warn The Council. But I don't want to create a panic. We have very little proof beyond a group of over-confident, arrogant, and newly made vampires who require severe discipline."

"And one too many rogues."

"Indeed."

Chaz rubbed his face with his hands and slid his hair back off his brow. "So, you think I should go to her?"

Sam's mouth quirked. "She needs you."

"She needs a man, not a vampire."

Sam shook her head at him, and he felt like a child again. "Should I let one of these imbeciles loose so they can kick some sense into you, or will you just listen?"

"I'm listening."

"She needs you, but you need her more."

Did he, Chaz wondered? He'd been alone for so long. Could that ever change? "You think?"

She laughed. "Of course, idiot."

Chaz sighed, reaching out to squeeze her shoulder. "Thanks, Sam. I owe you one."

"As you pointed out, I'll have plenty of time to collect. Go on. I can take care of these… imbeciles." She gave his hand a squeeze back. I'll let you know what I find out."

He did. He ran to Stacy's house using the exertion and the night air to clear his head. He liked her home. It was modern but homey. He remembered two bedrooms upstairs, especially the one downstairs, and what looked like a new kitchen. But the house had a feel to it, a vibe that made it quaint in spite of new siding and remodeling. She'd planted flowers in the front and placed little animal statues near them. Warmth and family, that was what he felt.

He found Stacy sitting in her car in her driveway under the carport next to the house. She lay slumped over the steering wheel, resting against her forearm, her face hidden until she turned her head. Her tears hurt him, tore through him like little knives. He knocked on the window, but she refused to acknowledge him.

"Stacy, please."

"Go away. Leave me alone."

"I can't."

"Please, Chaz just…*leave me alone.*"

"Stacy…don't make me shell out to have your car repaired."

"Have my car repaired?" she repeated in disgust. "Ooh, you are so annoying." She opened the door, catching him in the shin.

"Ow. That hurt." He lifted his leg to rub the abused area.

"Serves you right! You…you…"

Chaz only knew one way to shut her up. He kissed her. But, he didn't simply kiss her—he yanked her up against his body and engulfed her. Their tongues fenced and parried, searched, and steamrolled. She bit down on his lip, and the pain shot right to his groin. They bit, licked, and sucked, but they still couldn't get enough of each other.

She went wild on him, slithering and sliding up and down his torso. She grabbed at his shoulders and jumped up, wrapping her legs around his hips, which was fine by him except for one tiny detail. She still had her clothes on, and so did he.

Chaz pushed her legs down and forced her to stand in front of him. He continued to explore every crevice of her mouth with his tongue. He inched them both along the side of her car until he reached the door to her house. They staggered and broke apart as he pulled the screen door open, and she fumbled with the keys to unlock the door. At that moment, the world shifted.

Chaz smiled, took the keys, and once inside, pinned her against the wall and ground their hips together. He opened her jacket, popped open the first few buttons of her shirt, and lifted her breasts out of her bra. *Ah,* he thought. *Instant push-up. Victoria Secrets style.* Perfect for him to lick and suck.

He opened his shirt as fast as his fingers would let him and pulled her hard against his body. Was there ever a sensation as wonderful as that first skin on skin contact? Her nipples grew hard against his chest as he plundered her mouth. Chaz reached into every crevice he could find as he unfastened her pants. He wasn't surprised when her fingers began tearing at his jeans, trying to push them down his legs.

Chaz had been making love to women for nearly a millennia. At times he'd thought he'd go mad with boredom, but this night was different somehow. Maybe it was his grief. Maybe it was his shock at being attacked. Maybe it was the greedy little thing she'd become in his arms. No matter what, Chaz hadn't been this turned on in centuries.

He broke their kiss and licked his way down to her breasts—time for a little taste. To make her even hotter. His incisors grew as soon as the thought entered his mind. As he bit gently down into one of her breasts, he urged her legs apart with his knee. One hand followed and cupped her center.

God, you're so hot.

She moaned and urged him on. "Yes, please. That's it."

He swept a finger through her slit, and she rubbed frantically against his palm. She was wet and hot and, he could tell from the furnace surrounding his fingers very close, so Chaz knew he'd never get inside her before she came. He slid his finger inside her and bit down even harder. The act of drinking was like turning up the gas on a stove on most women, it just made them crazy. Stacy was no exception. She gasped, her moan loud and her juices flooded his palm with an explosive orgasm that seemed to last forever.

Chapter Fourteen

STACY

Stacy thought for sure she'd never stop coming. And she knew she was far from through. He let go of her breast and withdrew his hand, intent she supposed, on getting to the important part. But Stacy had other ideas first. She unzipped his pants, and Chaz sighed with relief. God, he was huge. She pushed his boxers down, and his hips pushed forward, seeking exactly what she had in mind. She kneeled down and licked the tip of his shaft. His penis jerked, and a small drop of fluid formed at the tip.

"Hello there, big boy."

Chaz urged her head forward, sucking in his breath in anticipation.

Circling just the head, she held the shaft steady with one hand and rolled his balls lightly with the other. Although there was a thatch of hair around the base, his wasn't a forest, and he had a unique scent, cleaner, sharper, not quite as musky as most men.

What a turn on.

Stacy didn't care that the wood of the floor bit into her knees. Or that her breasts were sore from his bites. As soon as she opened her mouth and drew his length down her throat, the pain disappeared.

Heat flooded her body as a live wire in a lightning storm. His hips pumped his full length into her mouth, hard but not out of control. She ran her tongue down the length of his shaft and over his balls, even taking one gently into her mouth. Then she sucked on the tip and let him slide in and out of her mouth. God, she loved the way he tasted—all kinds of salty and tangy and sweet at the same time. Then she looked up at him.

Chaz lifted her off her knees in one simple motion. His mouth engulfed hers as he lifted her legs with his arms as if she weighed nothing at all. He settled her in his arms, lowered her to the area rug in the middle of the room, and spread her legs. The tip of his erection teased her core. Her only thought was to be filled. She wanted his hard shaft pounding into her, filling her. He didn't disappoint.

He entered her in tiny, excruciatingly small movements. He seemed to be afraid he'd hurt her, but Stacy was different. Curse or gift, she'd never been certain, but her body could accept even his huge length.

She wiggled a little, twisted, and he slid all the way inside. She heard his breath catch and felt his balls tight against her ass. She smiled. Then all thought ceased as he began to move.

At first, he slid in and out like an experiment. Testing to see if something worked or didn't work. He spread her legs so he could go even deeper, and she felt the tip of his shaft touch deep inside. Then the base brushed her nub. He twisted, kind of like a corkscrew, and started pumping again. He was trying to make sure to stimulate every nerve cell she had.

He was doing a damned good job of it.

An incredible pressure built inside her core. Her internal muscles clamped onto his entire length and didn't want to let go. His breath caught again, so she kept squeezing and letting go. He moaned in her ear.

He started thrusting into her body as hard as he could. He was building, and so was she. "Yes, that's it. Harder. Oh, God, Chaz. Harder."

He obliged, and Stacy thought she would explode. She'd never built to such a crescendo before. With each thrust, he moaned, louder and louder until Stacy was certain they were going to wake the whole neighborhood.

She didn't care.

One thrust. Two. One last push, and she reached the highest peak. She groaned and shattered in a monstrous orgasm. A half-second later, he yelled, spurting hot jets into her body as they convulsed all around each other.

Stacy refused to let him go. He slid her hair from off her cheeks, fingers trailing gently down her skin. His gaze swirled with too many emotions. He buried his face in her neck as his short quick breaths slowed. He seemed to need her arms around him. She needed his more.

"I left most of my windows open, you know."

He grinned. "The neighbors will never let you live this down."

"After all that yelling," she continued teasing, laughter threading her tone, "they'll just be jealous."

"I'm sure they've heard the same before," he added to their by-play.

"We're lucky no one called the cops. I'd have had an awful time explaining."

Stacy pulled away gently even though it was the last thing in the world she wanted to do. She lifted herself off the floor, sighing with relief when he rose with her.

She feathered her palms gently across his cheeks. Although she hated their attitude towards humans, she knew he was hurting. He'd just lost his friend. "I'm sorry, Chaz. About Pitch. He was…kind. But he made no excuses for what he was."

The pain in his gaze made her hurt right along with him.

"Thank you."

They both reached for their abandoned clothes. After getting dressed, Chaz dug around in his pockets until he found what he was looking for. He opened his fingers to reveal a silver cross and chain. Very old looking.

"This belonged to the vampire who tried to kill me and left me for dead nine hundred years ago. How Mick got a hold of it, I don't know. I didn't notice it when he attacked you. Pitch must've pulled it off his neck as they fought."

Stacy sucked in a shocked breath. "Oh, God, Chaz. I don't know what to say."

"Hurts like a son of a bitch," he told her. "Big time."

Her stomach plummeted. "If I hadn't gotten into it as much as I did with those young vampires, you'd have had time to help Pitch destroy the rogue."

He sighed, and Stacy's heart went out to him. She urged him across the floor, not stopping until they were in front of the island in her kitchen. She made him sit down, and then she sat on his lap. Uncertain of what the correct vampire etiquette was, she offered him her wrist.

He pushed her arm away and buried his face between her breasts. She cradled his head and simply held him. Yet when he pulled away, he'd shed no tears.

"Not your fault, Stacy," he told her, leaning his head back into the crook of her shoulder. "Besides that was the plan, to begin with. There's more going on here than even I thought at first. And Sam agrees. I think we were set up."

"Set up? By whom? The bastard who created you?"

"I don't know yet, but the cross makes him a suspect." He paused. "Problem is, Sam's not sure either. One thing I'm pretty certain of, though, is you were a diversion tonight."

"A diversion?"

"Something we didn't plan on," he added with a nod. "I'm not one hundred percent convinced, but I believe the vampire manipulating us wanted me dead. Instead, it ended up being Pitch. "

Stacy didn't like the sound of that one bit. She jumped off his lap and started straightening already straight items on her counters. She put away dishes sitting next to her sink. Then she made some tea.

"Stacy, stop. We're both still alive."

She gripped the edge of the sink with both hands before whirling to face him. "Sort of."

"Not funny."

"But true."

He gave her a self-deprecating grin. "And that's the point. In a sense, we won."

"Or maybe Pitch was the intended target all along."

Chaz shrugged. "I don't know, but from now on, you're not leaving my side. And we're going to fight this thing together. Got that?"

"Sure."

He rose and started swaying on his feet. The sky had lightened considerably outside, and he was going to fall asleep soon.

"I've got some sick time," she began, a steely peace settling inside her. "I'm not going to just sit around and watch you try to get yourself killed. I'm going to call in with the flu. This way, I can stay home during the day."

"All right."

"Then I need to get into my lab. We'll have to do this at night when no one's around. So, before you decide to serve yourself up on a silver platter, how about you let me try and help?"

"That makes me sound like a piece of meat," he groused.

Welcome to my world. "I know the feeling. Is there a French word for a rogue appetizer?" she asked, trying to inject a little humor into the situation.

He gave her a half-hearted smile. "Don't think so."

"First, I need to figure out how to explain to my boss that I discharged my firearm."

Chaz shook his head. "First, they'll never find the bullets you put into Mick. Second, Sam will take care of the rest. Give me your boss's address. Sam will convince him that the next time he sees you, nothing ever happened."

"She's able to do that?" she asked, startled by their abilities, and beginning to rethink her position. Maybe she was trying to equate apples and oranges after all. The thought scored her insides.

"Yes."

He answered with such a matter of fact tone that Stacy realized she was back in Oz again.

Tongue in cheek, she added, "Think you can get me a raise?"

"Stacy," he chided, swaying as he tried to stand.

Stacy gave him a wry smile. "Can't fault a woman for trying."

Chaz threw her a look and made it to the couch just before he collapsed. She watched him fall into a sitting position on her sofa.

"The first thing I want to do is test you."

"Test me? Why would you want to test me? I already know how long I've been dead," he joked back. His words were already slurring.

Stacy shook her head. "Enough with the lousy humor."

He shrugged. "Actually, I really am curious."

"You'll find out soon enough. I need you to ask Sam if she can get me a tube of blood from the vampires that attacked me. I'm going to test your blood, theirs, and then test the cross and chain as a comparative. There's probably some of the rogue's blood on it. If there is one, a difference might give us a clue as to what happens to you when you go rogue."

"I already know how that happens. We call it blood fever. And once you've had it, you never forget what it feels like."

"All right," she sighed. "But something causes blood fever."

"Yeah. Starvation."

"What if there's something more?"

"More?"

"Of course. You said it yourself. Another cause. An additional cause. Or else something that can aggravate an already existing condition."

"I guess I never thought there could be something inside of us that would need to be triggered."

His eyelids began to droop.

"You wouldn't. You're not a scientist."

His mouth quirked. "About as far from one as a body can get." He rubbed his face with his hands. "Very well." He reached into his pocket and pulled out the cross and chain. "You won't end up destroying it, will you?"

"I'll take very good care of it. Promise." He started to lean back to lie down on the sofa when Stacy stopped him. "Hey, let's get you into bed."

He rose with her help, not an easy task. "Are you sure?" he asked, his gaze softening at the offer.

Stacy returned the look and nodded. He smiled, and she returned the expression. She drew his arm over her shoulder and helped him walk into the bedroom. "I'm going to take a shower, and then I'm going to join you. Later, I'll show you my domain."

He stretched out on the bed, and within seconds, he was out cold.

"My domain and perhaps a little more," she added with a soft smile.

Chapter Fifteen

STACY

CONTRARY TO TELEVISION POPULARITY, THERE WAS NOTHING glamorous about being a forensic chemist. And since Stacy didn't work for the FBI, she didn't have robotics and computer holograms and all those neat things that made droves of college students try to make sense out of organic chemistry and eventually give up trying. As Stacy had learned the hard way, with chemistry, you either had the knack for it, or you didn't.

And if you worked for the government with lots of money, your workplace would be a pristine, shiny lab with all the bells and whistles. Otherwise, your domain would look like hers: over-crowded equipment on every square inch of bench space, and folders and papers in organized disarray all over the space left.

"Hey," she told Chaz with an embarrassed shrug. "I call this home."

Usually, most of the staff worked normal hours unless there was an absolute rush on something. Besides, with budget cuts, no one wanted to pay for overtime. Hence, she figured by ten o'clock or so, everyone would be gone. She was right.

Chaz would be hard to explain.

Not that he wasn't anyway. And if Stacy wanted to try performing the scientific process on their relationship, she'd probably go nuts. Nothing logical applied to him. Or them. So, Stacy had decided, at least for the time being, to go with what was and just accept.

Not an easy thing for her to do.

He stood off to the side, looking a tad uncomfortable. Stacy started to laugh. "You won't catch anything, you know."

He smiled back at her. "Wouldn't anyway." She watched his smile fade. "I'm not real comfortable in tight spaces."

Really? she wondered, "Why not?"

He shrugged, but his gaze wouldn't meet hers. He took a deep breath and walked around, running his finger down the edge of the counter. He picked up a flask, only to set it back down. "Waking up in a coffin isn't fun."

Stacy couldn't imagine how that felt. The terror of not knowing if he'd be able to dig his way out. How far down under the ground was he, and— Stacy stopped her thoughts right there. She walked over to him and threw her arms around him, burying her head in his chest.

He sighed and wrapped her up in his arms. He kissed the top of her head and let go. "Thank you."

A fierce determination filled her face. She couldn't imagine that or the rest of his existence. What he'd endured made her want to know more.

"Do you know anything about your physical attributes besides the obvious? Hunter told me you lose about two pints of blood a day. Where does it go?"

"I have no idea."

"Haven't you ever been curious?"

"No. I've never thought of myself as a lab rat."

Stacy nodded. "Sorry. I forgot. Blacksmith, right?"

"Yeah."

"Hasn't anyone ever been at least curious?"

"Maybe, but most of my time, I can tell you, has been spent on trying to find my next meal." His gaze turned grim. "Don't forget, a lion doesn't think about what it is. It simply hunts."

"Is that how you see yourself? As an animal?"

He grimaced. "I don't know. I used the analogy because the lion has no choice. Either it hunts, or it starves. I'm sure that some of your books or television shows have described the need for blood. Well, I can tell you, it's far worse than anything a human can imagine. So no, I don't think anyone has had that much time on their hands to be curious."

Wow, Stacy thought, wondering if Chaz knew how bitter he sounded.

"I can hear your heartbeat," she answered, "which means it pumps the blood you drink, which allows oxygen to reach your cells and gives you the energy to move. That's important, isn't it?"

He shrugged. "It is now. To both of us. An army of rogues could destroy us all."

Stacy shivered. "You know, it's funny." She cleared out a space to work near her microscope. "I always thought a nuclear bomb was the worst threat to the human race."

The sadness in his gaze told her the truth. "Now, you know."

She shook her head, still unable to absorb the truth. Because it was also his truth. And Stacy still hadn't come to terms with that fact either.

"I guess I do." She sighed. "Come on, let's get to work."

Stacy thought her first step would be to see what rogue blood looked like under a microscope. So she created a slide and flaked off a tiny amount from the cross. What she found surprised her.

"This is interesting. I'm not really seeing anything unusual. Except that there aren't that many cells. I guess I was expecting something like a sickle cell or some sort of abnormality."

"So vampires aren't abnormal?" he joked.

Stacy didn't reply, which answered his question.

"I need a control," she said

"And that would be me, wouldn't it?"

She was excited by the prospect of discovery. "You betcha. You see, when you're trying to find out what's right and what's wrong in an experiment, you have to have some kind of standard to go by. Tag, you're it."

"You're going to use a needle?"

Stacy laughed. Who would've thought that the big, bad vampire would be squeamish around needles? "Exactly. So come here, big boy, and take your pinprick like a man."

When he saw how small the lancet was, he breathed a sigh of relief.

"You do realize this is going to hurt me way more than it will hurt you," Chaz teased.

"I'll kiss it and make it better."

His face tightened, and fear filled his gaze. "No, you won't. I have no idea what ingesting my blood will do to you."

"All right, all right. Take it easy. I was just joking."

He seemed to relax, and Stacy used the lancet to get his blood. Because he bled so much, just this one little stab enabled her to fill a small tube. From there, she put his blood on the slide.

Again, she found nothing unusual except that he had more cells than the rogue.

She sighed. "I'm not sure if I'm on the right track or not, but I'm going to hypothesize here for a moment."

"Hypo—what?" he teased again. "Scientists."

Stacy grinned. "Blacksmiths. Sheesh." She rolled her eyes and continued. "First, you bleed too much and too easily. That means you probably have no coagulants in your blood.

Maybe no platelets either. A pinprick or a tiny cut should be deadly. You shouldn't stop bleeding, but then you heal almost instantaneously. I'm not sure how you do that. but it is logical. And you slow rogues down by causing a bleed out."

Chaz turned serious. "Bleeding can be very dangerous. Even when we're not trying. In the 'old' days, swords. Knives. An ax nearly severed my arm once. I didn't think I'd make it."

"I get the picture," she grimaced. "Humans have blood types that react with each other when mixed," she continued. Stacy took out another slide and mixed both the rogue and Chaz's blood on it. After a few moments, she looked at it under the microscope. Nothing. No clumps.

Made sense. "When two different blood types react with each other, the cells clump together—they conjugate," she told him. "Antigens and antibodies. And that can be deadly. Obviously, you have no coagulants in your blood because you can't have them."

"That makes sense," Chaz said.

And the antigens and antibodies? Neutralized somehow? Stacy frowned and wondered. Logic. Follow the logic. "Now I know I'm trying to use human attributes and apply them to vampires, and that may be totally incorrect, but think about this: you used to be human. Somewhere along the way, that has to be the starting point."

"Starting point?" Chaz asked. "I'm not sure I understand."

Stacy chuckled, sure of herself in at least one respect. "Yes. In spite of being abnormal, you follow logic. Your morphology makes sense. You can't possibly accept all kinds of blood without keeping it moving in your system, so your blood hardly coagulates."

"A stake through the heart does create a total bleed out," Chaz told her, his tone thoughtful. "But that doesn't completely kill us. Eventually, our skin knits together. Even around the stake."

Wow. A little too much information there.

"Okay. So you live with a chronic condition I would term normocytic anemia. It means you have functioning red blood cells, just not enough of them. The fix for that is a transfusion. Which you do fairly often."

"Okay. I'm following so far."

"So, for a rogue, the blood cells can't be replenished fast enough, but whatever it is that makes you heal so fast, won't let a rogue die. Talk about a lousy Catch-22."

He stilled. In a soft voice, he said, "Now you know why we have to kill ourselves."

"Yeah," Stacy murmured. "You know, that makes me wonder. What about this rosary pea extract of yours?"

"What about it?"

"How does it function?"

"I don't know exactly. All I know is that the extract is the only thing that can slow a rogue down long enough for me to kill it."

Stacy flipped open her laptop. "*Abrus precatorius.* The seeds contain a poison called Abrin." She pulled up the chemical information on the poison. "It's pretty damned toxic. And you say you make an extract out of it?"

"Yeah."

"It causes bleeding of the internal organs when ingested." Stacy followed some more information. "Says here that it's also a protein synthesis inhibitor."

"What does that mean?"

Hmmm. Now that wouldn't work. Or would it? Wait a minute. Don't they? Stacy felt her heart start to speed up. "Chaz. Do you have any extract on you? I only need a drop."

He handed her his last vial. She took out a tiny droplet and put it on the slide with first his blood, then the rogue's blood. The rogue's slide turned clear almost immediately. His slide took longer but did the same.

"Fascinating," she murmured. "Of course," she breathed. "How else would you survive without a functioning liver? Or kidneys?"

"You lost me."

"What? Oh. Sorry. Okay, here's what I'm thinking. You have a mechanism inside of you. I'm guessing a protein, and I could be wrong, but I don't think so. When a red blood cell finishes its task inside your body, where does it go? You don't have a liver. You don't have kidneys. Well, you might, but they don't function. So what happens to the dead cells?"

"I don't know."

"Actually, I'm thinking a few things at this point. The phagocytes you ingest with whatever blood you take in aren't enough to take care of all the dead cells you create, so you use up everything you can get your hands on."

He shrugged. "Obviously. "

"And I'm thinking this protein, might be specific, might be more than one, and they help the rest of your cells heal really quickly. I'm not sure of the mechanism, but it allows your internal and external organs to stop you from bleeding. You always need to feed after you're wounded, and you need more than usual, yes?"

"Yes."

Stacy watched him start to pace then glance at his watch, then at her. With a concerned frown, he said, "We've been here an awfully long time. I'm not sure I like being this exposed, this open to attack."

Stacy looked around at her cramped, overcrowded lab, and smiled. "Open to attack?" she asked.

He threw her a look. "You know exactly what I mean. Think you can hurry this up a bit?"

Stacy shook her head. "I tried to warn you, Chaz. This may take a lot longer than you expected."

"The rogue has your scent, and more of those damned young vamps might try to find us," he protested.

"But I'm just getting started," Stacy complained. "Now, to continue. The rogue. He barely has any red cells in his blood. I'm not sure what could possibly do this, but his cells are being destroyed right after they get inside. Hence the need to gorge."

"Okay. That makes sense."

"And Abrin causes internal bleeding. So if the poison is creating an internal bleed out and the mechanism is out of control, well, now you know why it hurts a rogue."

"Stacy. Please. I think we should go now."

"Hush. Don't talk to me. I'm thinking."

He paced, and Stacy ignored him. She started researching proteins, but there were too many of them. After another couple of hours, she pinched the bridge of her nose and looked up. Chaz didn't look happy.

"Can we go now? Please?" he begged. "We've been here way too long. Staying in one place like this is simply too dangerous. I didn't think we would spend the entire night here."

"But—" she protested.

He shook his head. "No, Stacy. Long enough. We need to be smart about this."

"How? I'm the bait, whether I want to be bait or not. The rogue is going to find me whether we want it to or not."

He winced. "I know. So my job is to keep you safe until you can figure out what's going on."

"Is…is that all?" she asked, her stomach hollowing. "Is that all you need me for?"

"Of course not," he said. "Stacy, listen to me, this is the situation we're in whether you want us there or not. Now I'm using the word 'us,' here, got that?"

She nodded, feeling a little better.

"Good," he said. "Now we tried things your way, and that didn't work out too well, did it?"

"No."

"So let's try this my way. It's time to ask Hunter for his help. I think it's time for us to stay at the mansion for a while."

Stacy bit out a tight laugh. "I highly doubt that will be a welcome request."

"He'll have to deal."

Would he? Stacy wasn't sure she liked that at all. Since they were speaking of lions, going to Hunter's was like having one guard for the entire zoo. Not a situation that gave you a warm and fuzzy feeling inside. But as much as she didn't like it, Chaz was right. There was only one way to continue what she'd started. She needed time to complete her studies.

"What if Hunter decides it's too dangerous?"

Chaz shrugged. "Then it's too dangerous. We go to plan B."

"Plan B?"

"We'll figure it out."

"How? By keeping me somewhere I don't want to be?"

"That's not a bad idea."

"No, I want your promise. I want you to promise that you'll let me come back for a time every night and continue what I've started. I have to. It's the only way to find out what's going on. Otherwise, I'll come without you during the day."

"And get yourself killed? He'll pick up your scent here soon enough. Trust me on that one. I can't stay awake. You know that. Damn it, be reasonable!"

A secret warmth stole through her veins. Maybe, despite his protests, he really cared. "I am."

Suddenly, his face brightened. "What if I can get Hunter to set up a temporary lab at the mansion? This way, you can live and work there. It would keep the rogue off your trail for a while."

Stacy's jaw dropped. "Now you're really asking for the moon." Then the prospect of continuing her work made her heart beat faster. Hope seared through her. "Think he'll go for it?"

Chaz grinned, obviously liking the idea more and more. "I have my ways. And I have allies. If I can't, Sam will convince him."

"Knowing Hunter," Stacy said, "Even she might have trouble."

"Trust me. Arrangements can be made. Arrangements can always be made."

Chapter Sixteen

CHAZ

CHAZ HAD LEARNED TO IGNORE THE STARES A LONG TIME AGO. Ignorance and prejudice were universal concepts for humans and vampires alike. Most vampires hated him on principle, and some were even jealous. They never let him forget exactly what he was. Hunter might respect him, but only Sam truly accepted him for himself.

However, what they were doing to Stacy was unforgivable.

Damn if the woman wasn't a marvel. As they walked down a long corridor on one of the lower floors of the mansion, she held herself erect and faced down every stare with a strength he didn't know she had. She didn't deserve this kind of treatment. She was trying to help a race that thought of her as a piece of meat.

He tightened his hand on her shoulder and glared at one young soldier who had the audacity to allow his gaze to linger on her. He would have complained, but the next thing he knew, Hunter was standing in front of the soldier, nose to nose. The soldier didn't move a muscle, but Chaz could smell his fear.

His point made, Hunter stopped in the middle of the corridor and made his wishes clear. "The lady is my guest." Hunter didn't need to say more.

Chaz watched the tension drain out of her body as they walked past numerous doorways. Each soldier in the house had a small room where they lived, the higher the rank, the larger the room. The upper floors had more amenities and were reserved for the highest in rank. Then they came to the end of the corridor and stopped in front of a set of elevator doors.

Stacy stared up at him in surprise. "We're going down?"

Chaz nodded. Hunter explained. "The upper floors look like a human house. The main floor is made up of offices, complete with a cafeteria of sorts for the people who work here. Downstairs? I suppose I'll just have to show you."

"But I don't understand. Downstairs? We're on top of the Palisades. Even I know a rock when I sit on top of one."

Hunter smirked. "We can also be quite industrious when we put our minds to things. Although I've modernized much of the equipment such as the elevators, we spent years digging out the shafts ourselves by using modified mining techniques."

"Mining techniques? By yourselves?" she echoed.

Chaz smiled. "You'll see."

The elevator went down to what Chaz would have called the second basement. Two soldiers snapped to attention when they saw Hunter step out. The corridor widened into a gigantic room filled with banks of refrigerators lining the outside walls.

He watched Stacy shiver. "It's cold."

Hunter nodded. "It's meant to be cold. Less cost and stress on the refrigerators."

Stacy stopped dead in her tracks. "They're filled with blood?"

Hunter nodded. "It's not quite as much as you'd think, Stacy. We supply the entire East Coast of the United States."

"East Coast?" she echoed in awe.

"We have our own donation center. We take the people your blood banks won't. I, for one, couldn't care less if you've had cancer. Hepatitis? No problem. Most human diseases don't affect us."

"Makes sense."

"As I'm sure you're aware, most of our organs don't function anyway."

"Some do."

Hunter's lips quirked. "Indeed."

"You pay people to donate?"

"Of course." Hunter smiled. "Since certain issues keep people from donating in your world, but not ours, we have a steady supply. Our one pre-requisite, if you will, is that it will nourish us."

"Yeah," she agreed. "High liver enzymes. Lipemic blood. You wouldn't really need to use the serum anyway unless you need the volume."

"We occasionally do, and we do ask people not to go to a fast-food restaurant before they donate. But once the liquid and cells are separated, we have no trouble with any of that." It all made sense.

"I can tell if you're anemic a mile away," Hunter continued. Stacy watched Chaz nod in agreement. "And though we do need the real thing, the advent of the transportation of blood has made our lives that much easier."

"I have to say I'm impressed, but I already knew you were able to dine on just about anything."

"Not quite," Hunter corrected. "We screen out known drug addicts. We're still not quite sure whether drugs will have a lasting effect on us or not."

"What about HIV?"

"We're not sure, so we don't take that chance. Our screening process is pretty good. I'm sure Chaz has already touched your mind. So you know we can tell if someone is lying or not."

Chaz watched her throw Hunter a look. "I guess so," she said with a shaky laugh.

Hunter simply shrugged. "I'm not asking you to condone, Stacy. I don't want to step into people's minds, but I refuse to apologize for doing everything necessary to survive."

She nodded, not quite sure how to handle it all.

"It's a lot to swallow, Stace," Chaz chimed in. "We know that. This is just another reason why we try to remain invisible, but this is our world, and we do what we have to do."

"If it's any consolation," Hunter added, "our lives have never been this clinical before."

Stacy turned to him, and Chaz wondered at the thoughtful look on her face. "There were less of you before, too, weren't there?"

"Our mortality rate was much higher," Hunter answered. "If that's what you were asking."

Stacy nodded. "All right. Thanks for vampire lesson number two. So, this is where you want me to set up?"

Hunter nodded as they walked through a set of doors. "We will obtain all of the equipment you requested. We have wealth accumulated over the millennia, although I must admit, we don't have totally unlimited resources."

Stacy grinned. "I understand. I know where to get used equipment. Which will be fine for most of what I need to do. I'll make out a list."

"Not necessary. New will be purchased." Hunter bowed. "Is there anything else I can do?"

Stacy grinned. "Well, maybe one thing." Hunter lifted a signature brow. "Any possibility of turning up the heat?"

Chapter Seventeen

CHAZ

EVEN CHAZ MARVELED AT HUNTER'S EFFICIENCY. WITHIN HOURS, stainless steel carts were delivered and locked together to create temporary workbenches. Microscopes, racks, tubes, and Petri dishes arrived. A large crate was unpacked to reveal a machine that made Stacy extremely happy.

"A mass spectrophotometer!" she cried. "How did you manage?"

Hunter merely smiled.

A small refrigerator was wheeled off the elevator and placed in a corner while Stacy unpacked some more boxes. "Antisera. Western blot test kits. Everything I asked for."

Stacy walked over to Hunter and threw her arms around him. "Thank you."

Hunter looked uncomfortable as she leaned back and grinned up at him. That helped take some of the edge off his angst. As soon as they'd walked into the mansion, Chaz regretted his idea, unsure of which would be more dangerous—a rogue or a house full of unfriendly vampires. All of them wanting to take a bite out of Stacy's neck.

He also knew the sun would rise soon, and he wondered what

would happen to Stacy while he slept. Hunter seemed to be able to read his mind without having used the ability to do so.

"Sam will arrive shortly. I've asked her to keep an eye on Stacy while you sleep."

Chaz allowed some of the tension inside to drain out. No one would dare go up against Sam. "Thanks."

"But before you fall asleep, I'd like both of you to join me in my private chambers. I've asked Sam as well. I'm deeply concerned with these young vampires. She's brought two of them with her to question."

"I doubt you'll get anything out of them," Chaz scoffed. "They seemed unfazed by any of their actions. Or ours."

Hunter sighed. "The leaders of the other cells are extremely troubled by today's events. So am I. What has happened, what has been happening, is all very—the only word I can come up with is odd—out of character. You serve a distinct purpose, Charles."

"Tell me something I don't know," he muttered, watching Stacy unpack cartons like a kid on Christmas morning. He couldn't help but smile. Hunter followed his gaze. "She's pretty mean with a needle in her hand if that's any consolation."

Hunter tilted his head. "You seem quite taken with her, and though I understand the need for companionship, eventually, no matter how important she becomes to you, you know you'll have to let her go."

Chaz shivered, hating the cold ball of misery forming in his stomach. "I know."

Although Hunter hid his feelings well, Chaz sensed real regret in his gaze. "I'm sorry."

He sighed, fear melting the misery into a mess of emotions Chaz didn't know how to handle. "The rogue may decide to take that decision away from me."

As Chaz said the words, he realized he wished he could cry. The thought of not being able to watch her smile or scold, the reality of not being able to verbally spar with her, or the simple pleasure of holding her hand, let alone the intimacy they'd shared—all left him as cold inside as it was outside.

"Then Fate will dictate," Hunter replied. "I'm not sure which will be worse."

"You mean the part where she's really dead or where she's only dead to me?"

Which would be crueler, he wondered? Visiting a gravesite or sitting in the shadows watching her kiss another man?

Hunter raised a brow and crossed his arms. "I may not be able to understand because there's a difference between us." Hunter grimaced as though his next words would be distasteful. "There is a piece of you, inside, that remains human to this day. I do not carry that piece inside. I will kill without a second thought if I have to."

"I've never thought otherwise."

"Other vampires carry a part of their humanity with them. To different degrees, I admit. I had no humanity left inside me when I died. Not one ounce. Being a gladiator didn't allow."

"I'm sorry."

Hunter smiled, still cold but more—human—than Chaz had ever seen before. "Don't be. I have no regrets." He shrugged. "That which you carried over may make you able to love like a human. I don't know. I'm not sure it's something to hope for because of the pain that it causes."

Chaz was beginning to understand that. "Perhaps my existence is no better," Hunter added. "But that piece of me, the one that wanted, no still wants, revenge became the cornerstone of my survival. And that, I believe, is the key. I'll do anything to survive. And I'll do anything to protect my people."

"What are you're trying to tell me?"

"That when all is said and done, you can never have her."

Survival. The one and only thing a vampire really knew because of the need for blood.

Chaz walked over to Stacy and touched her arm. In light of Hunter's words and the reality he didn't want to examine, he knew that from now on, every touch would become special. She turned to him, giving him a brilliant smile. Why? After all they'd done to her, after the respect they hadn't shown her, she still wanted to save their sorry asses.

A soldier entered and whispered something in Hunter's ear. "Sam has arrived. Come."

Stacy flashed him a questioning look.

"Hunter would like us to join him for a meeting. To shed some light on these vampires and figure out why they're doing what they're doing."

"Of course." She looked down at her watch. "We don't have much time before you fall asleep."

"I know."

Chaz led her to the elevator, and when they arrived on the first floor, they walked down a corridor and into a large chamber. He was used to it being empty, but now a large table centered the room, and several chairs surrounded it.

He watched Sam nod, and Stacy smiled back. They might never be able to be friends, but Stacy had Sam's respect, which meant he would be able to count on Sam watching over her as he slept.

When everyone was seated, Hunter rose, leaning forward to rest his hands on the table. That was when he realized Hunter was on a video camera and the heads of the other cells worldwide were watching.

"We seem to have some very strange occurrences to contemplate, ladies and gentlemen," Hunter began. "Not the least of which are these young vampires in my custody. My first question is whether or not any of the rest of you has noticed any outright defiance by one or more members of your cells."

One by one, the members of the Council all answered in the negative.

"All right," Hunter continued. "Then you are now formally warned. Several young vampires within my domain have shown outward disregard for the rules that govern the cells. While we've experienced this type of behavior with newly made vampires, even young vampires realize that disobedience is not conducive to ensuring a continuous blood supply. Until we understand more or find the cause, any signs of unusual behavior must be contained."

"You speak as if this behavior is expected," Miklos, the leader of the Greek cell said, his tone haughty. "If a vampire in my domain knows what's good for him—or her—they won't disobey my rules."

Chaz watched Hunter hide his disdain as he answered. "This isn't about obedience, Miklos. We don't know why this is happening, but it is, and Samira and I both think it will get worse."

No one said anything in reply. "Use restraint, please," Sam requested. "There is a possibility that this behavior has been created."

"Created?" Dannika, leader of the Scandinavian cell, asked, her tone incredulous. "How?"

"We don't know that yet either," Hunter answered.

"Well, maybe we do, sort of," Stacy chimed in.

Stacy started as she became the object of everyone's attention. Hunter beckoned her over, so she stood in front of the camera. She swallowed but refused to show fear as she lifted her chin. His heart swelled with pride at her strength. "My name is Stacy Morgan. And yeah, I'm human, but I'm figuring you all knew that already."

He watched her take a deep breath, then continue. "I'm also a forensic chemist that used to specialize in blood banking. To make a long story short, which I'm also figuring you know, I'm the bait that will catch a rogue vampire terrorizing this area. But before you let him make me his breakfast lunch and dinner, you might want to start thinking about why vampires are behaving out of character and why, all of a sudden, you've had three rogues on your hands in such a short period of time."

"Going rogue can happen at any time to any one of us," Hunter told Stacy.

"I know you've told me that. You've also told me that it happens at the end of your life span."

"True," Hiroki, leader of the Japanese cell, answered. "But not always."

"Okay, look. I'm a scientist, and I know only one way to think when I'm presented with a problem—logically."

"Stacy," Chaz chided. "This isn't your meeting."

"It should be," she snapped back.

"Let her speak," Jason, leader of the West Coast cell, insisted. "If she has an idea, I want to hear it."

Chaz couldn't see them but, by their silence, knew they wanted Stacy to continue. He clamped his lips together and sat back in his chair.

"Thank you," Stacy continued. "Whatever is going on here, it directly links to your morphology. In lay terms, what makes you all vampires, which has a direct connection to your need for blood. Especially, what makes you go rogue."

"Why do you believe this?" Jason asked, his tone concerned.

"I was able to test a sample of the rogue's blood and compare it to Chaz's, sorry Charles' blood. There weren't enough blood cells in the rogue's sample to support life as you know it."

"Are you certain of this?" Dannika asked.

"Very," Stacy answered.

No one said anything for a long moment. "What makes you believe this, if I may ask?" Miklos growled.

"I believe there's a mechanism inside you that allows you to destroy used blood cells. I also believe you have a mechanism that gives you the ability to heal. My guess is that in order to create a rogue in a young vampire, one would have to speed up the need for blood cells like a hundred-fold. Make it run out of control. I need to prove that hypothesis."

No one spoke. Then Chaz remembered something. "She may be on the right track. The rogue threatening Stacy is Mikhail. He certainly didn't go rogue because of his age."

Silence fell around them. "I gave Mick, sorry, the rogue, a good mouthful of the extract. That should've crippled it, at least made it sick. Didn't do a damn thing."

More silence.

"How do we know we can trust you?" Hiroki asked Stacy, his tone filled with concern.

The tightness around her lips eased, and the worry in her face turned to eagerness. Stacy smiled. And Chaz knew she not only wanted to help them. She believed she could. "Because I'm trying to save my own life. Maybe, instead of trying to destroy this out of control vampire, I might just be able to cure him using science, something you folks seem to have forgotten exists."

No one spoke for a long moment. "An interesting concept," Jason finally replied. "And if you can't?"

Stacy shrugged. "If I can't, I'll be very grateful if you can kill it before it kills me." She paused and continued her tone, totally sincere. "I might be handy to have around, you know. If I can figure out what makes you all tick, I might just be able to stop you—meaning all vampires—from going rogue in the future."

Chapter Eighteen

STACY

MUCH TO THEIR CREDIT, THE HEADS OF THE OTHER CELLS AGREED with her, and then their conversation turned to the younger vampires who seemed to be rebelling against vampire social mores.

Stacy listened with half an ear. Her fingers itched to get at the equipment in the lab down below. Her heart sped up as she thought about the experiments she wanted to perform, but the rest of her body wanted to keel over and crash, her biorhythms were totally out of whack.

"I brought two of the young vampires with me for questioning," she heard Sam say.

"None of this makes sense," Dannika said, her tone confused and alarmed. "Throughout the ages, vampires have aligned themselves with each other, so they don't deplete blood supplies. Respect within a cell means order, order means survival. To have young vampires try to kill one such as Charles is unthinkable." Her voice trailed off.

"Jeremy's loss is painful to us all and quite unnerving as well," Hiroki added. "As is the possibility that this rogue was not destroyed. Most of all, that it was Mikhail."

Stacy watched Chaz throw a look at the laptop screen that said, "yeah, right; you're real crushed," before he turned back to the table. But then she heard the pain in the man's voice and realized the last part of Hiroki's statement rang true.

"For now, Ozzie knows he's in danger and will act accordingly," Chaz told them. "I've sent messages to the rest of the Paladin. They know to be on their guard. But if this escalates, if these young vampires start wreaking havoc, all hell is going to break loose. We're going to have to start taking them down."

Another long silence ensued. Hunter and Sam nodded, and Stacy realized she'd forgotten they had psychic abilities. The thought pricked at her. Here she was trying to save their sorry asses, and they still didn't trust her.

"Understood," Hunter sighed. "Are we in agreement then?" he asked the other leaders.

One by one, they gave their consent.

Then again, she realized, they didn't trust each other either.

Once the conference was over, they all rose. Chaz swayed a little but caught himself before she could help.

"A bedroom has been readied for you both," Hunter told her. "Although I'm certain you would like to go home, Stacy, Chaz won't make it there in time. I think it would be better to stay here and continue your work here for your own protection."

"No one would dare go up against me," Sam added. "But we mustn't forget there's an entire cell down there that would like nothing better than to feed on her."

Hunter agreed. "Duly noted."

"Hunter?" Sam continued.

"Yes?"

"I think it's time to issue an order of protection."

Hunter didn't answer.

"What's an order of protection?"

"She'll be safer if we stay on the move," Chaz argued, his words slurring a little.

"We can discuss this later," Hunter replied. He turned and added, "We often have guests from other cells who visit. We also have human technical representatives who fix our equipment that sometimes remain overnight. You can stay upstairs. And I'm sure you'll find the accommodations are to your satisfaction."

"No, wait a minute. Don't try to change the subject. I want to know what you're talking about," Stacy insisted.

Hunter turned to her, his face falling, his normally stoic countenance softening. He stared at her, hesitant to continue. Was that because he understood responsibility? Or perhaps he understood the need to be true to any and all obligations?

"An order of protection means that any vampire that touches you forfeits his life. It is the order we give with the humans that run the donation services. It should be given to you as well."

Stacy's insides hollowed. "Wait a minute. I refuse to be the cause of someone, anyone losing their life."

Sam frowned. "I don't make the suggestion lightly, Stacy. But it is for your own good."

"No. I couldn't live with that kind of order sitting on my shoulders. I work to save lives. I don't take them just because I exist."

"Very noble of you, but not exactly safe," Sam added. She cocked her head, and Stacy read the respect filling her gaze. "Very well. I'll agree for now. But I will give you fair warning; I may decide to do it anyway without your permission."

Sam bowed and went off to see about the young vampires, and Hunter gave her a thoughtful stare. Was that a tinge of respect lighting his gaze? Stacy would have to find out.

"I have only one request," he continued. "Please make sure that either Charles or Sam or I are with you at all times. I control my cell, but individual vampires are much like individual humans, they may say one thing and decide to do another."

"Even at the cost of their life?"

Hunter nodded, his gaze sad. "The blood," was all he said. He helped her get Chaz to their quarters, and they both watched him go out. Hunter seemed a bit uncomfortable, and Stacy hid a smile.

"I threatened your life not more than twenty-four hours ago, and yet here you are, trying to save mine. Why?" Hunter asked, his tone genuinely puzzled.

"I told you before, I have a personal stake in this. I want to live."

"Is that the only reason?"

Stacy laughed softly so as not to disturb Chaz even though she knew he couldn't hear. "What do you think?"

"I think, Stacy, that perhaps it is time for my people to begin to embrace change. Perhaps we should not fight so hard against it. But that requires a precious commodity."

"You mean, trust?"

"Yes."

"It's what I've been trying to tell you all along."

"Maybe, now, we will listen."

He bowed and shut the door to the bedroom with a gentle click. Stacy longed to get to work but knew she needed to sleep for a few hours. Chaz lay exactly as they'd placed him, clothes and all, which seemed uncomfortable.

Stacy watched Chaz sleep with newfound respect. So much had happened to them, between them, that she'd been unable to grasp the real Charles. Champion wasn't a word she used lightly, but the word kept pounding in her brain.

In her head, Stacy carried characters. Caricatures, perhaps. Vampires were cold, unfeeling creatures like Hunter. But now that humans and vampires faced a universal problem, she realized they were very alike. They simply wanted to live. They wanted even more to belong.

All Chaz wanted was to be a man. And when the need arose, a Paladin. A protector. So that his people could exist. So he could exist.

Stacy traced a fingertip over his brows, down the line of his cheek, and around the curve of his jaw. Fierce yet tender. Strong but capable of so much feeling inside.

She undid the buttons on his shirt and finally tugged and pulled the garment off. Then she undid his belt, unsnapped the clip, and shimmied his pants down his legs. Fierce yet tender, he seemed so much more human in repose.

Stacy yawned and let go of the tension keeping exhaustion at bay. She removed her own clothes and climbed into the bed next to Chaz. Would she ever get used to that first shock, the cool skin that heated quickly next to hers?

A reminder that they were different. Physically. And yet, she thought as she fell asleep, perhaps not so different after all.

Chapter Nineteen

CHAZ

WAKING UP NEXT TO SOMEONE WAS A PLEASURE CHAZ DIDN'T indulge in very often. Normally, he came out of the sleep, terrified of where he was, having fought his way out of a coffin and clawed his way up one too many times to forget that particular delight.

Her body curled around his, skin to skin on every possible place they could touch. Her hair still smelled of that citrus shampoo, making him think of freshness and light. He drew in a deep breath, inhaling her unique scent, which reminded him so much of spring.

Freshness and light. That's what she gave him. Strength. Honor. Fortitude. Intelligence. He could go on and on. And what could compare to the soft curve of her hip, the perfect taper of thigh to calf? God, she even had beautiful feet.

Uh-oh. Chaz clamped down hard on his thoughts before something else became hard.

Looking back through the past, Chaz knew his human life came when life was simple and centered mostly on survival. Indulgence was a word for the very few, the nobility, not a blacksmith and soldier. And cheap? A simple sword cut on the battlefield usually meant death. Childbirth was a gamble at best. Starvation was a general certainty more often than not within a lifetime.

And yet, there'd been joy. The moment when the sky lightened at dawn with streaks of pink fire, and the air smelled as crisp and clean as a mountain spring. The moment when he put away his hammer and let the fire die down, stretching sore muscles with an inner smile, knowing he'd performed a decent day's work—the laughter of children playing in the alley next to his smithy. As a human, he'd known peace. A quiet within his soul. Something he'd never been able to achieve as a vampire.

Until now.

A smile of wonder lit his face. Stacy snuggled closer to his body, seeking a warmth that would never be there. Not physically, anyway, and he asked himself the question he'd been dreading since they'd first met: Could she, no, would she be able to accept that?

He'd been alone for so long. To finally find someone who could fill the void only to know he would have to give her up?

Payment. He tightened his arms around her as he fought back the agony of his thoughts. As much as he didn't want to admit it, he couldn't deny logic, a life for a life. He'd caused Mary's death; he would have to give Stacy up as payment. He knew that now. And like the breaking of delicate glass, his insides shattered at the thought.

As a vampire, time was the one commodity Chaz had never thought about. Each moment they were together would carry a special meaning, become a treasure, be placed inside a box, and let out later when the loneliness got too hard to bear.

A gentle palm cupped his cheek. She looked up at him with a hint of alarm in her gaze. She sensed his dilemma but not his decision. And Chaz fell into the only place he knew that could totally banish the pain. She lifted up and feathered light kisses over his eyes, his nose, his cheeks, and his chin. Everywhere except where he wanted her to go. So he reached around, cupped the back of her head with his hand, and gently parted her lips with his. They'd made love fast and furious but never savory and slow, and Chaz wanted to imprint each millisecond in his memory.

He broke the kiss, leaning his forehead against hers, their breath mingling as one.

"Why, Stacy?"

She knew exactly what he was asking. "I don't know, Chaz, but I believe there are reasons for everything, and I'm not going to question that anymore."

"You've become the light in my very dark existence."

She gave him a sad smile. "Only because you believe it's dark."

She kissed him, her lips covering his, not allowing him to say more. Tiny bolts of lightning blazed up and down his spine urging him to forget all of his good intentions. Her tongue swirled around his and grazed each incisor on purpose, knowing what that did to him. She opened her neck as she opened her body to him, giving him everything within. He didn't deserve such generosity.

He wasn't about to say no. He twirled her nipples into tight little buds with his free hand; his grin grew as she moaned. He nipped his way down from the bottom of her ear to her shoulder, sorely tempted but not ready to accept the prize she offered.

Her legs kept trying to urge him on top of her, but Chaz was no fool. And he'd been making love to women for nearly a thousand years. This was one time when he was going to enjoy her moment as well as his.

He grazed her skin, roaming from her shoulder to her breast, replacing his fingers with his lips. He swirled his tongue around her areola, bringing her nipple to full attention before nipping gently. "Harder, Chaz. Harder."

He bit down, and she cried out, but he refused to draw blood. Amazement filled him at the oh-so-scientific chemist turning into the writhing woman who loved it hot. And he grinned.

She started playing with his nipples sending shots of pure pleasure into his cock. All right, she had him there. He could only stand so much before he gave in too, and when her hand closed around his erection, Chaz knew he'd have to speed up his timetable—a little. He slid down and began kissing her belly, his tongue swirling over satiny skin. And though it served no function at all, really, there was something outrageously eroge-nous about a belly button. Her quick indrawn breath told him so.

But that was not the prize he coveted. He swirled his tongue down over her mound, inhaling her womanly scent. His hormones pinged in answer, and he grew harder, a deep urgency to mate with her growing in his belly. She tasted salty and sweet; creating a hunger that could be quenched but never satisfied.

He lapped at her core, and she cried out. "Oh, God, Chaz. Don't. I want to—last."

He smiled and stopped, letting her rest until she regained control. He slid back up until their lips met and let her taste herself on his tongue. "You're so beautiful, Stacy. Inside and out."

Tears filled her eyes. "So are you, whether you know it or not."

He rolled her over on her back and spread her legs with his knee. He dared not believe that, not even for a moment. Instead, he stopped and rested just before entering her body. She squirmed and rocked, and he continued to tease until she reached the moment where he knew she would plead. Then he slid his cock just slightly inside. Her muscles clamped around him, and he swallowed hard.

Her eyes opened and swirled with heat. He found a gentle warmth, a special gaze that would only be shared by the two of them. With a single thrust, he filled her, and she cried out. Sweet heaven. That's what this was. Heaven. On earth.

Her muscles contracted all around his cock, and the time for slow disappeared. Chaz drew back and thrust into her body, taking care not to hurt her, but knowing she enjoyed his strength. Her eyes closed, and her body stilled, her face filled with pleasure. And just as she reached the pinnacle, just as her cries told him she'd reached the edge, Chaz sank his incisors into her neck. His body sang with her blood, and the knowledge that it was Stacy's blood only made the taste sweeter. He filled her, drinking only enough to make her pleasure that much more intense. Now was the time for giving, not taking, and so he thrust into her body and drew on her neck. And she climbed with him. Higher and higher, harder and harder, until she shattered for him.

Then all sane thought ceased. His body took over, his orgasm crested, and a wondrous thing happened. In the next moment, her breath hitched, and she started to convulse again, drawing an intense explosion out of his body. He withdrew from her neck, and their cries harmonized throughout the room until only tiny aftershocks remained.

Chaz pulled her tight against his chest as he slipped out of her. He listened to her swift indrawn breaths subside as her heartbeat slowed, and Chaz knew he wanted this moment to last forever. He wanted to drown in her warmth, her goodness, make the purity of her soul his. But he couldn't.

"Chaz, I—"

He placed a gentle finger against her lips. Now was the time for loving, for creating memories, not worrying about the future. He shook his head, hoping his gaze was as fierce as his emotions as he silently begged her to float with him, to remember that the only truly important moments were those they shared, that nothing could reach them until they opened the door.

She nodded, smiling as she snuggled deep into his body. Soon her soft breaths told him she'd fallen back to sleep. And for a little while, she would be his—only his.

Chaz waited until Stacy was deeply asleep before climbing out of bed. He stared down at her; his heart turned over in his chest. As a Paladin, he'd done what was expected of him. His eyes burned, dry, unencumbered. And yet, lying in bed rested the one person in this world he wanted to fight for.

No, die for.

Chaz turned away, stretching out his fingers. He hadn't even known they'd curled into fists. He cleaned up and dressed, trying to bury his thoughts. As he closed the door, he closed the gateway to his heart.

Chaz hurried out of the main house and crossed the grounds of the compound. There were several small houses scattered about the property, cottages actually, for every cell was honor-bound to provide shelter to lone vampires traveling in the area. Not every vampire wanted to be a part of society or owe allegiance to a cell.

He called out to Hunter. *Ozzie is on the premises.*

I'm aware.

I don't believe it's a social visit.

Nor do I.

Still our job.

Understood.

Chaz's mouth quirked. Communicating with Hunter was a courtesy, not a requirement.

The cottage stood at the very edge of the property closest to the woods. It still amazed him that there could be untouched land in the middle of one of the tri-states most affluent suburbs.

Ozzie rose from the bed as Chaz walked in. He didn't look too good. Ozzie didn't smile much, so his dark hair and dark eyes made him seem that much more taciturn. He'd been frowning, a normal pose for Ozzie, but Chaz sensed something was very wrong.

Still, they hugged and clapped backs. "If it isn't my old friend John Osmund."

"If it isn't my old friend Charles Tower."

They should have been smiling, happy to see one another, but circumstances dictated otherwise.

"He's here, Chaz. Close by."

"I figured as much."

"Never thought the day would come."

"Me neither."

Ozzie shuffled his feet and stared at the floor. "He used a couple tricks he taught us. Nearly lost him. Twice. And I vowed that would never happen again."

Ozzie finally glanced up, and Chaz sighed at the disbelief in his gaze. Chaz let go of the pretense of being strong, and his shoulders fell.

"I'm not surprised."

"The woman?" Ozzie asked, hope in his voice. "She's all right?"

"Yeah, she's safe. She's here. In the main house."

Ozzie's gaze fell to the floor again. His hands clasped together. "He knows she's here."

He watched his friend carefully. "The craving will force him to make a mistake."

"That wily old fox? Never."

"If he doesn't," Chaz insisted. "We'll have to make him make one then. She's dead if we don't."

Ozzie lifted his gaze in surprise. "That's not going to be easy."

"Tell me something I don't already know."

Neither of them spoke after that, the silence drawing out so long he could actually hear the sounds of the woods. "God. It's Mick. He killed Pitch."

Ozzie swung around. Chaz took one look and knew Ozzie was about to blow. He had to duck as his fellow Paladin pulled back his arm and made to punch the wall. Chaz stopped him just in time, but he could feel the muscles quivering with the need to explode beneath his fingertips. "We're guests. Not popular ones, either."

Chaz let go when he was sure Ozzie wouldn't try again. "Do you remember when we first met? In Boston?"

"I wasn't one for conversation." Ozzie fell into a chair, shoulders hunched forward.

"You still aren't."

"Mick looked at me. You remember how those bushy brows of his would draw together? Would make you feel like he could see right through you."

"Probably could."

"Asked me what I was searching for," Ozzie said. "It was him, Chaz. He was my teacher. My friend." The last came out just above a whisper. "My father."

"For all of us. But he's not Mick anymore. You'd better get that through your head. He's not human, not vampire. He's a creature. An 'it.' Period."

Ozzie winced with every word.

"And I need to know I can count on you when the time comes."

His fellow Paladin didn't answer, scaring Chaz.

"I loved him too. That's the problem. Ozzie, listen to me. I got up close and personal. That thing out there is pure need. You've had blood fever before. You know what that's like. We all have. Multiply that by ten thousand, and you still don't come close. I even got some extract in him. Didn't make a dent."

Poor Oz. By all accounts, a loner even among vampires. Especially among the Paladin. Mick was the one person in this world the poor bastard cared about. More than cared. "He'll kill hundreds of innocents."

Ozzie jumped out of the chair and glared. "I'll do my duty. Don't worry."

"I know you will."

Chaz reached out and squeezed Ozzie's shoulder. Ozzie shrugged him off and turned away.

"Do you ever wonder why we were created?"

Ozzie? Waxing philosophical? "I have."

"I don't want to anymore. I'm tired of having no choice, tired of having to do my duty." Ozzie faced Chaz again. Anguish swam in his gaze, one that seemed too heavy to bear. And seconds later, he stormed out of the cottage. Chaz followed with an empty ball hollowing his guts. In his beginning as a vampire, Chaz stayed near London. There were plenty of women looking for coin to satisfy his needs. Both needs. He would never forget the moment he met Mick.

"IF YOU TAKE MORE, YOU'LL KILL HER."

Charles swung around, staring at the intruder. He'd never seen another like him before. And that frightened him. "What business is it of yours?"

"That depends on how you want to be known. Somewhat human or truly vampire?"

"Vampire? What is a vampire?"

"What you are now."

"I don't understand."

"I know. I'm here to teach you."

"Go away. I need to drink." Indeed, the craving tore at him. Always the hunger.

"Do you? Or does the blood call to you?"

He'd never thought of that before. "Call to me?" he repeated. "I don't know."

"An honest answer." The stranger smiled. "Kill this woman, and you can never take it back. Never make it right."

Charles shivered. "I know. I—I killed my wife."

"Perhaps," the man answered. "Perhaps not. The sickness is coming. She would have died, and I fear, so would you." The man stepped forward. Charles

read compassion in his face. "There is a difference, my young friend, between what you can change and what you cannot. You can leave this woman and let her go on with her life, or you can end it. Your choice."

"Who are you?"

"I am Nicholai Alexander Mikhail Kirilenko, at your service, Charles Tower."

"You know me?"

"I know many things. One of them is that you are a Paladin. A protector. Not a murderer."

Charles let go of the woman after sipping one last time. That last sip seemed to make them go to sleep for a while.

"How am I able to make them forget?"

"One of your many gifts."

"Gift? You call this existence a gift?"

"Yes," Mick sighed. "And you have much to learn. Much to learn. So come my young friend. And I will teach you."

TEACH. CHAZ SHOOK HIS HEAD, COMING BACK TO THE PRESENT. The time for teaching was over. There could be only one ending to this lesson. Death.

Chapter Twenty

CHAZ

CHARLES WALKED BACK TO THE HOUSE WITH A COLD WEIGHT ON the back of his neck. Nothing about this situation was right, certainly not Mick. He'd never thought about it before—a final death. Just assumed that when his time came, most likely at the hands of a rogue, that would be it. The object of his demise was never supposed to be someone cared about by so many.

How he wished he could share Ozzie's anger. Just once, he ached, his hand curling into a fist. Just once. But this was not his home he noted once again, opening the door to where they were holding the young vampires.

So part of him applauded as he watched Sam bite down on her anger for the tenth time. She threatened, cajoled, even tried to use her psychic abilities to invade—all to no avail. Something, or someone, held these vampires with a will stronger than her own. Maybe she knew why. She kept glancing at them with something akin to fear in her gaze, and he'd never seen Sam afraid.

"Perhaps we should resort to force," Hunter advised, a gleam entering his gaze at the thought. He, too, looked weary of playing games.

"You know better than to ask me to go against everything I believe in, Hunter," Sam said.

"I have no qualms about hurting either of them," Chaz chimed in, his tone a tad too sincere. He stood with his arms crossed over his chest, his brows drawn together, and the twitch in his cheek vibrated as he clamped his teeth together.

Strange, just the challenge of a fight should have garnered at least a look, a flash of anger, something that would let them know these vampires were alive inside. They were, and yet, they weren't. And that made him wonder. They were behaving as if they were robots, automatons; as if they could go through the mechanics of life but had lost all emotion.

Hmm. Emotions. Vampires had less of them than humans. Because of the blood. Because survival was the name of the game, and the game demanded only the fittest endure. Were they hard? Ruthless? Hunter was a prime example. And yet, Chaz suspected beneath the armor, Hunter had a heart. He cared about his cell, did his best to make sure his people never suffered.

But despite their best efforts, eventually, the subconscious and the conscious met. Sometimes with disastrous results. After all, they still came from human stock. That was what Sanctuary was all about. Out of control vampires were a danger to them all. And rogues? Out in the world? Without control? Simply unthinkable.

Sam? Now, she was the oldest. And the most understanding. Perhaps time had a way of putting life into perspective. She counseled the weary, encouraged the time trodden, tried to inspire the bitter. And when a vampire began to go rogue, she helped them pass through this life, tried to replace the fear with joy. But these youngsters? Chaz watched her jaw clench. Harder than his. They were beginning to get on her last nerve, too.

"All right, you two. You have one more minute, then I'm going to hand you over to Hunter. You're not going to like his methods."

The first didn't answer. But the one called Donnie, he spat back, "You don't scare me, girlie-girl."

Affronted, Sam lifted Donnie by his shirt, shaking him as if he were a feather.

"Leave some for me," Chaz called out, a huge grin on his face.

"You need to stop being an annoying little gnat," Sam growled. Her fist closed, and the material tightened around Donnie's throat. "How dare you call me that! Girlie girl? Really?"

She tightened her grip. Donnie stared down at her, his gaze blank. No fear. He showed no fear. Was he that stupid—or....?

Sam let Donnie back down to the floor. She grimaced. "Hold him," she commanded.

Chaz grabbed the vampire's arms and watched as Sam opened his neck, and her incisors grew. He could feel the call of the blood echo in her veins just as it echoed in his. He could feel the thrum, the buzz. Sam reveled in the promise, her face tightening, filled with anticipation. Of them all, Chaz realized, only she knew the true nature of being a vampire.

"A long time ago, blood was given with pride, as a gift, for those who protected and served. I do not understand who you are. The song is dead and, in its stead, remains this murky darkness that I can only associate with evil. You've taken the children of this earth and made them into a mockery of what once was."

Chaz had no idea who she was speaking to, but she seemed to know.

"We are the descendants of a race as old as time. A magnificent race, brilliant in every facet of life. To see this mockery breaks my heart." She kept talking as her mouth neared Donnie's neck. "Our ancestors created marvels still talked about to this day. They created laws by which all vampires are governed. Drinking should never end in death. Ever. These are the laws our ancestors gave us. They forbade such cruelty, such disdain for life. Their laws, their lives, came from the beginning."

Chaz started to freak out a little. Who was she talking to? What was going on?

"But now they are no more."

As soon as she sank her teeth into Donnie's neck, Chaz knew something was terribly wrong. Sam reared back, horror and confusion swirling inside her gaze. An ancient scent, much like hemlock, burned through the air. Fear gelled inside her face turning it to marble. Chaz couldn't believe his sight. Sam feared no one.

She spit every drop out of her mouth, called for water, and rinsed again once delivered.

Chaz looked up. Hunter stared at her as if she'd committed a mortal sin.

In a sense, she had.

She wiped her lips with the back of her hand. Her cheek ticked. Her eyes, normally steady, shifted back and forth. And Chaz asked himself, *was someone trying to destroy them all?*

"Let him go," she commanded.

Chaz looked at her as if she'd gone insane. But he let go out of respect. Donnie started laughing. And it seemed that once he started, he couldn't stop. Which confused Chaz. It confused Hunter even more. Finally, Hunter backhanded the vampire to shut him up.

"What's going on, Sam?" Hunter asked.

"Yeah. Excellent question," Chaz agreed.

"His blood is contaminated," she answered, spitting on the floor in an obvious effort to try to get rid of the terrible taste in her mouth. "I'm not quite certain by what. Something that tastes very old and very bitter."

"Drugged?"

"More like acid. Poison."

"Poisoned? By what?" Chaz asked.

Sam didn't say anything.

"All vampires know to stay away from tainted blood," Hunter added. "We can smell it a mile away."

"I didn't," Sam told them. "And if I didn't, they won't."

Hunter frowned, and Chaz felt a tiny sear of fear seep inside. Sam simply wasn't, well, spook…able.

"Wait a minute," Chaz told them. "We heal each time we sleep. So, this is really weird. How could there be poison in his system?"

A good question. And still no answer.

"Do you realize we're talking about the impossible here?" Chaz asked Sam, his anger palpable.

Sam still decided not to answer. Was that because she didn't want to or because she wasn't sure?

"All right, let's take a step back and look at things logically," he continued. "The only reason we stay away from drug addicts is because we're not quite certain what the drugs will do to us, and out of control, vampires are very dangerous. If we didn't, we could have vampires trying to get high every night. Imagine that in a human night club."

Sam shuddered. Chaz felt a chill run down his spine.

"Imagine that night after night after night," Hunter added.

Obviously, none of them wanted to. The consequences were unthinkable.

Hunter started to pace. "So we have laws. Out-of-control vampires are put down."

"Destroyed. That's where I come in," Chaz said. "So why risk it?"

"What if they can't help themselves?" Sam asked. "What if they don't care?"

"A week ago, I would have told you that was impossible," Hunter replied. "Now I'm not so sure. Even you didn't know this vampire was —is the word sick?"

Sam shook her head and shrugged. She seemed to have no idea. Or did she, Chaz wondered.

"We don't even know how this happened," Hunter said. "Our best guess is that he was drugged, and that would mean from an outside source. If so, how? And with what?"

Not just a sear but a ball of fear formed in his belly that only grew colder.

"I don't know," Sam answered.

"Then the sooner we let Stacy do some testing on his blood, the better," Chaz said. "Maybe she can help us figure out what's going on."

Both vampires went silent until Sam said, "Agreed."

"And in the meantime?" Hunter asked softly, staring at her with a quizzical gaze. Even Chaz had no idea where to go with this besides Stacy.

"In the meantime, keep them away from your cell, and guard

them well," Chaz said. "And for all our sakes, we need to keep a lid on this. Until we know what's going on. We've warned the other cells that a danger exists, but I don't want to start a panic."

Neither Hunter nor Sam appeared to like that idea, but as he watched them process, they both realized they had no choice.

"They'll begin to ask questions," Hunter warned. "Sooner than you think."

Sam stared at both of them and sighed heavily. He felt the weight of her worry mantle his shoulders.

"Then we'd all better hope Stacy is as good at her job as she says she is."

Chapter Twenty-One

STACY

STACY PINCHED THE BRIDGE OF HER NOSE AND CLOSED HER EYES. Her brain had turned into mush, and her internet search hadn't produced any results. When she was in the lab at the mansion, Hunter or Sam would show up every now and then, making her feel terribly uncomfortable. Every time she asked Chaz what was going on, he'd get all stoic on her and shake his head.

The second part of all of this was the other vials of blood that they'd given her to test. Donnie and Nick. Stacy smiled. She kind of wished they'd let her draw them herself. Especially Donnie. She'd have made sure to dig the needle in extra deep.

Stacy got up from the computer and went over to the Liquid Chromatograph, Mass Spectrophotometer again. What she'd found was interesting. The rogue blood seemed to have some kind of a cyto-toxin in it. Which made sense. Any kind of toxin that would destroy healthy cells would obviously make the rogue want more blood. But the protein or proteins they made allowed instant healing. So there was a constant tug of war going on, but what was really interesting was that Donnie's blood had about the same amount of the cytotoxin.

"Stacy?"

"Hmm?"

"It's getting late. We should go back upstairs now."

"You go ahead. I still have more work to do."

He nodded. "Sam's busy right now. I need to stay with you. We have to go. I'm starting to get sleepy."

Stacy grimaced. "If you insist, but before we do, you need to listen to me."

He laughed softly. "Are you serious? You know I'm useless in here."

She laughed, "You're right. Besides, I need to tell Hunter and Sam. Donnie and Nick are starving, and they don't even know it. If they keep it up, they'll go rogue."

"Are you sure?"

"A mass spec doesn't lie, Chaz. They have some kind of toxin in their blood. I'm not quite sure what kind yet. I'll need to perform more tests."

"All right. I'll get word to Sam and Hunter. In the meantime, we need to go."

Stacy packed up her papers and printouts to study while Chaz slept. Chaz put his arm around her shoulders, pulling her tight against him. He looked down at her with such tenderness Stacy thought her heart would swell right out of her chest.

"I have a personal stake in keeping you safe, you know."

A soft thrill ran through her veins. "I know."

They walked out of the elevator into the hallway. Stacy stretched and felt the need for some fresh air. "Think we have enough time for me to go outside? I could really use some fresh air."

He smiled. "Not too long. I'm really starting to feel it."

"Just a moment. To clear my head."

"Okay."

They followed a sidewalk along a perfectly manicured lawn. Without warning, Stacy yanked off her shoes and stockings, running onto the grass with complete abandon, the grass cool and a touch damp beneath her feet. With a light laugh, Stacy ran over to Chaz and started to tug on his hand to join her. He shook his head.

"Come on. Try it. You'll like it."

Suddenly, Chaz inhaled. Deeply. He stilled. If a vampire could turn whiter, he did. All of the muscles in his face tightened. He bent down, sniffing the air.

Her heart in her throat, Stacy asked, "What's wrong?"

He ran down the sidewalk and pointed to the drops of pink salivate on the concrete. "Don't touch those."

"Like hell, I won't." She turned and ran over to her laptop bag.

"What the devil?" he cried. *"Where are you going?"*

"Inside my bag. I need a tube for a sample. I need to analyze that foam."

He rose and ran in front of her before she could take a step. "Are you freaking nuts? We're leaving. Now! The rogue might be anywhere on the grounds."

As frightened by the rogue as she was, Stacy held her ground. "No. I'm going to get a tube, and we're going to analyze that stuff. Or else we'll stand out here and argue about it until the rogue comes back. Which would you prefer?"

"God, woman, are you insane? Do you have a death wish?"

For a moment, even *she* wondered, but stubborn grit was a Morgan trait. "The longer we stand here arguing…"

He stepped towards her as if he was ready to physically pick her up and drag her inside, then he stepped back, his hands clenched at his sides. The entire operation took her less than two minutes, but even the walls vibrated with anger once they were inside.

"If you ever disobey my orders again, I'll lock you up. Do you understand?" He didn't shout. Didn't even get loud. Boy, did he mean business.

"Yes, dear."

He shook his head, his chest heaving. "You don't even have the common sense to be frightened."

"Who said I wasn't frightened?"

His fingers tightened on her wrist. "Then, you're just crazy."

"There's no need to get insulting."

"No…*no* need?"

Stacy hid a smile. He cared. The warmth in her veins was like armor against his ire. "We have an audience."

He looked up to see two soldiers staring at them. She thought her bones would crack beneath his grip. They arrived at their room in record time, greeted there by Sam.

"Hello. What's wrong?" she asked.

Chaz still looked ready to chew on some nails. And not at all sleepy anymore. "We went out for a walk and found signs of the rogue on the sidewalk of the grounds."

Sam frowned. "On the grounds?"

"I went back to get a sample of this." Stacy held up the tube for Sam to see.

Sam, it seemed, saw much more. "I understand. Thank you." She tilted her head at Chaz, and Stacy knew the priestess was daring Chaz to say anything.

After a long moment in which Stacy was certain they were communicating and not nicely, she broke the silence. "I need to get this downstairs into the refrigerator."

"I'll go with you," Sam offered. "Chaz, you look as though you're going to boil over or fall down. Why don't you go cool off then meet us back up here?"

He nodded and getting the message, turned on his heel, and left the hallway.

"He seems quite taken with you," Sam commented.

"I'm quite taken with him."

"Not a good place for either of you."

"No," Stacy sighed. As they stepped out of the elevator into her makeshift lab, Stacy turned her thoughts to the reason she was in danger.

"I told Chaz, so I might as well tell you. I've run the mass spec on both Donnie and Nick. They're starving, and they don't even know it. If they keep it up, they'll go rogue."

Sam stilled, her eyes widening. "But we've been feeding them."

"You have?" Stacy asked, a cold chill running up her spine. Then she chided herself for being melodramatic. But the more she thought about it, the clearer things became.

"Of course," Sam replied.

"Wait a minute," Stacy muttered, almost to herself. "Actually, that makes sense."

Sam frowned. "Why?"

For a tense moment, Stacy went over each and every one of the printouts in her head. No, she wasn't wrong. Which meant…Oh My God, no!

"Sam, listen to me. We have to get to them right away. Both of them, especially Donnie. They need to be removed from the premises immediately."

Sam looked at her as if she'd gone rogue. "What are you talking about? They're in a locked room guarded by several soldiers."

"Who will be dead soon if you don't listen to me!"

She watched Sam shake her head in disbelief but knew the priestess was smart enough to understand how serious she was.

"Please, Sam. I know I'm right. You can feed them until the next millennia, there's a cytotoxin inside their system. Kind of like the extract that kills them. Something that causes them to utilize the blood they take in too fast. They're already rogue. It destroys their cells before the blood they take in has a chance to do its job."

"Poison," Sam breathed.

"Yes. A poison. I'm not sure what kind yet."

Sam reached the elevator ahead of her and repeatedly jabbed at the button for it to open. Then she stopped Chaz from stepping out of the elevator doors just as he was about to start walking towards the lab. "The two young vampires," she shouted. "Stacy says they're already rogue. Whatever I tasted inside their blood. We have to get them out of here. We have to get them out of here and destroy them before they wreak havoc inside the cell."

Stacy made it into the elevator just before the doors closed. Chaz yelled to her through the opening. "I don't want you upstairs. Stay down here where it's safe."

She shook her head. She tried to stop the doors from closing by sticking her arm in between. He didn't give her a choice. He opened the elevator doors and pushed her back. She stumbled backward, and by the time she was able to scramble to her feet, the doors had closed again. Pissed off, Stacy slammed her hand against the metal.

"Damn you, you pig-head vampire. I can help."

By the time the elevator got back down, and she made it to the first floor, she realized Chaz may have been right. She stepped out of the elevator and into a war zone. Several wounded soldiers lay on the floor. She knelt by the one in the worst shape and offered her wrist. A strange light lit his gaze, but he shook his head. "I'll be all right."

Stacy rose and followed the trail of wounded out into the atrium at the front door. Donnie hadn't quite turned yet. He kept circling as if he didn't know what was happening to him.

Chaz and Hunter stood behind him, blocking the way back down the hallway and inside the mansion. Donnie started towards them. Hunter's legs braced, and Chaz steeled himself for the onslaught. At the last moment, Donnie halted. Sam opened the front door and stepped back. Donnie whirled and bolted for the door but then skidded to a stop. He turned and started going back toward Chaz and Hunter again.

Something seemed to be preventing him from leaving. As if he didn't have a choice.

Well, Chaz had told her she was bait. So bait she would be.

Very carefully, Stacy made her way along the wall as far away from Donnie as possible until she was close to the front door.

"Donnie? Hey, Donnie. Remember me? You said you wanted to taste my blood, didn't you? You remember that, don't you?"

Donnie paused and licked his lips. He snarled at her. With those lips pulled back in a feral snarl and the skin stretched taut against his cheekbones, Donnie reminded her of the last rogue she'd confronted. Mick. There'd be no reasoning with him.

Stacy lifted her gaze to Chaz. Fear etched deep inside his features, but Chaz wasn't looking at her. His total focus was on Donnie and the moment when Donnie would lose that last thread of control.

Good. "Come on, Donnie. That's it. Come and get me."

"Stacy! Don't!" Chaz cried.

Donnie turned in a circle. He started to drool, leaving a pink foam on the tile floor. Funny that she could even think it at a time like this, but Stacy wanted nothing more than to analyze that foam and compare it to the foam she'd gathered from the parking lot, knowing it might be the key to what was going on.

Of course, that split second of misdirected thought nearly got her killed. Donnie whirled and sprang straight at her. As he did, Stacy hit the afterburners and jumped through the doorway.

Donnie caught her with ease.

He picked Stacy up, lifting her like a piece of meat he was ready to feast on. His incisors sank into her flesh, and Stacy screamed in pain. *Oh, God, it hurt. It hurt.*

A roar filled her ears, the sound of fear and anguish and anger all rolled into one. Then the searing pain was gone, a dull, hot throb left in its wake. The wind whooshed out of her as she hit the ground and she couldn't breathe. Stunned, she would never be sure if what she saw was real or delusion, but she watched Chaz match Donnie, monster for monster. She watched Chaz lift the vampire up and throw him down with enough force to shatter rock. Then he pinned Donnie to the ground by driving a metal stake through his heart, so hard and so deep, Donnie couldn't move. Just as her eyes closed, she swore she watched him slice off Donnie's head.

Chapter Twenty-Two

CHAZ

CHAZ LOOKED UP TO SEE HORROR FILL STACY'S GAZE. THEN, thankfully, she passed out. He doused the rogue in oil and set fire to him, and Donnie faded into ashes. They brought Nick outside in chains. He hadn't reached the stage of blood fever Donnie had, but they all knew he would.

"You'd better tell us now," Chaz growled at Nick, knowing what awaited him when Stacy woke up.

If *she woke up*, a little voice inside his head added, making Chaz even angrier and more vulnerable.

Hunter joined them on the lawn. Several soldiers surrounded the young vampire who seemed totally unfazed by his predicament. He simply swayed and smiled, sometimes gently laughing to himself.

"Tell us who did this to you," Chaz commanded.

"Nirvana."

What? "Why have you been poisoned?" Chaz asked. "Who's been poisoning you?" He looked up at Hunter and Sam, his anger fading. He wanted nothing more than to go to Stacy, but her light breaths told him she was alive, and he'd have to accept that for now.

Hunter stepped forward and backhanded the young vampire. "Tell us why you've been sent here. Was it to destroy my cell?"

The vampire's lower lip split with the force of Hunter's blow. His tongue snaked out reaching for every drop of the blood. But he didn't appear to be the least bit bothered that he was dying. How was that possible, Chaz wondered in awe and fear?

"Nirvana."

No, true Nirvana was lying in Stacy's arms. "I don't think you'll get anything out of him."

"I may," Sam told him. "He hasn't quite gone rogue yet, but he will. Before he does, I'd like to try getting inside his head."

"Not one of your better ideas, Sam."

She nodded. "Go take care of Stacy, Charles. We'll handle this."

Chaz flicked his gaze to Sam then back to Hunter. "Vampire to vampire," Chaz said.

Hunter actually winced, hunching his shoulders, his gaze filled with regret. The vampire leader reached out and squeezed his shoulder. "Not because we want to, Charles, but because we have to. There's still some humanity left inside you. I wouldn't want to be the cause of its destruction. I don't think Sam would either. You were meant to live in both worlds, something we've been jealous of for a long time. Compassion is a word far removed from my vocabulary. I think Stacy has taught us all how great a mistake that was."

"We'll keep him away from the house, and when he starts changing, we'll call you," Sam said. "Until then, please take care of Stacy. She saved us all tonight."

Chaz nodded, his heart threatening to fall right through his stomach and onto the ground as he looked at the blood seep out of the holes in her neck. He walked to her, kneeling at her side. Even though she was in no danger of becoming a vampire, Chaz decided not to take a chance. He took out a vial of extract, placed a drop on his thumb, and put one on the first hole.

Chaz felt his insides constrict. God, the pain. His fault. He'd asked for her help and almost gotten her killed. What the hell was wrong with him? Was his race more important than her life?

Man. Vampire. Man. Vampire. How the hell could he possibly reconcile both now?

Taking a deep breath, Chaz repeated the action over the second hole. "I love you," he whispered, letting the air out slowly. The rogue blood sizzled, filling his nostrils with a stench. He hated the smell even more than her gaze of disbelief when he helped Hunter take Donnie down.

He'd lost something terribly precious tonight. He'd lost Stacy's innocent belief in him, her belief that the man overshadowed the vampire. For a sweet, short moment in time, he'd tried to make himself believe that was true, but the sad fact was he couldn't.

Vampire. Man. Vampire. Man.

Stacy was human. She lived in a world of fairy tales and dreams. For a split-second of his existence, he'd let himself believe in the fairy tale. He prayed that would last him for the rest of whatever life he was given. Because as sure as he was that he loved her, once this horrible mess was over, he'd never see her again.

Chapter Twenty-Three

STACY

STACY CAME TO IN FAMILIAR SURROUNDINGS. SHE WAS IN HER shore home, in her own bedroom. Her clock read 3:54 AM. Memories came rushing back at her, and she shut her eyes to keep them at bay. In spite of her efforts, her last vision of Chaz and the sickening thud of a stake driven deep into the ground still haunted her thoughts.

The door opened, and Chaz walked in. His face blanched, and his gaze darkened as he read the awareness in her gaze. Then he stiffened, his countenance turning bleak.

"You're awake."

She struggled to sit up against the pillows. The action bought her time, but not enough to reconcile the emotions swirling inside her. "Yes."

He held himself from her as would a stranger, and Stacy absorbed the blow, tucking it inside where it wouldn't hurt so much. He sat down, but she could already tell he wasn't really there. Not as he had been.

"I tried to warn you," he told her softly. "I am what I am."

"I know. I decided not to listen."

"There's only one way to truly kill a vampire. You watched me do that tonight." He sighed, resignation and sadness flowing out of him.

Part of Stacy could almost understand and accept. "I did." It was the brutality of his actions that she couldn't quite grasp. And reconcile with the man she knew.

Man?

"Sam and Hunter have decided it would be best for you to stay here and not go back to the mansion right now."

That hurt. "So all I am is bait again?"

He didn't answer.

"What do *you* want me to do?" she asked, trying to keep the pain out of her voice.

"The same."

"Very well. If you're sure, that's what you want me to do."

He steeled his features. "It is."

Stacy's insides shredded. "You tried to make me understand we're from different worlds. You are who you are, Chaz. I would never blame you for that."

He barked out a bitter laugh. "I blame *me* for that."

"You shouldn't."

He shrugged. "Can't help myself."

Stacy wanted to crawl inside herself and never come out. "So I'm to stay here and become a feast fit for a rogue? Is that it?" She'd never felt so cold, so alone before.

"No! We need time. Hunter needs to cool his people down. If you go back there now, you won't last two minutes. They're angry, and they're frightened. A lot of vampires got slaughtered on their own doorstep. That's never happened before."

"And I'm the inconsequential human, is that it?"

"No. Never," he protested. "Not to me, you're not."

Stacy laughed. "Poor Charles." She used his full name on purpose. "Caught in the middle as always, eh?" She shook her head, simply sad now. "Everything vampires do they do for themselves. That's what you've been trying to tell me all along, isn't it?"

He nodded, and she hated that he did.

"And you? What are you?"

"A vampire," he whispered.

God, that hurt.

He hesitated before sitting down on the edge of her bed. He reached out for her hand, and Stacy prayed he would take it. Perhaps his touch would banish the knot of misery inside her. His hand stopped just before reaching hers.

"Stacy, listen to me." He gave her a harsh half-smile. "We were a fantasy. Our time together was a fairy tale—a dream. One we can both cherish, but it was doomed from the start. I am what I am. I can't change that. More importantly, neither can you."

Stacy reached out to touch him, but his gaze told her not to. Crossing the barrier he'd created would be the ultimate betrayal now. "I won't accept that what's between us is simply a dream, or a fairy tale, or some kind of fantasy."

"You have to. You have to face facts. I'll protect you the best way I know how. I'll give my life for you."

God, that hurt even more than having her neck gouged by a fiend. "Once a Paladin always a Paladin. Is that it?"

"I'm sorry."

"That's all I am to you then?"

"Because that's how it has to be," he exploded, jumping up off the bed and raking his hand through his hair. He took a deep breath, began to pace, and stilled, trying to regain his composure. "You still don't want to understand! We're simply too unpredictable. Throughout all the millennia, we still haven't been able to figure out how to control ourselves, even me. There will always be the fear inside me. When will I lose control? When will I want your blood more than I want you?"

"Never."

He shook his head and refused to listen, his gaze a mixture of fear and self-loathing. "You don't think so? Right now, Stacy. Right here, right now. I can hear your heart pumping, the rush of blood inside your veins calling to me."

"Chaz, stop."

"No, it has to be said. When will the need overcome my will? While I'm deep inside your body?"

"I said, stop!"

He curled his shoulders, and his body caved in on itself. But one hand moved as if he needed to flay himself as if he needed to lash at himself until he exorcised his demons. "What about an innocent turn of your neck? Or how about when the deep pounding rhythm of your heart reaches that place, I try so hard to keep hidden from you?"

"Chaz, don't. Don't do this to yourself. Most of all, don't do this to us."

He whirled to face her. "*Us?* Is there really an 'us'?" he asked. "Can there ever be an 'us'? You seem to love denying reality, and I don't know how to get through to you."

He took a deep breath, and the words came out as he let go. Each one meant to be a wedge, a stake, driving deep. "I…am…a… vampire. I will always be a vampire. There will always be one thing that I'll want more than you."

"Blood."

"Yes!" he raged. "The animal, caged and held at bay, waiting to escape, wanting to ravage, and knowing nothing more than the desire for freedom. When I'm with you, I'll never be able to let my guard down. Not for a millisecond. Because if I do, I may not be able to stop."

"I don't believe that. I won't believe that. I've been in your arms. I've shared your joy and tenderness. You're more human than most humans I know."

He closed his eyes as if each word were the most precious gift she could give and yet, the sharpest knife. When he opened them again, she felt his agony as a physical force before his jaw clamped shut, and the muscle in his cheek twitched like a living being.

They stared at each other for a long time.

"I have to go."

"No, you don't. You simply refuse to believe."

"Believe what? In fairy tales? There is no happy ending."

"Because you don't want one."

His teeth clicked as she watched him bite down even harder. The muscles in his cheeks looked like they would explode. Until finally, he blew out a deep breath and rose. "I'm so very sorry I got you mixed up in all of this, Stacy. Now I have a job to finish. What I should have done originally. Go on the offensive. I need to go catch a rogue and kill it."

Stunned, Stacy had no idea how to answer. "So that's it? You're giving up?"

He shook his head no. Stacy didn't believe him.

"But you don't have to worry. There's a soldier from Hunter's cell. His name is Aidan. The one you tried to help tonight."

"I remember."

"He refuses to go away. So he'll be guarding you until sunrise."

"And you won't."

He ignored the finality in her statement. "Aidan will need a place to stay until the sun sets. He refuses to come inside, so I gave him the key to your garage."

"That's not necessary, you know."

"I do. He doesn't." Chaz sighed. "You're safe in daylight, and if you decide to continue your work at your office, just make sure you're back here before the sun goes down. I'll be back when I can."

He didn't say anything else, just continued to look torn as he tried to hold himself together.

"I won't let you change my mind. I won't," she said. "I may need some time to process all of this. But I refuse to let your vision of yourself denigrate what we've shared."

"Denigrate?" he whispered. "Never."

"Then stop this nonsense!" Stacy swallowed to hold onto her temper. "You're the one who's made the decision. Not me. Remember that."

He cocked his head as if to ask how he'd ever forget. His gaze told her the words he refused to repeat.

"I won't let you take my memories away. And I refuse to let you go."

He didn't answer. He didn't have to. She wouldn't have a choice.

Stacy refused to give up on Chaz. Simple as that. And if he wasn't going to admit she deserved a place—at least the right to remember—then she was going to force the subject. So she drove down to the hospital.

She wondered as she walked into the med-tech school lab if Tori was the right person to share her secret of the dead with. Tori had certainly lived with enough death to understand, and she didn't want to hurt her friend. She also didn't have a choice.

The picture on the desk was a cruel reminder of fate. One conference. One home invasion. Three dead and one life destroyed.

Life wasn't fair.

Stacy caught a hint of the same citrus shampoo she used in the air, which hit her nostrils like manna from heaven. Hospital labs never smelled good.

"Stacy?" Tori rose with a frown. "Hey! What are you doing here? Are you all right? When I called the office today about some missing paperwork, they said you were sick. Something about the flu. Maybe it wasn't something you ate after all."

"Hey," she replied. *Uh-oh.* Why did Tori look as if her problem meter was pinging a mile a minute?

Tori came around her desk, and they hugged. As she let go, Tori eyed her up and down and then commented, "I was going to call you tonight to see how you were doing, find out if you wanted me to stop by."

No. After seeing the concern in Tori's gaze, Stacy dared not risk putting her friend in that kind of danger. Then how the hell was she going to explain without explaining? Better yet, get the help she needed?

"But you don't look sick to me," Tori continued. "What's going on?"

"No. Not sick." Stacy shook her head. Every time she thought about Chaz going all noble on her, her stomach flipped. Was that fear or anger? "You wouldn't believe me even if I told you."

"Try me," Tori answered. "I've just finished another therapy session with Redmond. Suffice it to say, I know more about psychology than he does."

"Does it help?" Stacy asked, already knowing the answer.

Tori's face fell. "No."

"They say time heals."

"Bullshit."

Tori reached out to pat her arm to soften the blow as she walked around her desk. Then she indicated that Stacy sit down.

"I'll remember that." Hell, Stacy couldn't blame her. How could anyone bear losing so much and stay sane?

"So, what are you doing here?" Tori asked. "What's going on?" Tori paused, and Stacy figured if anyone would understand, Tori would.

"I don't know where to start."

Tori frowned, eyeing her up and down. "You...you're not pregnant, are you?"

"No, of course not!" Stacy cried.

"Phew!" Tori said as she swiped her brow with her hand. "At least you took that advice. I mean, he's gorgeous and all, but you need to get to know him first, no?" Stacy realized that her answer had been a tad too emphatic. Tori was way too astute not to know something was very wrong. Tori shrugged out of her lab coat and threw it over the back of a chair. Then her friend started rolling up her sleeves and started looking at her like she was an experiment just waiting to be dissected.

Double uh-oh.

Very well then, time to minimize the risk, and that was going to require some delicacy. She started playing with a test tube that was sitting on Tori's desk. That was when she knew Tori's radar started pinging. Stacy wasn't one to hem and haw about things, which was one reason they were friends. Whatever was going on, it had to be serious.

"You can talk to me, Stace. You know you can. I won't judge, simply listen."

Stacy sighed. "You wouldn't believe me even if I told you."

Tori shrugged. As curious as Stacy knew Tori was, Tori wouldn't press, but she'd always be there to listen. "Try me."

Something warm and fluid filled her. Kind of sweet, kind of sad, but also filled with irony. "When Charles picked me up at Adrian's, he didn't pick me up, he picked me out."

Tori's eyebrows shot up into her forehead then leveled. "Explain."

"He asked me for help. Said he needed me, needed a forensic chemist who specialized in blood banking."

Not many people needed someone like that. Ever. Unless the guy was a writer. Or— "He didn't want you to help him figure out how to murder someone, did he? I mean, you're a cop."

Stacy shook her head no and gave her friend an exasperated glance. "Look, I need you to promise me that you won't tell anyone anything about what I'm going to reveal to you, okay?"

"Then we need to go somewhere public, so we can talk in private," Tori replied. "The walls have ears around here. Which is kinda weird considering most of the people down the hall are dead."

Stacy's mouth quirked as she rose. "Right."

Tori grabbed her bag and hung up her lab coat. "I'm off duty now anyway. Come on, we'll go to Trattoria Rustica. Not as good as Luigi's, I'll admit, but decent."

"You feel like walking? I've been glued to a computer for what feels like a week," Stacy complained. Her neck popped a couple of times as she rotated.

"Long walk, you sure?"

Stacy nodded.

"So, what's going on?" Tori asked as soon as they were on the sidewalk.

"First of all, everything I'm about to tell you is hush-hush, okay? I'm not even supposed to be talking to you."

Tori nodded.

"I've been running some experiments on the side."

Stacy hesitated, and she pictured Chaz lying next to her, his hair spread against the pillow, watching her with that damned quirk of his lips that melted her bones. "Plus, I've got a non-disclosure agreement."

"Big pharma?" Tori asked, a light of understanding filling her gaze. "You're stuck on a problem, aren't you?"

Stacy's heart began to pound. Why hadn't she thought of that? "Charles works for a...a security firm. They're investigating a possible copy of a formula. He asked me to find out if the copy worked. The pharmaceutical firm can't do it without tipping off the suspect."

Tori lifted her brows and pursed her lips. "You're having trouble figuring out if it works?" she said.

"I'm afraid so."

They waited at a corner for a light to change and asked, "What's the first thing you were taught about the scientific method?"

"Use my experience. Consider the problem and try to make sense of it."

"And have you?"

Stacy laughed. But there was no missing the undertone of bitterness beneath her laughter. Tori flicked her a look.

"What I can tell you is that the formula I'm working on is for a blood disorder."

Tori's face cleared, and she lifted her hair off her shoulders, settling them beneath her coat. "Makes sense. Were you able to create a hypothesis?"

Stacy's mouth quirked, but she couldn't hide the far off look in her eyes that told Tori there was more to the story than her friend would probably ever find out. "To a certain degree."

"And were you able to form a conjecture?"

"Yes."

Stacy watched Tori rub her chin as she thought about that for a moment. "Then, your testing isn't going right."

Stacy nodded. "I just wish I knew what I was doing wrong."

Tori smiled and looped her arm through Stacy's, giving it a gentle squeeze. "Maybe, instead of trying to prove the hypothesis, you should try to disprove it."

"You mean, work backward?"

"It's been done before."

Stacy gaped in stunned silence for about a minute. "You're a genius."

"I've always thought so." Tori beamed with pride. "Goes for the other problem you're having, too, with Charles."

Stacy thought she was going to choke. "Am I that transparent?"

"Of course not, but I'm your friend. If it hadn't been for you and

Kelly and…" Tori swallowed hard. "Let's just say we've weathered a few storms together, now haven't we?"

"Yeah." Stacy grinned. "I guess we have."

Tori snared her gaze. "Are you in love with him?"

How did she answer that? She wasn't even sure she wanted to acknowledge the question. "I don't know, but I've never felt this way about anyone before."

Tori smiled. "Damn. This is one man I have to meet again." Her friend's smile faltered. "You do realize it's way too soon, don't you? A little brake pedal could be a good idea, no?"

Stacy wasn't sure and looked down at the sidewalk, so Tori wouldn't see the anguish in her gaze.

Horror spread through her insides like a slow-moving poison, forcing her to stop dead in her tracks. Their arms pulled apart as Tori kept walking.

"Stacy?"

Stacy didn't answer at first. Then she turned and started walking very fast in the opposite direction, her eyes never leaving the ground.

"Stacy? What's wrong?"

Stacy ran. She could hear Tori behind her.

"What in the hell is going on?"

Stacy dared not answer. She ran as fast as she could as fear started bubbling up through her stomach. Finally, caught by the elbow, Stacy pulled around and stopped.

"Will you answer me, please?" Tori cried. "What the hell's gotten into you?"

Stacy stared at her friend, not knowing what to say. Did the rogue have Tori's scent now too? She'd never been this frightened before.

Stacy drew in a deep breath and let the air shudder out, trying to stay calm, knowing Tori knew she'd lost that battle before it began. "I need to take a rain check on dinner."

"Rain check? We're half a block from the restaurant. Well, maybe a block now."

"Tori, listen to me. I can't tell you what's going on. Something occurred to me while we were talking." Stacy grimaced. "I can't elaborate, I'm sorry. You do understand, don't you?"

Tori stared, trying to read the emotions flying across her face, and Stacy clamped down on them. "Yes, and because I can't help myself, I'll ask. Do you need my help in any way?"

Shaking her head, she reached out and squeezed Tori's shoulder, but then Tori pulled her into a quick hug. When they pulled away, Stacy had her emotions under control again and even managed a quick smile.

"No, but thanks for asking. You go have dinner. When this is all over, maybe we can try again, my treat."

Tori couldn't argue. Well, she could, but that wouldn't be fair. Above all, they trusted one another. "All right. It's a deal. You'll call me when you can, right? So I know everything's okay?"

"You bet."

Stacy stared down at the drops of pink salivate on the sidewalk, her stomach swimming with worry. Tori had hugged her, so now Stacy's scent was on her friend. They used the same shampoo, the one Tori had recommended. Oh, no. *What have I done?* She needed to call Sam immediately. *Stupid, stupid, stupid.*

Interlude

Tori couldn't shake the worry that crept into her chest as she watched her friend walk away. Stacy was off her game, and that notion more than anything else had her turning just a half a block after she left her friend. She wanted to make sure Stacy would honor her promise.

Surprise filled Tori as she watched Stacy bend down and peer at something on the sidewalk. Totally focused on what she was looking at, Stacy didn't seem to see Tori watching her, or that she'd crept back. Stacy took a tube out of her pocketbook and swabbed the sidewalk.

What the hell?

Why was Stacy using an evidence kit in the middle of the block, and what the hell was that pink goop she was putting in a test tube to analyze?

Chapter Twenty-Four

STACY

STACY GOT OUT OF THE CAR AND WALKED UP HER DRIVEWAY, staring at the evidence envelope in her hand. Her fingers itched to tear the damned thing open and get to work on it. She wanted to drive straight to her lab to start analyzing the salivate, but she owed Aidan a check-in first. After all, he was putting his life on the line for her.

"Aidan! Aidan!" Stacy cried as she ran up the steps to her home.

A shiver ran down the back of her neck, and she paused on the porch. Where was he? Normally, he would come out of the shadows and let her know he was there.

Stacy turned in a small circle. The silence seemed to close in on her. She scanned the street, the other yards, but nothing seemed amiss. She pulled out her key to put it into the lock.

She stopped. With the lowering of the sun, the temperature had fallen. A cold wind whipped her hair against her face, but that didn't come close to the icy dread inside her belly at the thought of the rogue being so close. Or Aidan not being here.

"Aidan?" she cried again.

When the vampire still didn't appear, Stacy's heart started to pound. She turned to open her front door and found she didn't need to use her key.

And she realized she wasn't wearing her gun.

She crept through the doorway, trying to still her frantic heartbeat. If the rogue was nearby, the sound would be like a homing beacon. She hated that she had to go back to her bedroom to her gun safe but breathed a sigh of relief when she made it there. In several seconds, she had the safe open, her gun clip loaded, and a back holster clipped to her jeans. As she crept out of the house, she scanned the floor looking for pink salivate but found none.

Since her block was fairly short, Stacy tracked the sidewalk in front of her house first. She didn't see any sign of the rogue or any other sign for that matter. All was still and quiet. Too still. Too quiet.

A crashing metal garbage can sounded behind her, followed by a low grunt. Stacy ran towards the alleyway between the two houses across the street. She followed a trail of pink droplets on the ground. The rogue crouched over a body, but she couldn't see who it was.

Rather than fire her weapon, Stacy ran full tilt and jumped on its back. The smell of decay made her gag, but she hung on, bringing the butt of her gun handle down on the rogue's head as hard as she could. Once. Twice, with enough force to at least stun the damned thing.

The rogue shook her off as if she was a feather and Stacy went flying, slamming into the side of one of the houses. Her shoulder took the brunt of the impact, and she felt it pop.

Oh God, the pain. Stars danced inside her brain. Fire radiated down her arm and through her chest, but that didn't stop her from rolling to her feet and preparing to fire. "Come on, you little bastard," she cried. "I've got a bunch of bullets here for you."

The rogue twisted, greasy tendrils of hair swinging to and fro. Blood covered its mouth, the tatters of its shirt spotted with red. It growled with ire, intent only on finishing its meal. Then it straightened, twisted, and started moving towards her.

Stacy wrapped her finger around the trigger. She wouldn't be able to steady the gun with her other arm, but she was certain she'd get in some pretty good shots.

Scrape-drag. Scrape-drag. The rogue almost crawled towards her. Then he hesitated. He cocked his head and leaned forward, almost as if he were trying to see something. The creature lifted up. He stilled, seeming to fight with himself. He seemed eager to drain her dry, but something held him back. It almost seemed as if he was staring at something. Stacy tightened her hand, ready to shoot. Then the rogue turned and sprinted off once again, leaving her with one question pounding through her brain.

Why?

She latched the safety on the gun and bent over to slip it inside her back holster. Then she realized. She'd worn the silver chain and cross for safekeeping so she could give it back to Chaz. Some good had come from it after all—it had just saved her life.

With only one useful arm, Stacy ran to the person lying on the ground. *Aidan.*

"Aidan? Oh, God. No." The rogue had been feeding on Aidan. "This is all my fault."

He couldn't talk. His throat was pretty torn up, but he shook his head. His gaze filled with gratitude and something even more important—respect.

"Aidan. Listen. I have to be able to use my arm to help you, but I can't. My shoulder is dislocated. I need you to help me put it back in place."

He saw her arm hanging by her side and nodded. He lifted his hand and grabbed her wrist. "On the count of three. You pull, and so will I. One. Two. Three…."

Stacy screamed as pain shot through her shoulder, but as soon as Aidan let go, her shoulder popped back into place, and the pain subsided to a dull throb.

"Come on. Now I can help you get back to the house. I have a couple of blood bags for you."

He shook his head. His throat was already healing. He beckoned her to come closer. "You must help me die," he whispered.

Stacy reared back in horror. "No. You're going to be fine. You're going to…."

He moved his head side to side. "Kill me. You must. Before I go rogue."

"But you can't. You need to stay alive. You need to stay here. Protect me."

His gaze told her the terrible truth. The blood fever was already trying to engulf him.

"I can cure you. I just need time."

"No more time. You need to kill me." He pointed to the rake on the ground. "I can break the wood and use it as a stake. I will help you."

"Aidan, no. Oh, God. No. Don't ask me to do this. Please. I can't."

As his throat healed, he was able to speak in full sentences. "You're a very strong, very brave woman, Stacy Morgan. At first, I wanted to guard you because I wanted to understand why you offered your blood to me. As I grew to know you in that short time, I've found you to be a very unique soul. You carry within you a generosity of spirit, something my kind needs very badly. I thank you for sharing that spirit with me. At times, you made me remember what it was like to be human."

Tears filled her eyes. They slipped down her cheeks even as she smiled. "That's because you've all forgotten where you really come from."

He shook his head, his gaze wry and sad all at the same time. "Perhaps you're right."

She held out her wrist again. She hadn't been there when Pitch died, at least she could be here now. "Please, Aidan."

His eyes closed, and he swallowed hard. When he opened them again, he said, "I was not a very noble being in life. At least let me be a noble being in death."

"But I'm a police officer. I protect people. I've never killed anyone before."

"This isn't exactly murder. You must save my soul now. Please," he begged. "I would be honored."

Oh God, how could she say no to that?

Stacy rose, her heart breaking, and went to get the rake as he'd requested. As she returned, he swallowed again, and she saw that the pink salivate was coming from his incisors. He snapped the wood in half, already regaining his strength. Time was running out. She took the rake handle and positioned it over his heart. He lifted his hand and gripped the wood.

"There is only one true death for us, Stacy. You must make sure someone takes my head. Otherwise, I'll wake up, and be a rogue."

Stacy nodded, and he pulled down on the rake handle as hard as he could, grimacing with the pain. Stacy made sure the wood went all the way through his body. His breath came in short gasps as he continued.

"Thank you."

Tears dripped down her cheeks as his blood ran out onto the pavement.

"Don't grieve. Please. I'm happy."

She nodded and watched Aidan close his eyes, never to open them again. His chest stopped moving, and she felt a sigh, a rustle along the wind, the same as she had the night Pitch was killed. She hoped it was his soul parting this world and going on to the next.

Chapter Twenty-Five

CHAZ

CHAZ FOUND STACY KNEELING BESIDE AIDAN. HE TOOK IN THE scene and in seconds, realized what had happened. He sent up a prayer of heartfelt gratitude that Stacy was still alive.

"Stacy." He bent down next to her. "Stacy." He put his hand on her shoulder. "You have to let me finish."

"He died trying to protect me," she told him, her grief evident in her tone.

"I know."

"He wouldn't let me try to heal him. Why?"

"We all have our reasons. I guess he decided it was his time."

"He was so decent, so gallant," she whispered, her indrawn breath suspended for a moment then releasing in a pent-up rush. "He wanted to die a noble death. With someone who cared at his side."

Her shoulder started shaking beneath his fingers, and Chaz lifted her up and into his arms. She simply stood there without moving. But when she lifted her face to his, the tracks of her tears tore at his heart.

"Go inside. I'll follow in a few moments."

"No. He deserves an honor guard and medals and accolades. But most of all, he deserves respect. Do what you have to do."

"No. You had trouble handling the last one, remember?"

"I'll be all right," she insisted.

Chaz frowned. "I don't think that's a good idea."

"Just do it!" she cried.

Chaz wanted to keep on arguing, but time was of the essence. He drew out a very wicked looking dagger from his coat and knelt by Aidan's head. The smell of the vampire's blood licked like liquid flames at his intentions. He drove the need back with an iron will.

He looked up to see Stacy kneel beside the body and reach out. Her tender touch against Aidan's cheek tore through him. He caught her gaze, letting her see how conflicted he was. Jealousy had no place in this moment, yet he couldn't help himself. In the end, he knew Aidan would have appreciated the gesture. Because he'd learned. From Stacy.

She stood and stepped back. Then she closed her eyes and nodded. Chaz severed Aidan's head from his body. By the time Stacy opened her eyes again, Aidan was gone. There was only fire.

She turned from the flames without a second glance at him and started walking towards her house. "I want to be alone. No guards, no vampires, just alone."

He ran to catch up with her. He knew she was hurting. The question became, was there such a thing as too much reality? "I can't let you do that."

"Damn you, I can take care of myself."

"No, you can't. Especially now. "

Stacy whirled and started pounding on his chest with her fists. Then she groaned and buckled her arm, clutching her shoulder.

"What happened?"

"The rogue dislocated my shoulder. It's all right now. I'm just sore."

Chaz wanted to wrap his arms around her and draw her close, comfort her, get her to snuggle her head right in that special place in his chest, and never let go. Then he wanted to punch holes in walls, tear down trees, and break anything he could get his hands on. He drew in a shuddered breath.

Now that's just wonderful. "You went after the rogue? Without Aidan's help?"

"Yes. Was I just supposed to let him lie there and get drained dry?"

"Damn you, Stacy. You can't go up against a rogue!" he roared.

"I can't? Well, I just did. Again." She whirled away and started marching up the sidewalk, but then she stopped and faced him again. "When are you going to trust me? When are you going to believe in me? When are you going to have faith in me?"

He didn't know how to answer that question. "You're not the problem. I am."

"When are you going to trust yourself? When are you going to believe in yourself? When are you going to have faith in yourself?"

"Never," he said. "I told you, I am what I am."

"No, you're not!" she yelled back, running towards her home. She stopped when she reached her porch, her chest heaving as if she were trying to outrun her own pain. "You're what you let yourself believe you are. There's a difference."

Agony raced across his features. "I know." He sighed, following her up the steps to the porch. "Let me in, Stacy. I have a story to tell you. Maybe then you'll understand."

She threw him a look. "I'll let you in, and I'll listen to you, but you're never going to understand until you realize that you don't have to explain."

He shrugged. "I've denied the truth for far too long now. I've wanted to believe that because I chose to die that I deserved redemption. I don't. Because I can't deny what I am. I'm a vampire."

"Remember you said that word, Charles Tower," Stacy replied, throwing his words back at him. "Not monster. Got that?"

"Once you hear what I have to tell you, I think you'll revise your opinion."

"I doubt that very much."

Interlude

Blood fever.

Charles, First Guard of the Tower of London, didn't understand what had happened to him. One moment he was staring at the stone wall of the prison waiting for death to overtake him, the next he'd awakened in the stable under a pile of hay mixed with manure.

Night had fallen, and as he staggered to his feet, Charles felt a strange strength flowing through his veins. He could hear people talking across the courtyard. He could see well beyond them, even through the darkness. The scent of manure, usually not at all bothersome to his nose, nearly gagged him.

As he emerged from the stable, he realized he wasn't far from home. He walked to a trough and sluiced water over his face and hands. Shaking off the excess, he wondered why he wasn't home, and as soon as he thought about being there, he was.

Was this a dream? Or a nightmare?

Charles opened the door to his home, afraid of the answer.

Mary was bending over the hearth, stirring a pot of stew. The stew smelled better than the air inside this tiny hovel, and he wrinkled his nose at the assault on his senses. Still, he'd been a soldier once, and nothing stuck with a body more than the stench of a battlefield.

Mary straightened and gaped as he stepped inside. "Charles?"

At first, he was certain he saw joy on her face. Then her gaze raked him, and her mouth narrowed, her features turning stern.

"It's been three days, Charles. Where have you been?"

Three days?

Charles shook his head. Nothing made sense.

Tears filled her eyes as she whispered, "Did it matter to ye that I have been out of my mind wit worry?"

Three days?

She started towards him and stopped. Her arm lifted, in greeting, he assumed, but fell to her side as if something inside her didn't want to touch him. The thought amused him. He wouldn't want to touch these clothes either.

They stared at each other for a long time. Hurt replaced the anger in her gaze, and the resignation in her posture tried to cut him. But he felt as if he were living outside his body now. Nothing meant anything. As if he was dead inside.

"Was the drink so important to ye then"?

A roar built inside his head. It sounded like the ocean. He'd seen the ocean once. When he was young, he used to marvel at its enormous power, the water's sheer expanse stretched as far as his eyes could see.

Charles didn't know what to say. He looked down at his hands as if they belonged to another man. He shook his head. Suddenly he realized everything was off-kilter, out of sorts, just plain wrong. He stared down at the rushes on the floor, his insides empty—dead almost, when he should have felt remorse. Should have felt something. Anything.

"So, ye refuse to deny it."

The roar continued to build like water flowing fast downstream. At first, Charles ignored it.

He choked and coughed as if he hadn't spoken in a long time. "I don't remember takin' one drop."

She nodded as if this made perfect sense. "Ye wouldna, now would ye?" Her shoulders slumped, and she turned away from him to stare into the hearth. "Was she very pretty then?"

The next thing he knew, Charles was standing behind her. "Mary, luv." And yet, as the word left his lips, the truth crashed down upon him. He didn't love her. In fact, she meant no more to him than a favored horse or dog, and that made no sense at all.

"I would never betray ye. Ye know that."

"Do I?" Her tone was filled with bitterness. She lifted the strands of her hair from her shoulder. "I have eyes, ye know. I see that I am getting old." Charles remembered their wedding day. How beautiful she looked in the spring sunshine with flowers in her hair.

"Ye know that I dinna drink like other men and ye know that ye're not old. Stop this nonsense this instant."

She turned back to him with a gaze filled with hope. His face softened, and he knew he eased her fears. Then the roar in his ears exploded. Charles lifted his hands to cover them. He doubled over, not in pain, but because of a terrible knowledge invading his soul—the one he no longer had.

"Charles?"

Her voice sounded far away. He heard the concern, but the emotion never reached him. He lifted back up to hear her swift, harsh, indrawn breath. All that mattered was the pulse throbbing in her neck. His gaze fixed on it as the pumping of her heart throbbed in his ears.

Hot juice filled his mouth, and something strange happened—his teeth. Two of them grew. Long and sharp. His tongue explored, and he winced at the sharpness of one.

Blood.

His insides clenched with need. This was far worse than hunger, and he knew hunger. Had lived most of his life in hunger, but this need, this need was different. This was one hundred times worse than anything he'd ever experienced before.

He couldn't answer her. Better yet, he didn't dare.

Bits and pieces of a terrible dream-like reality passed before his waking gaze: a guard with his throat torn to shreds; watching a man break in half with a single blow.

No. This was witchcraft. That's what this was. He'd been bewitched. These nightmarish pictures came from one of the damned. Charles closed his eyes trying to convince himself of the truth. But the terrible truth was he'd become one of the damned.

When he opened them, Mary stared at him as if he'd grown hoofs and horns. He didn't care. He reached out to draw her to him.

"Charles. No. Do not do this."

Blood. He could see right through her skin.

"I am a good wife to ye. And yer not yerself. I can see that now."

His hands wrapped around her shoulders. They tightened as they would around a hare before he broke its neck.

Fear filled her voice. "Yer hurtin' me, Charles."

But still, she trusted him. Her mistake.

Charles felt as though he'd stepped outside his body. He could see the pinch of pain on her face, knew he was the cause, yet he didn't stop. Not until her body was touching his. His shaft grew in response to her, but even that held no meaning for him.

There was nothing but blood.

"Charles. Yer face. Oh, God. Yer face."

What of it? What did this insignificant little human mean to him?

Charles shook his head again. He nodded as a truth wound its way into his non-existent heart. A final truth. The one he had refused to accept until now.

He was dead. Yet not dead. And there was nothing left except the blood.

Mary stilled in horror as he turned into his true nature. A part of him didn't care. A part of him cared too much. His incisors grew until they could grow no longer, and he welcomed them. He ran his face up and down her neck, catching the delectable scent of her blood through her skin. His tongue snuck out once or twice to taste the salt on her, but salt was not what Charles was after.

He knew that now.

One arm banded about her shoulders to keep her still.

"Dear God, help me. He's gone mad. This is not my husband," she cried.

Too late, Mary must have realized her danger. She began to fight him, to struggle for her life. The hunter in him responded, delighting in the challenge of submission. He wanted her to know his power. He wanted her to know she could never escape.

He bit down into her soft flesh, and blood swirled inside his mouth as she screamed. His hand covered her mouth so no one would hear. Which opened her neck even wider and allowed him better access.

His incisors drew in deep draughts of sweetness. Her fists pounded on his back, her body flailed from side to side. He lost his grip and had to release her, her blood squirting all over his face.

He lapped his tongue out against each drop.

Sharp and rich with metal, his nostrils widened to breathe in the luscious scent of her blood. He sank his incisors back into her neck.

"Oh, God, Charles. You are hurtin' me. Do not do this. Please stop."

Her pleading became weaker, her struggles slowed, and he shifted her in his arms to get a better angle. He drank and kept on drinking. Power swelled inside his body, his muscles quivered with the strength flowing through them, his fingertips tingled with heat. He wanted to run ten miles, jump over walls, and race with the wind.

With a jolt, Charles realized Mary had stopped moving.

A last sliver of humanity invaded. There was blood and nothing but blood, and from now on, there would only be blood. But that did not mean he had to kill. From somewhere deep inside, Charles found a will to resist the evil he'd become. The need to drain her body dry welled from the very depths of his being. He wanted to keep going. He wanted more.

There was blood and nothing but blood.

This was a fight he would have to win every day for the rest of his existence.

Chapter Twenty-Six

STACY

STACY STARED AT HIM. SHE DIDN'T JUDGE. JUST GAVE HIM THE space to continue. "Mary died a few months later, broken in body and spirit. At first, I ran, not knowing where to go. But I knew I had to watch over her, so I kept going back every so often to check. I watched her die knowing I was the cause."

"I thought time healed old wounds," she said, trying to comfort him.

"Didn't you hear a word I said? I tried to drain my wife dry! Because of that, she succumbed to the fever and died."

His outburst made her shiver, but not from disgust, from fear. Stacy worried he'd never forgiven himself. What he refused to understand was that he had no way to prevent what happened.

"From the way you're telling me the story, you didn't even know you were a vampire."

"That's not an excuse."

"Whatever."

"Stacy, even if you don't want to understand, you have to listen," he said. "Even if I'm able to destroy the rogue, even if you're able to help figure out what's causing these young vampires to eventually go rogue, even if we get the entire leadership of the vampire world to accept you as you are and not make you forget, we're still an unmatched pair. We can never be together. Because the day will come when I'm faced with a choice—to give in to my nature or not. I won't put you in that kind of jeopardy."

Stacy opened her mouth to retort then took a deep breath, letting the air out slowly. "So I get no say in the rest of my life, is that it?"

"The kindest way to deal with this is to make you forget all about me."

Oh really? "And who's going to make *you* forget?"

"No one. I accept my penance."

Damned noble fool. "For what? Becoming something you didn't want to be? For using your existence for good and not evil? For trying to protect the rest of a race—the rest of *your* race—that hates you because you're different? God, Chaz, I don't think it's that you *have* to be a martyr, I think it's that you *want* to be one."

He blanched. "No, I don't. I want to protect you from your worst enemy. Me."

"There goes that 'T' word again, right out the window. Did it ever occur to you that I don't want your protection, don't feel I need your protection? That I *TRUST* you not to hurt me?"

He stared at her, his chest heaving as if he couldn't catch his breath, as if she'd given him the ray of hope he kept insisting he didn't deserve. "But the way you looked the other night."

She shook her head at him in total exasperation. "Didn't I just prove to you that I can handle anything you can? Try to at least be fair. I'm not even allowed to wrinkle my nose when I see something horrifying?" She rolled her eyes. "How the hell did you expect me to react? You cut off a man's head. You turned him into ash. I wasn't watching a television show, it happened right before my eyes. Don't you think I'd be horrified if I watched a fellow police officer gun down a perp right in front of me? I'd be watching him take a life, something that can't be given back, no matter whether his death was deserved or not."

Chaz didn't answer.

"Do you know why I went into forensics and not medicine, Chaz?" He shook his head. "Because I was terrified I'd end up making a mistake. I was scared to death that I would end up taking a life instead of saving one. Because, in the end, I let myself be a coward. Don't let yourself be a coward, Chaz."

Stacy wanted to reach out and touch him. She wanted to wrap him in her arms and never let go. She wanted to force-feed what she'd just learned—that nothing is more important than being true to the being inside. Be it vampire or human.

No one was more surprised than Chaz when Stacy threw her arms around him and planted her lips on his. But this kiss was different. The rules of the game had changed. They both knew the consequences of their actions.

It seemed a lifetime ago that Chaz sought her out. Perhaps he'd known all along they would come together at this moment, in the truest sense of what two people can call together—no pretense, no games, just truth, and reality. She realized this was why he fought so hard against her. They were from different worlds. Each of them had to accept that.

But Stacy knew the real fight, the harder fight, the one that would keep them together and not apart. Now she asked him to take that final step, to discard the past and look to the future, a future that might contain just the two of them.

He drew back, loath to let her lips part from his. "I told you once that you'd become the light in my very dark existence. I was wrong."

"Wrong?" Her insides blanched, turning bleak, and she stiffened.

"You've become my very existence."

Thank God. Her stomach settled, but he held up his hand, and her angst came back tenfold. As they stared at each other, her shoulders fell. She shook her head at him as reality—sorrow and disbelief filled her face.

"I'm sorry, but nothing has changed. We're still from different worlds. I'm still this far from becoming that monster. There will never be an 'us.'"

"Then you're taking the easy way out."

Her words cut them both to the quick. "Easy? You think standing here and telling you I can never have you is easy? Guess again."

He spun away and walked slowly towards the front of the house to leave. She watched each step rip apart something inside him. He'd have to learn to live with the pain—that was all. She refused to.

"No right, no wrong, just what has to be," he told her as he opened the front door. He turned one last time to look at her, and she braced herself. She lifted her chin and squared her shoulders, daring him. He opened his mouth as if to tell her something. Was it to tell her he loved her? How she wished. But his lips closed it before he admitted anything. Obviously, the truth would be too cruel to tell. The lock clicked shut behind him, and she knew every day from this day forward would be the worst kind of torture.

Chapter Twenty-Seven

STACY

STACY EMPTIED HER VACUUM INTO A BAG AND STUCK HER FACE IN the dust. Since she was allergic to dust, she came out looking like she'd been sick for a week. When she got to work, everyone gave her a wide berth and left her alone.

She threw herself into her problem with a vengeance. If she could prove to Chaz that he'd never go rogue, he might decide to rethink his position regarding their relationship. So instead of trying to find out what was wrong with their blood, she took Tori's advice and tried to find out what was right. The good news was that Chaz's blood exhibited the correct responses for antibody-antigen reactions.

Her lips quirked in sad memory as she picked up a tube of Aidan's blood.

"Aidan. Come here, would you please?" she had asked him the day he died.

Aidan had come closer but didn't reply. She'd gotten used to his silence. *"I need some of your blood. To test."*

He'd nodded his consent, and she used a lancet to fill up a tube, amazed yet again, at how fast his skin healed. But with Aidan, she also noticed something else. He wasn't very good at hiding his reaction to the smell of his own blood.

Embarrassed, he went outside to guard her door. Stacy followed. *"Is it always like that?"*

He started at her question, then a light of respect entered his gaze. *"Yes."* He paused. *"Worse, sometimes."*

"Chaz tried to explain."

His gaze turned sad. "You could never understand."

"I guess not. Are you ever sated?"

"No," came his blunt reply.

"Are you hungry?"

"Guarding you leaves me little time to feed."

Stacy went into her downstairs refrigerator and gave him two expired units. He stared at her in surprise. "Thank you for watching over me."

He'd nodded and smiled. Then died trying to save her life.

Stacy sighed and went back to work. She found that Aidan's and Chaz's blood exhibited the same properties, but with Donnie's blood, there was no reaction at all. So something had caused the death of the red cells in Donnie's blood.

But what?

The second step she took was to find out if there were DNA markers for vampire blood by using a Western blot test. And here she found something very interesting: the DNA markers for Chaz and Aidan were exactly the same. Which surprised her at first, then didn't. Vampires weren't exactly alive. They were alive only because they used a living substance to survive. So it would make sense that they would take on the attributes of the person whose blood they ingested, but they also needed that substance to be universal. They needed to be able to drink just about anything.

So Stacy set up a second blot to compare all three vampires, Chaz, Aidan, and Donnie. Donnie's test didn't work. Discouraged, Stacy thought she'd hit another brick wall. Then she remembered that Sam had said Donnie was regularly feeding. So there should be residual DNA strands somewhere. She tried again.

Nada. Zip. Zilch.

And that made her realize something. Something was destroying the cells inside Donnie's blood. Because when she flooded Chaz's blood with heparin to make it like Donnie's and then tested it through the blot procedure, she got separated bands of DNA.

Time to start using the mass spec. Time to find out what was causing all of this. Because whatever the agent was, it was damned nasty.

Stacy set up a broad-spectrum analysis and felt lighter than she had in days. She let the mass spec run, hoping the analyzer wouldn't require any babysitting, took her paperwork home and stopped for Chinese. She was on her third bite of Peking duck when her cell rang.

"Hunter? What's wrong? Is Chaz all right?"

"I need you to come up to the mansion. There's been a... development."

She set her dinner down, her appetite gone. "I'll be there as soon as I can."

Chapter Twenty-Eight

CHAZ

S<small>TACY STOOD IN THE FOYER OF THE MANSION WHEN</small> C<small>HAZ WALKED</small> in. Hunter greeted him, feet braced apart, as if he was ready for anything that might arise. Chaz found that stability comforting.

"Good. You're both here. So is Sam. We need to make some decisions."

Chaz stiffened as Stacy brushed past him to follow Hunter. He caught a hint of her citrus shampoo and his insides clenched with need. He watched her walk in front of him, her lithe form enticing him from behind. Chaz admonished himself in stern tones and clamped down on those thoughts.

"Members of my cell managed to capture two more young vampires. Sam's been working with them. They're being held outside the house but on the grounds. I need you to come with me and see this for yourselves."

This was an excellent precaution considering the last ones they captured.

"They all respond to the word Nirvana," Sam added as they approached a small barn.

A guard opened a door and let them in. One side of the barn had large stalls with barred doors meant for horses, and heavily wrapped chains and steel braces kept the door locked.

The vampire inside the stall circled the area, and Chaz knew he was just about to go rogue.

"We won't let it go that far, Chaz," Hunter told him. "We'll destroy him before he goes rogue."

"Can't we help him?" Stacy asked.

Sam replied. "No, Stacy, we can't. Watch."

They all watched Sam approach the stall. The vampire ignored her presence. Until she said, "Nirvana."

Then, the poor creature flew to the door, trying to claw his way through the bars, his hand outstretched as if he were trying to get at whatever Nirvana was. He seemed like he was totally addicted to a drug.

"Stacy, you had the idea that this Nirvana might be some kind of drug they've been given. As you can see, you were right."

The captured vampire started begging and pleading, scraping his hands against the wood, trying to climb out of the stall, anything to get the Nirvana he so desperately craved.

Chaz shook his head. "What the hell is going on here?"

"We don't know for sure," Sam replied. "But I think Stacy may be able to help us with that. Let's go back to the mansion so we can talk in private."

When they reached the conference room in the mansion, Hunter grimaced as he sat down. "Stacy, I think I'll let you have the floor. Yours is the most important news of all."

He watched Stacy nod and lean forward. Despite how tired she looked, excitement radiated from her gaze. "I've been performing different analyses of different samples from these vampires and analyzing what was left of Donnie's blood. And I was able to analyze the saliva from the rogue that's been trying to kill me."

She dared Sam and Hunter to ask how that went with a quick look. They were both aware of Aidan's demise.

"So far, I've come up with at least one compound—a cytotoxin. A cytotoxin is a poison that destroys cells in the body. I've also found that you have no antigens and antibodies, or platelets, save those that you ingest. I believe this is at least part of what keeps all your blood moving. I've also completed some blot testing. There are no strands of DNA in the rogue's blood that I can quantify."

Stacy just happened to be watching Sam when she said this. Sam blanched but covered up quickly. Chaz wondered why. "Last but not least, because we believe there is some kind of drug that probably contains the cytotoxin, I'm running a mass spec on Donnie's blood. If you think of it Nirvana sounds like something off the street."

Sam nodded. "That's very possible."

"I'm not so sure," Stacy said. "I can't imagine a street drug being this specific." She shook her head. "None of this makes any sense. Why put a toxin in a street drug when vampires don't drink from a human that's high?"

Chaz was glad she had them thinking. "No. I believe this Nirvana, as they're calling it, has been engineered. So let's take each step logically if we can. Even if you ingest a drug, all things being true and the sleep being curative, its effects should be neutralized by the time you wake up. Instead, this Nirvana is acting like the most powerful of addictive drugs. Obviously, that should be impossible. Whatever is causing the cells to be destroyed, once the process starts, it won't stop. Maybe the other part of this, I'm not sure what to call it, is some kind of hallucinogen? To brainwash these young vampires into believing that what they're doing will give them—well, they keep telling us— Nirvana? Not death?"

No one spoke.

"The mass spec analysis may take a while, but we should have an answer on what compounds this stuff is made of soon."

Chaz saw the impact of her findings as he looked around the table. Hunter appeared to be plain old angry by the set of his mouth and the tic in his cheek. Guess he didn't like the idea of vampires being brainwashed. Chaz also figured Hunter didn't like the idea of his brothers being used as guinea pigs. And how did *he* feel about all of this? Chaz didn't appreciate the idea that someone was creating rogues on purpose. After all, he was the one who'd have to hunt them down. With his guts in a knot, Chaz glanced over at Sam. Now, this was strange. Sam's eyes were wide and wouldn't quite meet his gaze. She looked frightened, and all Chaz could do was ask himself why?

"They don't even know they're being starved. And I'll bet—" Stacy continued, "—that if you question your guards, Hunter, they'll tell you they drank those blood bags, not Nick and Donnie."

"Why do you say that?" Hunter asked.

"Because anyone can be brainwashed, even a vampire. If this is as powerful as I believe it to be, and the response we saw was created, Nick and Donnie would only drink when allowed to do so. Not only that, but from a specific source. I think they attacked me and were told they were only allowed to drink my blood. My guess is that they've been so brainwashed, they don't even know they're starving."

No one said anything for what seemed like forever.

"Who would have that kind of power?" Hunter finally wondered out loud.

Stacy flicked her gaze over at Sam and watched the elder vampire shudder and swallow hard. Hunter caught the action too and tilted his head in question. Sam waved away his concern with an arrogant flick of her wrist.

"No one that we know of," Sam replied, her tone vehement. "So, for now, our priority is to cure these two young vampires as we can all be sure there will be more of them in the future."

"Can you continue to help us, Stacy?" Hunter asked.

"I can try."

Sam's countenance softened. "Thank you."

"I think you're going to have to strap them down and force-feed them," Stacy added. "I believe that's going to be the only way to save them."

"They seem to be able to resist every measure I try," Sam added, her tone too neutral. "I can't get through to them. So, whoever or whatever is holding them is very powerful."

STACY LEFT THE ROOM. SHE MUST'VE KNOWN THEY WANTED TO talk among themselves.

"All the more reason, then, for Stacy to keep trying to find out what's going on," Hunter said.

"Agreed," Sam said.

As much as he wanted to go after Stacy, Chaz waited until Hunter left, then he walked out with Sam.

He reached out and gave her shoulder a quick squeeze. "Whatever it is, Sam, remember we're all with you. You're not alone."

She looked stunned for a moment, then she smiled. The smile didn't quite reach her eyes. "I know, Charles. I know."

"Is there anything I can do for you?"

She shook her head. Then she paused. "Perhaps one thing."

Surprised, Chaz wondered what kind of favor he could do for such a powerful vampire. "What's that?"

Her mouth quirked. And this time, her eyes softened in genuine amusement. "What I told you to do before. Go after her."

"I can't."

"Why not?"

"I love her."

Sam laughed softly. "I've known that since the very beginning."

"Then you also know why we'll never be together."

Sam shook her head at him. "No. I only know that there are exceptions to every rule. You're the exception, Charles."

"Am I? And what happens when I believe that?"

"What do you mean?"

His angst bubbled up from a cauldron of misery. "What happens years from now or months or days? When my guard slips? When I fall into that—that black hole?"

"Black hole?"

He shook his head, wondering if she was being deliberately obtuse. "What happens when I can't break away, when I can't stop drinking her blood?"

Sam frowned at him, her countenance turning stern even as her gaze grew warmer. "You already know the answer to that."

"No, I don't."

"Then let's start with the obvious. You don't trust yourself."

No, he didn't. "Stacy said the same thing."

"She did? Good for her, but that's not the second part of the problem."

Chaz frowned. "Second part?"

"You don't trust your love for her."

"She doesn't know."

This time, Sam reached out to comfort him. "Don't you think you ought to tell her?"

"And make losing her even harder?"

"The only reason you're going to lose that woman is because of you, not us," she scolded. "I'll make sure of it."

"Get real. What about Hunter? Better yet, you're going to be able to convince Miklos? Hiroki? Somehow I don't think that's possible." Sam started to raise her hand to cut him off, and Chaz grinned. "Okay, okay, I get the message. I don't doubt you, Sam. Honest."

"You doubt yourself."

"Yes."

"I could tell you not to, but you need to figure that out on your own. But I will tell you one thing. You're an honorable man, Charles Tower, and I've known that for the last nine hundred years. Give or take a few."

"You think so?"

"I know." She smiled at him. "Go after her. Follow your heart."

Could he?

Sam walked away, and Chaz could feel his heart expand with hope and contract in fear. He wanted so much to believe. Sam kept trying to tell him that the darkness was only in his mind, conjured by guilt. And yet, he knew the truth. Stacy needed an order of protection from him just as much as any other vampire walking the earth. The blood would win. The blood always won.

He could try to fight the blood. It would be a constant battle. Was he up to that task?

Chaz left the mansion in a quandary. "Ozzie?" he asked as the phone picked up.

"Yes?"

"Do you have her?"

"I am not in the habit of letting anyone down. You should know that by now."

He sighed. Ozzie could be—trying at times. But he was still one of the best trackers the Paladin had. "I'll be there soon. Just don't let her out of your sight, got that?"

"I understand. I won't let any harm come to her."

Chaz went to his home in the city to think things through but found no solace there. He'd heard it said that the city never slept. He'd found that to be true for no matter what hour of the night, there were still sirens sounding in the distance and the rumble of a car going past. Streetlights never darkened until the sun rose. He looked out through the arched window set with brick wondering why he didn't feel comfortable. Even in his worst moments, Chaz could look out at his neighborhood or at the wall filled with books gathered through the years and find solace. Not tonight. The walls felt too devoid of life. Characters weren't people. The pages brought them to life but only in his head. Not for real.

Suddenly, Chaz felt the walls start to close in. So he grabbed his car and drove up along the coastline of New Jersey to West New York. River Road. At first, pure Jersey suburb with houses and malls and way too many apartments built too close to the Hudson River. Then up the hill to a much more urban, street-wise section where bodegas and stores sat beneath more apartment buildings on one side of the road and the river bordered the other. Scattered between the road and the river were patches of trees and grass, snippets of nature for families to use. Next to one, he found a parking spot and got out to sit on a park bench. He stared out at the lights of the greatest city in the world.

There was no way to describe the sight. On a clear night like this one, the lights reminded him of diamonds and stars, painted on a black background. If you stared long enough, the outlines of the buildings faded, leaving a panorama of jewels for the eyes to drink in.

Never in his wildest dreams as a human could he have imagined such a sight.

But the visual hid what lay beneath: the strength, the determination to survive, the need to grow and create made New York City the greatest city in the world. Perhaps this was the treasure of time.

Such a marvel would never have been conceived of when he was a human being. The entire modern world would have been unfathomable. Which made him wonder, for a moment, where the years had gone. Looking back, his time on this earth had been but a blink of an eye. And yet, the years also seemed beyond endless. Depending upon which way he chose to see his existence.

But there was one fact he couldn't deny. For all their faults, humans had indeed grown in-depth and in knowledge, which made them closer yet even more frightening than ever. Man's thirst for knowledge had brought the human race to the point where they were this close to truly accepting the idea of vampires' existence. Would they be able to go beyond a television series and the movies? Would they be able to accept fantasy as reality?

Remaining invisible had protected them for so long. Even Sam couldn't deny that an absolute total disaster was possible when the shadows were removed. And yet, she was making him an offer he couldn't refuse. She was telling him she'd protect Stacy as an equal.

The choice was his.

He leaned forward and rubbed his face with his hands. The right thing to do was guard Stacy until he killed the rogue and then make sure she remained safe. The noble thing to do was make her forget all about him—the vampire with the bloodstained hands. The decent thing to do was make sure she understood that a vampire and a man were two different entities and that she belonged with a man, not a vampire.

The easier thing to do was drive a stake through his heart and not rip the damned thing out. Then let Ozzie take his head.

God, he was so toasted. Because he still didn't know what to do. He wanted to love her, take the opportunity Sam offered, but he also knew the day would come when he would try to drain her dry.

Would he be able to stop? Would his love for her overcome the all-encompassing need for blood?

Like Sam said, the choice was his.

Chapter Twenty-Nine

STACY

STACY SLAMMED THE CAR DOOR CLOSED, GUNNED THE ENGINE, AND told herself speeding ticket be damned. She was that pissed off. Of course, half a mile later, she slowed down, but only because being caught would be embarrassing.

There had to be something that would push Chaz over the edge, forcing him to admit she was worth fighting for. But what?

Become the bait and flush out a rogue.

Yeah, and maybe get herself killed in the process.

Oh, well.

She reached the shore too quickly and pulled into O'Reilly's, shuddering as she remembered the last time she was here. She shivered, remembering the way Nick and Donnie circled her like a piece of fresh meat. She remembered the rasp of Donnie's tongue on her flesh. But in the end, that's exactly what she was, what she'd agreed to be—a piece of meat. Stacy got out of the car and walked into the bar, feeling as though she'd never be safe again. Then she realized there was only one place she'd ever truly felt safe. And that was in his arms.

"Haven't seen you in a while," Pat remarked. "You okay?"

She slid onto a bar stool, grappling for a moment of normality. "Yeah, I'm fine. I've been busy."

Pat nodded and pulled out a bar rag, which meant she was going to get an earful. "Told your Dad I'd keep an eye on you."

"I know,"

"Guess you're old enough to take care of yourself." He didn't say anything else right away, just kept wiping. "Makes me damned proud to see what you've done with your life."

"Thanks, Pat." Stacy smiled, thinking back to her idea. "Might amaze you yet, you know."

That surprised him enough to get him to look up at her. "Oh, yeah? How?"

"I've been thinking about going to med school."

The bar rag stopped rotating for a second. "Bet your Dad would bust if he were here."

"I've always wanted to help people. I thought maybe I could do that if I helped catch the bad guys. I guess it's not enough. I want to save lives. Not take them. Came way too close last time I was here."

Pat nodded but seemed to understand this was her talk, not his, and that Stacy owed him an explanation about the night of the fight. "I'm sorry I couldn't tell you about what was going down the other night, Pat. I was working an angle for the department," she answered, embellishing the truth a little.

"I had a feeling." The bar rag started swiping the counter again. "Don't remember too much. Mike doesn't either. Hope we put those youngsters in their place a bit before they got their licks in."

Stacy's heart warmed. "You are awesome." It was comforting to know there were people around her who would always have her back. Of course, she didn't dare tell Pat the truth. "Those two young punks were part of a drug sting."

Pat grimaced and nodded. "Never did like you carrying a gun. Kinda figured you'd leave that to Mike. But when I found out you worked in a lab, I was okay with it," he groused. "You're gonna give that all up if you go to med school, aren't you?"

"Yes, I'll give it up," she laughed. As she sobered, she reached out to give Pat's hand a quick squeeze. "They wanted someone familiar with the area, and I was available. No harm, no foul."

Pat seemed to accept her explanation. He threw the rag down and frowned. "You hungry? You look like you've lost weight."

Stacy shook her head. "And you sound like my mother."

Pat laughed. "Sue me."

"Let me have a glass of the Pinot. The *good* Pinot and a burger." She wrinkled her nose at the irony of becoming a piece of meat and eating one.

Oh well.

"Coming right up."

Stacy enjoyed her meal, the first one she'd noticed eating in days. She watched part of a baseball game on the television behind the bar, drowning in the normalcy of the night. And she wondered. Would there ever be a time when she could do this with Chaz? Would he ever be able to accept that they could live in both their worlds?

If there was ever to be an "us" or any kind of a semblance of an "us," Stacy had to prove to him she could function in his world. More importantly, that she could stand up to anything vampires could dish out—even rogue vampires.

So that meant she needed to make her presence known.

Stacy thought about walking then got into her car and drove the short distance to the warehouse, where she'd first encountered the rogue. And her first vampire lesson. Sitting in her car and staring at the empty parking lot, she replayed the entire night, realizing that he'd been trying to save the man's soul, not take his life.

What a fine line between truth and deception.

Stacy laughed softly. The same could be applied to her own predicament. No one would ever be able to know Chaz existed. She would never be able to bring him into her human world. He would never truly be able to bring her into his. Her life would become part of his darkness, she would become isolated, what little piece of the vampire world that accepted her would be the only piece they could share. She had to accept that. In fact, she had to embrace it. Otherwise, she would never be able to accept the loneliness.

And yet looking back on her life, Stacy still felt out of place. Even though people like Pat and Tori and Mike cared about her, Stacy felt insulated. She didn't want to say alone, but rather, she used the word singular. She'd never fit in. She was a scientist, a geek, a geek cop in a world that seemed to accept one or the other but not both. The only time she felt whole was when Chaz was with her. She needed him. Being with him made her come alive in the truest sense of the word.

Stacy had scoffed at the line, 'you complete me.' She'd never thought that plausible, let alone possible. Now she knew how wrong she'd been. Chaz was her other half. In the truest sense of the word, they were soul mates, because there wasn't any other way they could truly mate.

The last question remained. What was she going to do with this knowledge? Logic dictated that she run as far away as fast as possible. The future with Chaz loomed uncertain and frightening. But then there was the flip side to that coin. The future without Chaz was simply unthinkable.

She loved him.

And maybe, someday, if she was lucky, she might tell Pat and Mike all about the vampire who was more human than most humans. Until then, she'd simply have to go it alone.

So Stacy got out of the car and walked around. She picked up pieces of garbage, ran her hands over the railing, and rubbed her palms on the pavement.

She yelled, figuring it wouldn't help but knowing she had nothing to lose at this point. "Come and get me, you murderer! Come on!"

And she took a box cutter that she kept inside her purse for emergencies and cut her finger, pushing out several drops onto the pavement. She thought of them as tears of absolution because the protectors of the innocent were never fully appreciated.

"These are for Pitch!" she cried, hoping wherever his soul landed, Jeremy was happy.

She walked across the parking lot and pushed out several more. "These are for Aidan." Who deserved a second chance for trying to save her life.

"These are for Chaz," she whispered, knowing how much he'd suffered, believing he'd killed his human wife.

Stacy lifted her gaze to scan the entire industrial park. "Here it is!" she yelled. "Nice and warm. All ready for you. And so am I."

"Well, I'm not!" a voice exploded from behind her. *Chaz*. She whirled around to see one very agitated vampire stalking towards her. "Are you freaking crazy, or do you simply have a death wish?"

He looked ready to have a heart attack. And since that was one of the organs she knew actually worked inside his body, Stacy decided to hang onto the snide reply. Instead, she asked, "How did you know I was here?"

"Ozzie. Did you think I'd ever leave you unguarded?" he exploded. "And just what in the hell do you think you're doing?"

"Saving both our lives."

"More like trying to get both of us killed!" he yelled, reaching out to grab her shoulders. At the last moment, he must have thought better of that action because his arms fell to his sides, and his fists tightened into knots of sinew and muscle.

"I have no intention of dying."

"Really?" he asked, his tone telling her he couldn't believe she was that stupid. "You've seen a rogue in action. Explain that one to me."

"And stand in the middle of a wide-open area while I do? Now, who has the death wish?"

He drew in a deep breath while his pale cheeks suffused with red. *Fascinating*.

"Damn it, woman, get in the car! Now!"

The scientist in her wondered how high his blood pressure would go. The woman simply stood her ground. "No."

"You have half a second."

Threats? Had he just threatened her? Good. Then her plan was working.

"Make me."

"With pleasure."

Stacy hid a smile. Then the air whooshed out of her lungs as he literally picked her up and threw her over his shoulder.

"You.... could...have.... been.... more.... gentle.... about.... that," she choked out, unable to draw in a full breath as his shoulder bit into her diaphragm.

He set her down next to the passenger door, threw it open, and then shoved her into the seat. He looked ready to put a hole in her car with his fist, so Stacy held her tongue until he'd climbed into the driver's seat.

"Where are we going?"

"Home."

"Mine or yours?"

"Yours."

"Isn't that kind of like leading the fox right to the hen house?"

"Doesn't matter now."

"It doesn't? I don't understand."

She didn't like the marble caste to his countenance at all. But she wasn't about to back down. He had a choice. Now or never.

"You will, Stacy. You will."

Chapter Thirty

CHAZ

CHAZ HAD NEVER BEEN SO ANGRY IN ALL HIS LIFE. NEVER. NOT even after he'd found out, he was a vampire and could never die. He'd never been so scared either. Not even after he'd woken up buried underground for the tenth time and had to claw his way through the damp earth to freedom.

A hot knife seared his insides, slicing away at his guts. He kept telling himself she couldn't be that dumb; she couldn't believe she could ignore the danger she put herself in. Better yet, she couldn't be so naïve as not to care.

"What the hell is wrong with you?" he asked after carrying her inside the house and slamming her front door closed. Then he dumped her on the couch like a sack of potatoes. She jumped up, fist drawn back, ready to punch him. If the whole fiasco hadn't been so unnerving, he'd have started laughing.

"Wait a second. This is my home. My turf. I didn't ask you to come here; I didn't ask for your help back at the bar."

He drew in a deep draught of air and held onto it for a few seconds so that his insides wouldn't meltdown. "Then you really are crazy. You've got a death wish."

"No, I'm finishing this disaster once and for all. Then you can take your vampire friends and all your vampire games and go jump in the lake for all I care. I've had it. I'm tired of being treated like a piece of meat, the cheese in a trap, and a pile of crap all at the same time."

She couldn't mean that, could she?

"Stacy, wait." Chaz started to pace, not knowing what to do with himself as he tried to figure out a way to get her to change her mind. "I know we've been a bit arrogant. I know we've been selfish. And that we haven't exactly treated you with the respect you deserve."

"*We*, Chaz?"

Her question dumped a bucket of cold water all over her anger. "All right. I haven't either."

She nodded in agreement. "You bet your sweet ass, you haven't."

Frustrated, Chaz raked his hands through his hair then threw them up in the air. "What would you like me to say? I'm sorry? Is that going to change anything?"

She folded her arms across her chest and stared at him, her countenance stern. "It would be a beginning."

All right then—"I'm sorry."

"Are you, Chaz? Are you really?"

The raw hurt in her voice grabbed at him. "You'll never understand."

"Try me."

"Humans have emotions. We have shadows."

She frowned, considering his words. "Are you saying you can't feel or that you won't?"

"Both. Neither. The point is that whatever is lacking enabled me to drain Mary to the point of death. And don't forget, I was only a few days removed from being a human. Only one thing stopped me."

"What was that?"

"What was left of my conscience."

Her forehead furrowed as she tried to understand. "Are you telling me that you have no conscience left?"

"No," he denied, ready to tear his hair out in shreds. He stormed over to her, then stopped, wanting desperately to reach out and hold her and know that everything would be all right. But it wouldn't. "I'm telling you what little conscience I do have left may not save you. Or sustain you."

She didn't answer right away. "Shouldn't I be the judge of that?"

"Yes. And no."

That made her rear back in surprise. "I think you'd better explain."

"It's rather simple. A vampire is as close to an inanimate object as a living being can be."

"Says you."

He threw her a look and continued. "Vampires have no feelings, no emotions, and they don't expect to have any. They are pure selfishness, not because they want to hurt others but because they don't see themselves as selfish. They live to survive."

He paused to find he wasn't getting through to her. So he added, "Look at Hunter. He'd have had no trouble killing you when you first met."

She gave him a weary smile that said she knew something he refused to see. "But what about now, Chaz? What about now?"

He shrugged and refused to answer.

"Don't you see? Hunter's changed. Not a ton, I'll grant you that. But for the better."

"He's a vampire, Stacy. And so am I. That's what I've been trying to tell you."

"But he's learned to respect me as a human being," she said. "And he's smart enough to know that there are other humans in the world that can be beneficial to vampires."

Could they coexist? It was the question that haunted him. It was the question that became the key to whether or not he had a future with Stacy.

Very slowly, Stacy undid the first two buttons on her shirt. The sight tantalized with promise. But then he watched as she lifted the silver chain and cross from around her neck.

"This belongs to you. I think it saved my life with the rogue. I could be wrong because all bets are off when it comes to them. But it doesn't belong to me. I want you to keep it." She held out her hand

and dropped the chain in his palm. "Because it represents all the good and all the bad in our future."

A future he now knew he wanted very badly. He closed his palm around the metal, and a voice came to him out of the past. A conversation with Mick. His mentor. His friend. On a night much like this night, with a hint of promise in the air.

"You, my young friend, are unique," Mick told him.

He frowned, having no idea what Mick was talking about. "How so?"

"Of all of us, you have come closest to becoming rogue. Of all of us, you have the most understanding of what that feels like."

Terror gripped his insides. Dark memories flooded his brain. "Which is why they must be destroyed."

Mick nodded in agreement. But a curious gaze caught his. "Do you not feel pity, my apprentice?"

"Yes, of course, I do. But pity is a human emotion. Vampires lose their humanity when they turn. And to some extent, we have as well. Even you and I."

"Perhaps."

Chaz remembered his heartfelt sigh. "And now, as centuries turn into more centuries, it seems as though my emotions are becoming harder and harder to find."

"Aye," his mentor nodded. "That is true. But must it always be so?"

At the time, Chaz thought long and hard about that question. He wanted to believe that he retained part of his humanity, that there was goodness still left inside him despite what he'd done and been forced to do since. That he could make up for his mistake by keeping humans and vampires safe from a greater evil.

But the sad truth was he was still a vampire, and that would never change. So he told Mick the truth. *"As long as we remain vampires, I believe it does."*

Now Stacy was asking him that very question. He'd thought nine hundred plus years had destroyed the very essence she was seeking. And yet, stubborn as it was, the will to live not simply exist, the desire to do the right thing, the goodness inside him refused to be destroyed.

Like a plant in the desert, it kept adapting, changing, shrinking and growing, whatever it needed to do to survive.

And he realized how wrong he'd been. No matter what they were or had to become, the choice to be good or evil rested inside the individual. As did the strength to resist temptation. But most of all so did the ability to love and be loved.

A great weight lifted off his shoulders. He smiled and opened his arms, knowing he couldn't stand another second of not holding her. His arms banded about her shoulders, and she burrowed her head deep against his chest.

"You do realize the odds against an 'us,' don't you?"

Her shoulders began to shake. "You mean, besides the rogue stalking me? And young vamps going zombie on you?"

"Yes."

She lifted her face, and Chaz knew exactly where his emotions were. Better yet, where they'd always been.

Chapter Thirty-One

CHAZ

Chaz bent his head. Her lips feathered across his. He wanted to take his time, go slow, and savor the moment. But he couldn't. It felt like years since he'd last held her in his arms and eons since he'd last kissed her.

"Make the world go away," she begged. "For just this moment, make the world go away."

That, at least, he could do.

Chaz bent down and captured her lips with his. She opened her mouth, and his tongue dove inside. She fenced with him, and a fire erupted inside. Part of him wanted this moment to go on forever. His lower half had an altogether different opinion.

The kiss deepened, and they both staggered backward, needing support from absolute free-fall. The kitchen counter finally stopped their progress, allowing them both to come up for air. But only for a moment. They tried to inhale each other. He tightened his arms around her back in his need to become one with her. Her fists kneaded the flesh surrounding his shoulder blades with the same idea in mind. They both broke apart, knowing they were both beyond slow and gentle.

Chaz let his feelings shine through his gaze as it roamed every inch of her face. He traced the outline of her cheek, and jaw with his tongue and she growled with desire. He reared back, knowing there was a forbidden place nearby that he didn't dare go near yet and focused on the rest of her body instead. He ripped her blouse out of her pants and pushed her bra up to get at her breasts.

His thumb and forefinger worried first one nipple, then the other while he captured her lips again. He swirled his tongue into her mouth, and she moaned. When he tore his mouth from hers, gasping for breath, she wrapped her hands around his neck, but now they sought his flesh too. His shirt buttons popped open one by one, and he couldn't get over the sensations when she returned the favor.

With trembling fingers, he helped her remove her blouse. Then she reached back with her hand and unsnapped her bra. His inability to get the hang of doing that was damned funny. His answer to her now was a quirk of his lips and a what-did-you-expect-from-a-guy-born-before-the-damn-thing-was-ever-invented look.

She smiled back at him. Chaz knew, at the moment he saw her walk out of the room with Hunter, how much he loved her. He knew she stood up to Sam. He knew most of all, when she insisted she was strong enough to continue with their insane plan, because the thought of losing her, of her not being there, of not putting his arms around her became an emptiness too stark to bear.

That smile, this moment, filled that emptiness back up. In fact, his heart started to overflow. Tears formed in his eyes, something a vampire couldn't do. Another gift? He wasn't sure. The only gift he knew was holding her in his arms.

Bending down, Chaz licked his way down the valley of her chest. H then he began to suck on her nipple. She moaned, which did funny things to his insides. He turned his attention onto the other, and her hands started clawing at his belt. Once they reached the prize, he was a goner.

Thoughts of taking her right there on the counter-top entered his mind. But that wasn't what he wanted to share with her. He wanted warm and, yes, slow had gone out the window a long time ago.

Lifting her up, Chaz carried her into the bedroom. They both undressed with fumbling fingers. They fell onto the bed.

She urged him to roll on top of her, but he wanted to savor one more kiss. He slid his tongue over her lips, and when her mouth opened, he explored every crevice inside. He could feel every beat of her heart, wanted to sink himself into the life within her. But all he could do was sink himself into her flesh and come as close to being alive as he would ever get.

Chaz rolled on top of her and lifted onto his arms. He slipped inside as if he were meant to be there. She wrapped her legs around him, and he held still.

"Stacy, I love you."

Another hope flared, one that she would return the sentiment. When she didn't answer right away, a shaft of disappointment seared his guts. What had he expected? That she would simply say she loved him back? That she had automatically followed suit?

Not everyone fell in love at the same time.

What she did do was to draw his head down to hers and give him a searing kiss that left him breathless. He began to move, tried to go slow, but his body was firing on all eights. He spread light kisses all over her face and began to love her. Harder and harder until there was no other reality than the joining of their bodies.

She writhed beneath him, begging for more. He gave it to her. He let his love for her shine through. He brought her to the brink first, then held his breath. He opened his eyes. Her rich, bronze hair scattered in magnificent disarray all over the pillow. Sweat beaded her face. Her head thrashed back and forth. And he watched her shatter completely. For him.

Then his own release followed. He cried out as the reflex of his body pumped into hers. He moved until every pulse was gone, reveling in the sensation, until he collapsed on top of her.

Chaz pulled out of her knowing what he had to do.

But that would mean trusting himself. Could he do that? After being the cause of Mary's death? After trying to absolve himself for over nine hundred years?

He dared not open his eyes for fear she would see.

Terrible memories surfaced. Watching Mary grow haggard and frail. But most of all, seeing the light of life die in her eyes. She'd always remained young to him because of her soul. She loved to tease, she lived in the moment, and she took pleasure wherever she could despite their meager existence.

On a night he'd rather forget, Chaz took that all away from her. Because he had no willpower. Could he find it within himself to flirt with the brink of disaster now that he'd found the one true love of his life?

Stacy was willing to lay down her life to save his. Could he do any less?

With his head on her chest and her heartbeat pounding in his ear, could he resist the temptation and not cross the point of no return?

He thought back to the rest of the conversation he'd shared with Mick that night.

"I would answer your question with one of my own. Can the most terrible of acts, the taking of another life, ever be redeemed?"

Mick shrugged. "I do not know, but every day I exist, I seek that redemption."

Now was the time to find out the truth of that answer.

A core of steel formed inside his being. Chaz knew he'd have to be stronger than he ever thought possible to do what he'd set his mind to do.

He lifted his head and pinned Stacy's hands to the bed as he shifted his body up a little. Then he began nuzzling his way over to her lips. He seared his way through her mouth, plundering, tasting, and invading until she was breathless. Her body writhed beneath his seeking a satisfaction only he could give.

He tore his mouth away and sought first one breast, then the other, but these were not light kisses, they were demands. He sucked, he teased, and he worried her nipples. He even bit them a little until she became a wild woman underneath his body.

Then he spread her legs. Letting go of her arms, he captured her thighs so she couldn't move. He lifted her core to his tongue and lathed the outer regions then plunged into the furnace that awaited him. She cried out, but she was nowhere near where he wanted her to be. Not yet.

He lapped at her nub until she reached the brink then backed off, kissing and licking the inside of her thighs until she cooled off. He repeated the stroke until she was nearly mindless, begging him to take her, growling out demands he finally wanted to meet.

Without waiting, he let go but kept his hands under her legs. He centered himself at her core and thrust his shaft deep inside, holding her captive. Her legs wrapped around his back and he pinioned her hands again against the bed. He began to thrust, so hard she would have moved up the bed if he hadn't held her steady. She began to build, he could see it in the tension in her face. As she did, he responded to the call inside his own body.

Chaz let the river of her blood pound with the beat of his heart. He could hear the rush of the fluid, taste the coppery tang on the tip of his tongue.

Just as she reached her pinnacle, Chaz sank his incisors into her neck. The sensation floored him. Her life ran into his, singing through his veins. Energy flooded his system, and as she screamed her release, he reached his. He pushed and pumped as her blood became his as he drank. He had to drain her to the brink and then stop. Because he knew it was what he had to do.

Chapter Thirty-Two

STACY

SOMETHING WAS WRONG. STACY COULDN'T RIGHT HERSELF. THE world kept spinning out of control.

"I'm sorry, Stacy."

Her body still pulsed with the aftershocks of an amazing orgasm, but she couldn't get the room to balance, she felt drunk, higher than a kite. Damn him, he'd used the thrall.

"I won't let you sacrifice yourself for something you should never have been involved in."

"You won't what?" Stacy tried to lift her head. The room tilted when she did. "You bastard," she cried, realizing what he'd done. "You...you didn't..."

Such sadness. After such pleasure. "Not exactly."

Stacy tried to gather her thoughts. As she did, he covered her with a sheet and rose. She'd never seen such steely determination in his face before. "You're going after him by yourself."

"To keep you safe."

"That's not your choice."

"It is now. I drank enough of your blood so you won't get out of this bed and try to be a hero."

"Did you really think that was my only motivation? That I was doing this to be a hero?"

He stared down at her, his gaze unchanged. "You'll be all right after you sleep it off. Go to sleep."

"No, I won't."

She struggled to sit up and fell back onto the bed, too weak to get up. She tried again, only to have the room spin out of control.

"Why?" she asked, her thoughts a mass of contradictions.

"Because I love you."

She watched Chaz turn on his heel and leave the room. She had to close her eyes again to get the room to stop spinning. She could hear him throwing his clothes on in the other room. Then she heard him stop in the doorway.

"I'll never forgive you," she said, her tone flat and her stare hard as she opened them. He was leaning against the doorjamb. He looked anything but nonchalant.

"I'd never forgive myself if something happened to you. So we're even."

She read the regret in his gaze and pushed it away.

"You'll never pull it off without me."

"Guess I'm gonna have to try." He lifted off the doorjamb, turned, and walked out of the house.

"You are such a *man*, Charles Tower," she cried out after him, slamming her hand down on the bed, which didn't do much for her head.

Chaz had forgotten exactly who he was dealing with. She might be weak and woozy, but she was smarter than him any day of the week. There was no way she was going to get up at this moment, so resting came first. She closed her eyes, picturing Chaz in her head. Damn him! He had no right. This was her fight just as much as it was his. She'd put herself out there for him. The least he could do was respect that.

Not quite sure how much time passed, Stacy finally felt the world begin to steady. She lifted her head off the pillow and swung her legs over the edge of the bed. The room tilted. She closed her eyes, breathed deeply, and then opened them—one step at a time. First, an ice-cold shower, a fast scrub dry, clean clothes, and yes, a short rest on the side of the bed. After that, she made it to the kitchen using the walls as a guide to get there. Then a bottle of Gatorade, the last few swallows joined a double dose of her iron supplement to put some life back in her veins.

Then another rest in a kitchen chair. That freaking vampire! Stacy ended up having to put her head between her knees for a couple of moments. He was going to get more than an earful when she found him. She lifted up. The room swam a little then just started to rock. Okay. How about some coffee? Caffeine would certainly help. After finishing half a mug, Stacy started to feel more like herself again.

She looked at the wall clock in her kitchen. The process took longer than she wanted, but a couple of hours later, at least she was on her feet. Functional? That remained to be seen.

Stacy knew where Chaz was going and drove as fast as she dared; the other cars' movement tended to make her dizzy. She stopped at a convenience store for another cup of coffee and decided she needed another dose of sugar. A package of cupcakes did the trick. She got back in the car and drove until she reached the warehouse.

As she drove, Stacy tried to imagine herself with an unquenchable thirst. She thought about Jim and wondered yet again if she could have saved the security guard's life. Knowing what she knew now about vampires and the tightrope they tread, she realized Chaz had been right. There had been no right or wrong that night, only fate. The rogue had a choice. He chose the security guard and not the cop.

Now she had a choice. To offer herself up as bait or let another innocent, no make that a whole lot more than one, die. When put that way, there wasn't a choice at all.

Stacy pulled into the warehouse complex and drove around for a few minutes. She pulled into the center of a parking lot and turned off the car. For a moment, the world tipped and went black, and Stacy cursed Chaz for his damned nobility. She sat back, trying to get her head to clear and get the warehouse in front of her to stop spinning. She leaned back and let her head fall onto the headrest.

The loud thump on the roof of her car made her jump. Then a fist tried to smash the windshield. Cursing herself for her stupidity,

Stacy fumbled for the starter. The engine roared to life, and she threw
the car into gear and floored the gas pedal. Then she swerved into a
circle to throw it off.

Tires squealed, but she couldn't shake the creature, so she pulled
down the alleyway into a larger parking lot. She thanked every star,
God, and anyone else she could that cell phones in cars were a way of
life now. And that she'd memorized his cell number and entered it into
her car before she'd left. "Call Chaz cell."

She tried the swerve technique again, but it had no effect. Instead,
she revved up the torque, peeled out again, and then threw on the
brakes. The creature lost its grip and fell forward over the hood.

Stacy slammed the car into gear and tried to run it over, but it was
too fast. It scrambled out of the way.

The line opened. She could only pray he heard her. "Dandridge.
Warehouse. NOW!"

Not sure where the instinct came from, Stacy hit the brakes again
and put the car into reverse. She hit the gas, and the car lurched
forward as she hit the creature. Then she shifted into drive and tried
to get the hell out of there.

An angry vampire is something a human doesn't want to deal
with. An angry rogue vampire? The driver's side window shattered
with the force of its fist. That same hand reached out and wrapped
around her throat.

Already weak, Stacy did not need her air supply cut off, but she
had enough adrenaline pulsing through her system to know that she
might just be able to knock the rogue off using the wall of the warehouse. So she swerved back through the alleyway and deliberately ran
her car up against the building.

Sparks flew, and so did the creature as it jumped off her car. But
now Stacy was going the wrong way. She was going into the complex,
not out. She tried to pull the car around again, but it jumped onto the
roof. She pulled her gun out, and as it tried to catch hold of her
through the window, she fired. She missed, but at least the creature
was aware she had another weapon at her disposal.

She fired again as soon as she saw it, but by looking out of the window, she missed the alleyway and rammed the car into the side of the building. She tried to get it to start. It wouldn't.

The hand that grabbed her throat meant business, but with her seat belt on, it couldn't pull her out of the car. With one hand, she clawed at the vice-like grip. With the other, she groped for her firearm on the car seat.

Talons. That's what its fingers were. They were digging holes in her neck, and the smell of her blood was driving the creature mad with hunger. It kept trying to pull her out, pulling flesh and blood to its mouth.

Then she found her gun.

She fired four successive rounds at point-blank range into what she thought was a face. The rogue screamed in pain, and let go and then the thing was gone.

Chapter Thirty-Three

CHAZ

CHAZ STOOD ON THE ROOF OF THE WAREHOUSE. HE'D FIGURED THE rogue would go back to the warehouse parking lot after Stacy left every sign imaginable. As he waited, he realized it seemed nearly a lifetime ago that he watched Stacy stare down a creature worse than her worst nightmare.

His stomach plummeted when he watched her car pull into the lot. Sheer horror filled his belly when he realized Stacy had been followed. The rogue jumped from out of the shadows and pounced down onto the roof of Stacy's car. His guts liquefied, and his feet slid on the roof as he ran towards the edge where her car was. Just as he was about to leap off the roof and get the rogue away from the car, Stacy peeled rubber and swerved. She was trying to shake the creature off. When she slammed on her brakes and quickly rammed the creature with the car, he wanted to applaud. He skidded to the edge of the roof. He was ready to fly down to the ground when his cell buzzed his leg. He didn't dare answer. Instead, he opened the line so Stacy would know he'd gotten her message.

And then her predicament became his. He jumped and rolled to the ground, ignoring the pain as he edged around the corner of the building. He needed an opening to get the rogue away from her, and she was doing her damnedest to keep him from helping. His heart lodged somewhere in the middle of his throat as he watched her car arc in a half-circle. She was facing the wrong way. She needed to turn around…

"Oh no," he whispered as her car smashed into the wall and refused to start.

Chaz died a thousand deaths as he ran towards the car, seeing the rogue bend through Stacy's car window. He was just about there when he watched in absolute amazement and terror as she fired a bunch of shots right into it, and that was all he needed to see.

With the determination of a madman, he hauled the creature off the car. He stared at the missing face with immense satisfaction as he swung his fist right into a mass of tissue and muscle. Blood went flying, and pain scorched through his arm. He could have cared less.

He lifted the rogue by its torn shirt and tried to smash what was left of its face back into its brain. Again, he ignored the pain his right hook caused and watched with glee as the rogue went flying.

With the strength of ten men and the determination of a man who'd nearly lost his life and his love, Chaz lifted the rogue as he'd been lifted and threw his nemesis as hard as he could down onto the ground.

"You are not going to kill one more being, you monster!"

But the rogue wasn't done yet. It managed to crawl to its knees, its lust for blood, any blood, overcoming the agony coursing through its body, and Chaz realized he needed an edge.

"Do you remember this?" he cried, pulling out the silver chain and cross.

The rogue hesitated and cocked its bloody head. It took a step towards him. "Do you remember, Mick? You had a heart once. You cared."

Scrape-drag. Scrape-drag.

Was there something pitiful in the way the cross mesmerized the rogue?

"You killed him for me, didn't you, Mick? The vampire who made me?"

Scrape-drag. Scrape-drag.

"You avenged five good men the day you did that, but you aren't Mick anymore, are you?" Sorrow filled his soul. And yet, there was no pity left inside. The rogue had tried to kill Stacy. It needed to die.

Never before in all his existence, had Chaz seen a vampire so decimated. Unsure what he'd need to use to kill it, Chaz pulled out the syringe of extract with his other hand and hid it in his palm. Any and all ammunition welcome. He waved the cross on the chain in front of him, drawing the rogue ever closer. The rogue licked its lips, pink spittle flying from its mouth as the desire for blood fought with the prize he held in his hand.

With one great leap, it flew through the air, arm outstretched to seize the cross. As soon as it landed, Chaz took the syringe of extract and jammed it into what he hoped was the rogue's heart. He couldn't tell because it didn't have much of a head left to use as a gauge. With one mighty push, he dispensed the fluid into the rogue then ripped the needle out. It screamed in absolute agony as the fluid burned a hole through its chest.

"I am what I am because of you, Mick. I'll be forever grateful. But there's nothing of you left." Tears filled his eyes. "You had a choice. You should've gone to the caves. And for that, I'll never forgive you."

All the fear, all the anger, all the knowledge that this thing had to die helped Chaz keep the rogue down on the ground.

"You had a choice not to kill. Instead, you've murdered, I don't even know how many innocent people. I don't know why. I'll never know why. I'll always hate you for what you've done."

With all his might, he drove his fist into Mick's unrecognizable face, and his arm jarred from the impact of the rogue's head hitting the macadam of the parking lot. He held the creature pinned to the ground so it wouldn't escape.

"Charles. Chaz. It's okay now. It's over," Hunter said, lifting him off the vampire while several soldiers surrounded the body.

He tried to fight off the arms that held him. "No! It's not. I have to finish this."

Hunter forced him to look at him. "It's over."

Chaz drew in deep draughts as he broke away and stared at the monster lying on the ground. "Not until I take its head!"

Hunter shook his head, and for the first time in his life, Chaz watched Hunter's gaze soften. "You let me take care of that."

"No. He betrayed us, Hunter. Mick was a coward, but he betrayed me most of all. He was a coward." Chaz spit the word out as if it burned his tongue.

Sam stepped in front of him, her gaze solemn. She didn't say a word. She simply handed him her knife.

"But worse than that, he tried to kill Stacy. For that, he dies by my hand and my hand alone."

His heart threatened to pound out of his chest. His rage became a living thing. A roar in his ears blocked out all sound. The same roar he'd heard nearly a thousand years ago when he'd nearly drained Mary dry. The roar wasn't the sound of her blood; it was the sound of his. The roar was his terrible need to end another life. Only this time, he recognized that need for what it was.

With a sudden jolt, he stopped. A quiet calm filled his being. With it came sorrow and a realization. A life should never be taken out of anger or need, only out of necessity.

"I'm sorry, Mick," he whispered. Perhaps this was the final lesson. He didn't know.

He lifted his gaze to Hunter and Sam, and they nodded. They understood.

Taking a deep breath, Chaz kneeled by the rogue. "You were my father, my mentor," he whispered, letting the air out slowly. He brought his arm down and sliced off the rogue's head. "You were my friend."

A sigh rustled through the wind.

Chaz lifted from the ground. He handed the knife back to Sam, who received it with honor.

A few moments passed, and then Sam said, "Go take care of Stacy."

Stacy? The sound of her name inside his head made him turn and run towards her car.

So pale, he thought as he fumbled to get the door open. And her head was just lolling on the headrest, tiny rivulets of blood dripping down her neck. "Stacy? Darling? Oh my God, Stacy. Talk to me. Please."

He ripped at the seat belt, finally getting it unfastened. Then he lifted her out of the car as if she were made of spun glass. He set her down on the pavement.

At first, he had no idea what to do. After all, she was the scientist. Stacy knew about medicine more than he did. He thought about tearing open his own wrist for a split second, but again, he was learning. If Stacy wanted to join him in this life, then that was a choice she'd have to make for herself. Instead, he fumbled for her pulse.

"Lower, bonehead. Closer to my wrist."

Oh, God. Thank you.

"Damn it, woman," he cried, not knowing whether to kiss her or strangle her.

She opened her eyes, both shining with suppressed laughter.

"How in the hell did you manage to fight off a rogue all by yourself?" he asked.

He didn't go on. He didn't have to. He knew damned well. She was one in a million, this woman of his. "I'd have told Hunter and Sam to take my head if I'd lost you."

She tried to laugh, but the sound didn't go too far. *Her* throat was in pretty bad shape. "No, you wouldn't," she choked out in a hoarse whisper. "Because you're like me, Charles Tower. We're bound by pride and duty and by something much stronger. Love."

Did she mean it? Under the circumstances, he shouldn't doubt her. But he wanted to hear her say it. At least once. "Say it," he commanded.

She smiled. "I feel like a thousand-ton truck ran over me, and like my throat has been inside a vice, and you want me to tell you that I love you?"

"Yes."

"I love you, Charles, first guard of the tower. Forever and always. As long as you never, ever do that to me again."

He laughed and pointed to the car. "As long as you never, ever, do *that* to me again too."

"No promises," she whispered.

"I know."

Chaz refused to move her until he performed the rites on her neck. Then and only then, did he lift her and carry her to his car. After setting her inside, he told her he'd return in a moment and walked up to Sam and Hunter.

"How is she?" Hunter asked, the concern in his tone touching Chaz deep inside.

"Her throat is swollen, but I already know she won't let me take her to the hospital."

"More important, how are you?" Sam asked.

"I think I'll be all right now."

Sam grinned at him and nodded.

"She's more than proven her loyalty to us," he told them, still uncertain if they'd agree to accept her into their world.

"Indeed, she has," Hunter said. "I've never met a woman with her strength of will."

He swallowed hard, his gaze turning solemn. "Will you accept her as my mate? Will you allow her to remain with me?"

This time Sam answered. "She earned that right the night she saved us at the mansion, Chaz. Tonight was simply icing on the cake."

"And the other leaders? I won't rub anyone's nose in our business, but she's going to want to continue her work, and I think we should let her."

"Question already posed and answered," Hunter said. "With a unanimous vote."

That thousand-ton weight slid off of him. "Thank you."

"When she's healed and ready, we need to know more about Nirvana. Both Dannika and Jason have advised that they have had to imprison a couple of these drugged vampires inside their cells. The problem seems to be growing."

"Understood."

Sam smiled up at him. "She's an exceptional lady, Chaz. We are honored to call her a friend."

Hunter agreed. "Every member of my cell has voted to guard her with their lives if necessary. Of course, not every cell will agree."

Chaz nodded. "I know, but it's a beginning."

He walked back to the car and got in, lighter in heart than he'd been in centuries. He decided not to take her back to her shore house.

"Where are we going?" she choked out

He smiled. "We should be going to a hospital, but knowing you'll fight me tooth and nail, I figured I'd take you to my place. It's safer."

She didn't answer. Taking her to his home meant he was letting her inside himself. He hoped she understood what opening that door meant.

Once he had her tucked safely on his living room couch and sipping on a cup of tea with some honey for her throat, Chaz realized they had a few mountains to cross. He clenched his fists as he watched the purple bruises grow on her neck. Then he realized he had to let go. She had the right to live the way she wanted to live. He sat down next to her.

"You nearly lost your life, Stacy. As proud of you as I am, I'm not sure I can handle going through something like this again. There'll be other rogues in the future. You have to promise me there'll be only one rogue hunter in this family."

She shivered. "I'll leave them to you. I promise."

All right. At least she wasn't arguing.

"Now we need to talk about family and who we are. What we'll become. This is only the beginning, Stacy. Perhaps even the easiest part. I'll never truly be a part of your world. You'll never truly be a part of mine."

"Don't you think I already realized that?" she asked.

"Did you also think about the children you'll never have?"

"Yes." She took another swallow so that her voice would come out close to normal. "Did *you* think about me growing old while you remain young?"

"Yes."

"Then you know that the answers to all of our questions lie in the future," she told him. "We have to take that future one step at a time. I'm willing to do that. Are you?"

"More than willing."

"And as far as both our worlds, we'll figure that out too."

He smiled, lifting her onto his lap. She snuggled into his chest, and

He swallowed, knowing she was in no shape for what his lower half had in mind.

Clearing his throat, Chaz continued. "That may not be as far in the future as you think. It seems you've made quite an impression. All the vampire leaders have agreed to let you stay in our world. I'm sure Sam had a lot to do with that, but I'm not complaining."

She stilled a moment, then her shoulders started to shake with laughter. "And here I thought it was because of my charming personality."

He laughed with her. "Don't think so."

"My keen wit and sharp scientific mind?"

"Maybe." He sobered. "You've even won over Hunter. He said to tell you his cell will guard you with their lives."

"Wow."

When she didn't say anything else, Chaz couldn't believe his ears. He didn't think anything would render Stacy speechless.

"Hunter also said that he would very much appreciate it if you'd consider continuing the work you've begun. I guess we were wrong after all. We need to find out what's going on with those young vampires. We still need your help."

She hesitated, and Chaz frowned.

"Something wrong?" he asked. "I mean, after the way you've been treated, I wouldn't blame you for not wanting to help."

"What? Oh, no. It's not that, but coming close to death has also made me realize how important life is, and that I was meant to follow a dream."

"What dream?"

"I want to become a doctor."

"A doctor? Really?" Chaz thought about that for a moment, realizing she belonged in that profession.

She nodded and burrowed deeper into his chest. "So I'll have to work around my classes. Do you think Hunter will be okay with that?"

"Shouldn't you be asking me that question?" he fired back at her.

She looked up at him with just a hint of guilt. But the excitement in her face gave him her answer. "Yes."

He smiled down at her. "Whatever you want to do is fine with me as long as we're together. And we're together, right?"

"Always."

And that was good enough for him. He bent down to give her a kiss with a rogue's gleam in his gaze. Her vampire. For as long as she would have him.

THE END

Thank you for reading! Did you enjoy?

Please Add Your Review! You can sign up for the City Owl Press newsletter to receive notice of all book releases!

And don't miss more paranormal romance like MY SONG'S CURSE by City Owl Author, Poppy Minnix. Turn the page for a sneak peek!

Sneak Peek of My Song's Curse

BY POPPY MINNIX

Being a siren sucks.

Every customer stares at me in attentive silence as I sit at the least conspicuous table in the back corner of this mom-and-pop Italian restaurant.

Well, excuse me for clearing my throat.

Going out in public wasn't the best idea, but this afternoon, I held a heated conversation with the actors on my television. They apologized to each other with caresses and phrases of sweetness, but I ended up on the floor, hugging a pillow in the empty silence. When a show becomes my reality, it's time to leave the house.

Now, as usual, I've enthralled the humans. *Whoops*. They study me as if the next thing I do will make their lives complete. The attention is normal, but I'm the last being they should covet, because there's much more to my species than being a lust magnet. A few more words from my hypnotic voice and they'd lick my shoes if I asked them to. Not that I would.

So now, it's time to return home. I push my chair back, but a shadow obscures the dim glow of overhead lights.

A man looms over me, dark and decadent, oozing charm with his confident smile. Well, hello, handsome. Other diners stand to follow him toward me.

"Stop," I tell them. "Return to your seats. If you work here, continue your duties." I bring my gaze to his. "You stay."

Even though our conversation will be as fake as the actors I argued with earlier today, my heart thumps an excited beat. It's been months since I've sat with someone.

I slide the empty chair out from under the table with my foot. "Sit." I keep my voice quiet and controlled, but it's a deep purr of promise.

He does what he's told, waiting with a familiar expression of hope mixed with dedication plus a dash of do me. Poor humans are so easy to captivate.

I let my fork drop against my bowl of pasta primavera, creating a loud clang that shatters through the room. "Name."

"Jordan Oltier."

"Okay, Jordan..." I draw circles on the checkered tablecloth with my fingertips. "Tell me three things about yourself."

He concentrates, lips pursed and eyes to the ceiling. "I play basketball, own a dog named Maizy, and I'm a nurse at Grison General in the pediatrics department."

Wow. Mr. Oltier sounds perfect. I dig deeper just for giggles. "Do you have a wife, fiancée, or girlfriend?"

"No."

"Boyfriend?" I ask, taking another bite of pasta.

Unlike most humans, his focused pucker relaxes into a grin. "No."

His big hands rest against the cream-colored tablecloth. They'd unzip my dress, and splay across my back, hot fingers digging into neglected skin. Eagerness flares in his eyes.

I haven't invited someone in for a long while. Each move we'd make would play out in a script with me as the director. Except I'd force my leading man to do whatever I wanted, unsure if he enjoyed himself or what he'd do if he had free will. After, he'd return to the humans, used for a night with fuzzy memories of me that would fade by the hour, while I'd hold on to every fake touch because it's the closest thing I have to life in an empty room of endless time. I don't want that for either of us.

Still, what's the harm in talking about it?

I prop my elbow on the table, cupping my jaw. "What were your thoughts when you saw me? Before I spoke?"

"You were the most beautiful woman I'd ever seen. Confident and brave. Maybe a screamer." He lights up like the thought delights him.

He wouldn't enjoy my screams, but his comment makes me grin. I ask him my favorite question. "What do you wish to do with me?"

"Kiss you, then tie you up . . ."

Yum. I didn't peg him as the type.

He shifts forward, his stare hard and unwavering. "And run a knife down your sternum thirty times, cutting deeper each time until I could touch your bones and play with your heart, the slickness of your blood—"

"Stop."

I hate it when this happens.

Chilled silence reigns in the restaurant, not because of creepy confessions but because my voice is a beacon to every creature that isn't a siren. They stare, not at this serial killer but at me. They should rage, call the police, or run for it. Instead, they wait for my attention, hanging on each sound. I wish they wouldn't.

"How many have you killed?" I ask.

"None," he replies.

Relief replaces the tight hold of terror in my chest. "Do you want to kill someone?"

"Yes."

His enthusiasm still simmers, but I don't appreciate this brand of passion. People tell me odd and honest things, but his confession is one of the more disturbing ones.

I lock onto his dark eyes, and my voice shifts into a deep and deliberate tone. "You will never kill. Think of how to help others instead of harming them. Pay for your dinner and leave."

Wannabe-serial-killer Jordan walks to an empty table near the front of the room, places bills down, and glances at me over his shoulder. He nods before exiting.

Odd. They rarely look back after I order them to go.

The room is so quiet, chills raise on my arms. I'm tempted to break a plate or turn over a chair to make a racket. Even the prep workers stare, frozen in the kitchen doorway.

A man and woman walk in, stopping short in confusion. The couple follows everyone's gazes to me, and the man give a low whistle, earning a smack on the chest from his companion. With a chuckle, he presses his lips to hers.

I want to sigh or say aw, but I bite my lip and keep quiet. I won't ruin meaningful kisses for those able to enjoy them.

His hand sneaks around her waist, and she melts into his embrace as the world shushes, leaving them alone to savor each other. He chooses her above others, even a siren, and his body language is a gift of insight into his mind.

Lucky humans.

Eyes follow my every move as I pin money under my plate and make my way to the exit.

Squeezing past the couple, I snatch a few buttermints from a dish on the hostess stand and call over my shoulder, "I was never here."

As I step into the warm night air, the chatter inside resumes. The customers and staff won't recall that I took over their dining experience, and those who see me around town will remember me, but I'll be nondescript. Forgettable. I'd love to understand why I'm this way, but even my most knowledgeable sisters tell me, "Just because, Lu." It's like they don't care to find out our history and where the three original siren mothers went.

Nonetheless, my ability is as frustrating as it is a comfort. I may not have friends besides my sisters, but I've altered wannabe-serial-killer Jordan's brain to a normal, human mode . . . or he may go insane. He won't kill anyone, though. Win? I shrug to myself.

Not ready to return to my empty house, the endless downtown sidewalks beckon me. Couples file out of bars and head home or to the beds of others. They talk in loud laughing phrases about human world things—friends, politics, and pop culture, until they notice me and staring replaces the conversation. The urge to speak up is unmanageable; *I enjoyed that movie too. Yeah, the new governor is a douche, except he has good educational policies. Your girlfriend has princess syndrome.*

A hush falls over the city this time of night, leaving me to meander in relative peace. The rhythmic clack of my heels echoing off brick and concrete soothe me and send my thoughts wandering to the human culture I've experienced this evening.

My phone buzzes in my purse and I drag it out as I check if anyone is within earshot. Few people walk the streets. Smiling at Amah's name, I answer in a whisper. "Hello, Ma."

"You sound happy. Why are you whispering?"

I wince. I nicknamed my oldest siren sister 'Ma' for a reason, not just because it fits her real name or because she's the closest thing I have to a mother. Amah makes sure we take care of ourselves and behave. I'm one for two. "I'm walking downtown."

The tap of her nail clicks against metal. "Tell me about tonight's outfit" she says, toneless.

I glance at the sheath dress that clings to my every curve like a warm hug. "Sweats."

"Liar."

"Fine. My favorite green dress. I went to dinner, had primavera, stopped potential crime." Ma won't appreciate that. She takes a natural approach to the mortals. Farm what you need from them, then set them free.

"Oh, Lula. Only you. Let's see it's . . . my goodness, eleven where you are? Darklings and otherworldlings may be out. Please go home soon."

The memory of my first darkling encounter makes my steps slow. Lena's death was more than a century ago. It's over. I shove away sad thoughts. It's my night out on the town, my time to pretend I belong somewhere. I'll save heartbreak for when I'm alone again.

"The otherworldlings fit in with the humans," I say, clacking along the sidewalks. "They won't make a scene, and I can control them if they do. Plus, the streets are empty." Eerily so, even for the late hour on a weekday.

"I know. I just worry. Have you spoken to Gerty or Venora lately?"

"I spoke to Gerty last month, but Ven and I chatted two weeks ago."

"Gerty isn't returning calls. Ven's in love, again, and has been hard to catch. She tells me he's intense."

"Intense?" Venora's the romantic out of my seven sisters. I'm happy for her if she's found another to keep her warm and off the phone, but she holds onto her sweet, doting men and women a little too long before setting them free. "Not her typical choice of companion."

"No, he's not. He withstands her thrall well, but she claims he's human."

"You think he's an otherworldling?" The non-human species resist our ability better than humans, but they eventually succumb.

The chipped sidewalk catches my heel, and I stumble before a boarded-up building. I've wandered into an area of town that would terrify most people.

"I should go," I whisper.

"Let me know if you hear from them."

"I will. Love you, Ma."

"Love you, too." We hang up, and I pivot, put my phone away, and walk the direction I came.

"Mm, now there's a fine piece." A droning voice close behind me grabs my attention.

I spin and get a glimpse of green spiked hair before a fist rams into my midsection, and the air rushes from me in a harsh 'whoosh.'

Crumpling, I gape my mouth to inhale, but can't get a breath.

Two pairs of scuffed boots and three sets of colorful kicks step closer. Straightening up shoots a pang through my gut. The five men circle—sharks scenting fresh blood. Each is menacing, with piercings, scars, and bared teeth. The same devil face tattoo marks their necks. Their sick laughter promises hate and pain, and I need to speak right now. A couple puff up, jerk toward me with aggressive movements, closing in to block my exit as I gasp to find my missing air. Nothing happens but a wheeze. Not good.

"On the corner tonight, sweetheart?" One harsh voice says. "I could use a good workout." As if I needed clarification, he steps closer to brush his hardness against my side. I move to hip check his crotch, but he hurries back, barking a laugh.

"Got a little fighter here," he says. "Fun, fun."

Balling my fists, I struggle to growl, but nothing comes out. I'd command them if I could only get a breath. These the type of beings that need to be enthralled for good.

Someone jerks me upright as the man with hair like spring grass steps close, inches from my face, and shows off a cracked incisor. "What's a high-class bitch like you doing on our turf?"

His voice is a low growl. Demon? He'd be a runt if he were. My nose tingles with lack of oxygen as I gulp at the night air that can't find room in my lungs yet.

"This is our street, Mama. Ain't nobody gonna save ya. Ready for me? Hmm?"

A man jogs out of the shadows. "Let her go." He strides forward into the dim light, his jaw clenched tight. He's wearing a plain gray tee, no tattoos cover his neck, and the ferocious scowl he wears tells me he doesn't belong to this group.

The man next to me gives a dark chuckle, reaching into his pocket for what I'm sure is a weapon. Finally, I inhale enough air to speak. "Step . . . back."

The three that haven't yet spoken walk backward in sync. My thrall and I have a rocky relationship. This is a proud, appreciative moment.

The one holding onto me releases my arm, but Grass-head in front of me only twitches. It's as if his body wants to move, but his mind fights it.

Coughing forces more air in, then out of my burning lungs. "Go home."

This time, four turn and walk away without another word. The stubborn fifth remains. Some humans have more resistance than others, and since otherworldling species hold out long enough to harm those around them, I always work fast.

I hum, though it's shaky. Three seconds of my note, and he drops his proud stance. He swallows and blinks several times, then raises his smitten gaze.

Placing my hands on my hips, I straighten, so I'm as tall as he is. "Are you listening now?"

"Yes." He nods, a tapped bobble-head doll, and relief loosens the tension in my back. At least until I notice the onlooker still stands ten feet from us. My ability should have seeped through, even if he were deaf.

Witnesses are an issue, but sometimes life throws you gang members and you have to make community servants. Or liquified bad guys. It can't come to that, though. Not here.

I'll handle the other man in a moment, but first, my focus falls on the enthralled asshole. I should make him jump in the sewers and let the wildlife deal with him. My sore stomach aches under my hand. "Treat women with respect. No punching, name calling, and no grinding against unwilling participants, got it? That's just gross."

Past his shoulder, spray paint and neglect touch everything, but between two boarded-up buildings lies a big dirt lot under a street-light. There's potential to give someone the purpose they need.

I point. "Start a community garden. Get your people involved and donate extra food. Go make plans."

He scurries away, leaving me with the stranger.

The streetlight illuminates him, a spotlight on a golden-haired movie star. Tonight must be tall and handsome night. This guy better be less psychotic than Wannabe-serial-killer Jordan.

I ball my fists and shove my resurfacing libido aside. My body is so desperate, it has already forgotten the punch. "Did you not hear me? Go home."

He ambles toward me. Stubble lines his sculpted jaw. It's been far too long since I've experienced stubble burn. He halts a foot from me and stares with rare golden eyes. The color is inhuman. My hands fall from my hips, power stance forgotten.

"I heard you fine, Firecracker." His voice soothes, even though his powerful frame and towering height tempt me to step back. "Are you okay? I can't believe they punched you. That shouldn't have happened."

My eyes widen. No one resists my power except my species. There are no male sirens, right? I play over every detail of siren history. The three mothers exiled from Olympus only gave birth to females then disappeared. I'm the fourth generation from the line of Agalope, second youngest of eight sirens, so I'm aware that I don't know everything about our species like Amah does. I'm soulbound to my species though, I'd connect to this being, wouldn't I? I've learned much in my hundred and eighty-two years, but a resistant male is new. He appears concerned for me. Maybe he's slightly enthralled?

"I'm fine. Leave."

His furrowed brow smooths to an amused angle. "Care to explain how you turned a gang of felons into future gardeners?"

What? Wait. How? *Words, Lula, you can do this.* "Why aren't you headed home right now?"

"Because I'd rather be here, making sure you're safe. Are you okay?"

I should run. I have no weapons beyond my voice. Amah has warned me time and again that my curiosity will get me killed, but I have to figure him out. "What's your name?" He doesn't look like a Grizaldak the Torturer.

"Call me Alex."

That name works for him. I deepen my timbre, letting my vocal cords relax into each word. "Leave, Alex."

He tilts his head and perfect lips purse. "I'm not sold that you want me to."

This isn't right. I review my list of otherworldlings with the ability to disguise themselves as human and dismiss each species that doesn't match—no fangs, no fur, no tail. Tall, but not giant height. Two stunning gold eyes. I narrow the possibilities to a few choices. Shapeshifter, Nephilim, or incubus. Bad, worse, or worst.

I can't deal with this tonight. If I sing my siren song, even the saintliest among beings would murder for me, but after a verse, they become sleepy and unaware that their organs are dissolving. If I hit the chorus, there's not enough of them left to order around anymore. But releasing my power hurts even if the creature's evil. They scream in agony, and I have guilt-laced nightmares for months.

No, thank you.

This one tried to help me though and doesn't appear to be a

danger to humans. I pivot, and the sidewalk leads me from the friendly enough bad guy.

"Hey, hold up," Alex calls.

"Go away." I break into a tiptoe run.

"Hey, wait." A hand snatches my forearm within a second, and Alex spins me. I slap at him, but he snags my wrist in mid-air and plants my hand against his chest, ducking his head, face level with mine. "I won't harm you."

"That's what incubi say before they suck out someone's life force."

The ancient song etched in my DNA spills from my lips in a rush of power. It's a cadence from celestial tongues, except the heavenly notes bring death.

Alex's eyes widen. Under my palm, his heart thuds a peaceful rhythm.

My voice carries with more strength, pulling deep from my soul. Releasing it makes my body hum, but my thoughts seize up as I wait for the disaster to come. When I get to the chorus, he bites his smiling lip, and the song dies in my throat.

"Beautiful. You're a siren."

He knows what I am, and he's still standing. How in the hell is he still standing? His face isn't showing pain. He's grinning like the guy at the restaurant did at his companion.

Oh, shit. Not good.

Fear sends tendrils of tightness to every muscle in my body. Black spots threaten my vision as my overwhelmed mind merry-go-rounds, and the ground sways. Alex moves in, supporting me with a strong arm. "Hey, it's okay. I won't hurt you."

He must have calming pheromones because the heat of his skin calls to mine and I sink into his hold, breathing in his sweet citrus scent. Focus, Lula. Incubi are masters of seduction, but even an incubus wouldn't smile at my song. They wouldn't hold me as if I belonged in their arms, because they'd be busy on the ground, having their insides liquefied.

"What are you?" I ask.

Alex's amused expression falters, sending tightness through me again. I try to jerk away, but he clings and blurts out, "A demigod."

No way. A deity on earth? There's the slightest glow to him, a confident golden hue that draws me to him, telling me he's here to help. No otherworldling has that.

My palm lies over the heart of a god.

I've never met a deity. Amah says they abandoned the Earth long before I was born.

He—Alex—observes me, squinting. In the old days, people worshipped the gods that visited Earth in preposterous ways, right up to tossing themselves off cliffs to gain the divine's favor. Three decades ago, a nymph told me she came across two and tried to please them, but they wouldn't accept anything from her, only wanted to talk about humans and otherworldlings. Maybe this deity has questions too.

I breathe slowly, attempting to tame my speeding heart. "What's your real name?"

He leans forward, millimeters from my cheek, warm breath brushing my ear. "Alexiares."

I shudder, letting that information settle. I've studied him—the demigod who wards off wars. The son of Hercules, and grandson of Zeus, the king of Olympus. Damn.

My eyes wander his features, searching for any clue to the phenomenon that is this deity. "I don't affect you?"

"Oh, you affect me."

Unable to keep the sarcasm at bay, I groan and step back from him. "My ability, I mean. Siren, remember?"

"Did you just eye-roll at a deity?"

I grin instead of performing the thousand apologies I'm sure he's expecting. My power doesn't work on him. I'm still wavering between belief and impossibility. It's a flaw, a dream, a crazy oasis mirage envisioned in a desert when I need it the most, except I'm not thirsty for water. I've never had an honest conversation with a male.

His full grin is disarming. "No, your ability doesn't affect me. You could ask me to kiss you, and it would have no impact on me."

Intrigued, I eye his lips. "Really? Kiss me."

With a step forward, he cups the back of my head, fingers threading through my hair, and peruses my features with intent I've only seen in romance movies.

I'd contemplate that look, but he inches forward. Chills rise in response to the electricity shifting between us. I didn't believe he'd kiss me.

He's a deity.

He's also a stranger, and I should pull away.

"No impact, huh?" I whisper.

"Just a taste. Tell me to stop." His eyes search mine.

He radiates warmth, smells like my best dreams, and for one moment, I want someone to kiss me because they want to.

I relax into the hand cupping my head, tilt my chin up . . .

And wait.

Don't stop now. Keep reading with your copy of MY SONG'S CURSE by City Owl Author, Poppy Minnix.

And find more from Linda J. Parisi at www.lindajparisi.com

Want even more paranormal romance? Try MY SONG'S CURSE by City Owl Author, Poppy Minnix, and find more from Linda J. Parisi at www.lindajparisi.com

---

Ultimate control has its downside, especially when it comes to romance. But will it be enough to keep them together?

As a siren Lula Aglaope can bend anyone to her will with the smallest whisper, but she'd give up her power for one meaningful, honest conversation.

She wants a normal life, like the open, true connections the humans seem to pull off with such little effort.

When she meets Alexiares, God of Warding off Wars, all thoughts of normalcy fly out the window. The beautiful demigod cannot be controlled! He's frustrating, irresistible...and utterly off-limits.

Alex has watched Olympus slowly fall apart. The old gods continue their archaic control of the Universe, denying the progress of humans and other deities. But Alex has plans to repair the damage, and Lula is a major player.
She just doesn't know it yet.

Falling for her is the worst idea. And just when things move in the right direction, danger arises that no one expects, plunging the sirens into the deadly Olympian spotlight.

With Lula's sisters missing, and a pile of broken laws surrounding them, will Alex and Lula change the Universe for the better or destroy it?

Please sign up for the City Owl Press newsletter for chances to win special subscriber-only contests and giveaways as well as receiving information on upcoming releases and special excerpts.

All reviews are **welcome** and **appreciated**. Please consider leaving one on your favorite social media and book buying sites.

For books in the world of romance and speculative fiction that embody Innovation, Creativity, and Affordability, check out City Owl Press at www.cityowlpress.com.

Acknowledgments

I'd like to give a heartfelt thank you to Eva Scalzo, my wonderful agent at Speilburg Literary, for helping make my creation a reality.

A special shout out to my CP's who've read this book in all its versions: Chris Clemetson, Gwen Jones, and Gretchen Weerheim.

A huge hug to MaryAnn Johnson for always loving my vampires, and for being the first person to read this book in its entirety.

A very special shout out to NY Times and USA Today Best-Selling Romance Author Caridad Pineiro, whose insight got me on the right track.

Thank you to my co-workers, Barbara Phillips BSMT ASCP, and research scientists Jessica Brady and Anjana Nair, for helping me fine tune my science and for listening to all the crazy ideas rolling around in my head for way too many years.

Last but very not least, I'd like to thank my husband John for putting up with all the years of my writing books. You are and will always be, my HEA.

About the Author

As a major in biochemistry with a minor in English literature, LINDA J. PARISI has always tried to mesh her love of science with her love of the written word. A clinical research scientist by day and NJRW Golden Leaf award winning author by night, she creates unforgettable characters and puts them in untenable situations, much to their dismay. Choices always matter and love conquers all, so a happy-ever-after is a must. Linda is the current Treasurer of Liberty States Fiction Writers, a past board member of New Jersey Romance Writers, and long time member of Romance Writers of America. She lives in New Jersey with her husband John, son Chris, daughter-in-law  Sara, and Audi, a Cocker Spaniel mix who had her at *woof!*

www.lindajparisi.com

 twitter.com/ljparisiwrites
 instagram.com/ljparisiwrites
facebook.com/lindajparisiauthor

About the Publisher

City Owl Press is a cutting edge indie publishing company, bringing the world of romance and speculative fiction to discerning readers.

www.cityowlpress.com

Made in the USA
Middletown, DE
08 September 2020

19007825R00158